MURDER AT HOME

As Caprice and Roz headed for the kitchen, they had to pass the sword room. Caprice didn't give it much notice . . . just kept walking. But Roz suddenly stopped.

Caprice turned around.

Roz stood in the doorway, looking puzzled.

"Is something wrong?" Caprice asked.

"The curio case is open and—"

Roz took a step inside and . . . screamed. It was a bloodcurdling scream that shook Caprice to her core.

Hurrying to her friend, she stepped into the room and couldn't believe what she saw. Ted Winslow lay on the floor, one of his prized daggers protruding from his back . . .

Staged to
Death

KAREN ROSE
SMITH

KENSINGTON PUBLISHING CORP.
http://www.kensingtonbooks.com

KENSINGTON BOOKS are published by

Kensington Publishing Corp.
119 West 40th Street
New York, NY 10018

All Kensington titles, imprints and distributed lines are available at special quantity discounts for bulk purchases for sales
promotions, premiums, fund-raising, and educational or in-
stitutional use. Special book excerpts or customized print-
ings can also be created to fit specific needs. For details,
write or phone the office of the Kensington Special Sales
Manager, Kensington Publishing Corp., 119 West 40th Street,
New York, NY 10018. Attn. Special Sales Department.
Phone: 1-800-221-2647.

Kensington and the K logo Reg. U.S. Pat & TM Off.

ISBN-13: 978-0-7582-8484-6
ISBN-10: 0-7582-8484-5
First Kensington Mass Market Edition: December 2013

eISBN-13: 978-0-7582-8485-3
eISBN-10: 0-7582-8485-3
First Kensington Electronic Edition: December 2013

10 9 8 7 6 5 4 3 2 1

Printed in the United States of America

*This book brought back memories of "home"
and childhood for many reasons.
I dedicate it to my mother, Romaine Arcuri Cacciola,
my grandmother, Rosalie Caltagirone Arcuri,
and my aunt, Rose Marie Arcuri Rigelhof,
for giving me a love of cooking
and a true sense of family
as aunts, uncles, cousins, and friends shared meals.*

Acknowledgments

Thanks to my agent, Evan Marshall. With his support, my mystery series became a reality.

I also want to acknowledge the experts who helped in my research: Tony J. Little, M.A. Taylor, Officer Greg Berry, and Officer Jeffrey Leer.

Chapter One

"That's highway robbery!" Isaac Hobbs protested.

Isaac was a tall, husky man in his early sixties. He was staring down at Caprice De Luca as if she'd pulled one of those antique knives from the locked case by the door and threatened him with it.

His antique store, Older and Better, was one of her favorite places to shop for her home-staging business. But she and Isaac always bargained like two thieves.

"Give him the seventy-five," her sister Bella advised her from across the shop, stuffed with furnishings and memorabilia. "The tapestry is pretty, and you know Roz will like it. It really goes along with your Camelot theme. Who wouldn't want to be a lady with a knight in shining armor at her feet?"

Caprice wouldn't want to be that "lady." Give her an ordinary guy who could be a partner in life, and he could forgo the armor as well as the white horse. In her thirty-two years she hadn't found anyone to fit that bill, though she'd thought she'd come close once. Her two sisters and brother had a lot to say on the subject of her criteria. Actually they had a lot to say about everything.

Except for today.

Bella had been way quiet on the drive here. She hadn't commented on the Saturday traffic, or their sister Nikki's latest catering job or their older brother Vince's dating habits or even her husband and kids.

"You talkin' about Roz Winslow?" Isaac asked. "That mansion has to be as drafty as a castle. I guess a Camelot theme suits."

When the economy headed south, Caprice had transformed her interior design expertise into a home-staging enterprise. Her specialty was themed stagings for high-end clients. But she'd take any job, big or small, simply because she loved mixing colors, textures, and styles. Her latest client, a long-time friend, had decided on a Camelot theme. Caprice hadn't told Isaac whose house she was staging, simply asked him to keep his eye out for specific Old World pieces. But word carried in Kismet, Pennsylvania, just as in any other town. It was no secret that the Winslows wanted to sell their faux castle-mansion and downsize. At least that's what Roz had told Caprice. The house had been on the market six months before they'd hired her.

"They went to school together," Bella told the shop owner.

"Went to school with Roz, huh?"

To her chagrin, Caprice guessed Isaac was comparing her to Rosalind Winslow in his mind's eye. And, yes, they'd been friends in high school and different as night and day. Roz was tall and willowy and had blond hair. On the other hand, Caprice was barely five foot four and was ten pounds overweight, with long, sleek, dark brown hair in a style straight out of the seventies era she loved. Well, she loved anything retro, from her vintage clothes to the lava lamp in her living room. But Roz . . . since she had married Ted Winslow, she was sophisticated elegance all the way.

"Yep, went to school with Roz," Caprice verified to Isaac. "Her open house is Sunday. So . . . are you going to give me that tapestry for seventy? It smells a little musty and—"

"Seventy-two," Isaac countered, cutting her off.

"Done!" Caprice agreed quickly, knowing her budget as well as the Winslows'.

Wealthy folks might spend more, but they still counted their silver dollars. Ted Winslow had been adamant about sticking to the contracted amount. Even though she didn't much care for Ted, even though Roz's marriage to him had interfered with their friendship, Caprice respected the financial terms of their agreement.

"Caprice, come look at this. I think it's Nana's pattern. Mom would love it. Her birthday's coming up, and we could go together."

"I'll roll the tapestry. You look around and see what else you'd like," Isaac offered with a wink.

Caprice smiled. Isaac knew she couldn't resist a good bargain. She stowed extra pieces she suspected would be useful someday in a rented storage compartment.

After threading her way around a Boston rocker, a pine dry sink that held a green-glazed ceramic pitcher, and an oak pedestal stand topped by a friar cookie jar, Caprice crossed to a primitive apothecary cabinet where a crystal bowl sat. She picked it up.

"Careful," Bella warned her. "My credit card is maxed out from buying Megan and Timmy spring clothes. I don't need a broken Fostoria fruit bowl charged to it."

After examining it, Caprice called to Isaac. "Navarre, right?"

"Sure is. One of the most delicate patterns from the forties."

"I'm sure Nana didn't have this in her collection."

Caprice and Bella's paternal grandmother, Celia, had moved in with their parents a few years ago. She'd sold or given away many of her belongings. However, she'd handed down her crystal and sterling silver to their mom, who'd appreciated the beauty of it for years. There was no doubt Nana Celia had excellent taste. Often she gave decorating pointers to Caprice that she actually remembered and used.

"Do you have any more pieces?" Caprice asked Isaac.

"Not now. But I'm headed to an auction in York and one in Harrisburg later this week. Do you want me to keep you in mind?"

"Are you thinking of pulling in Nikki and Vince?" Bella took the bowl from Caprice to examine it more carefully.

"A few pieces would make a wonderful present. We might even want to think about a surprise party." To Isaac she said, "You have my number. Give me a call if you find more of the pattern. I'll make a list of what our mom has so we don't duplicate anything."

Barely twenty minutes later, Caprice climbed from her restored yellow Camaro and headed up the flagstone path to her Cape Cod style house. The end-of-April day was gorgeously sunny. With Bella following close behind, Caprice appreciated her home, which had been built in the early fifties and nestled between a crimson maple and a white birch in one of Kismet's older neighborhoods. Mostly brick, with stone around the unusual arched door and copper roofing above the porch, it gave off a warm, homey air that had appealed to Caprice from the moment she'd seen it. Pink azaleas just starting to bloom under the dining room's bay window made her home look dressed up for spring.

A tall privacy fence stretched on both sides and surrounded the backyard with poplars practically hiding it.

As soon as Caprice's foot touched the porch, a wild yipping began inside.

"Another stray?" Bella's question seemed to carry a tad of censure.

Caprice knew why. Her sister had been a beauty from the moment she'd been born. Not that Caprice remembered the event. She'd been two. But Bella's curly, black hair, perfectly oval face, and huge, almost-black eyes had earned her smiles and pats on the head from an early age. Vince was the brainy one. Nikki was the practical one. And Caprice was the curious one who asked more questions than anyone had patience enough to answer. But Bella, short for Isabella, liked her hair perfectly curled, her house straightened up, and her life in order. That was tough, with a husband and two kids, but she did a good job of it. That kind of life, however, had little room for strays.

"A neighbor found him. She was going to take him to the—well, you know. I couldn't take that chance. He's really adorable. You'll see."

"That's the whole point," Bella protested. "I don't *want* to see. Every time Megan or Timmy visit you, they come home whining that they want a dog or cat. Honestly, Caprice. Why do you put yourself through getting attached and the—"

Ah-hah! That was the real reason Bella didn't want a pet. Attachment.

Caprice unlocked the door and pushed it open.

Dylan was black and white and fluffy-furred all over. His name had been easy. She'd been listening to Bob Dylan when her neighbor had brought the dog to her. He weighed about ten pounds and had a tail that could practically dust her mosaic-topped coffee table in one sweep.

Ecstatic to see her, he barked and jumped up and down while Bella just shook her head and ordered, "Down, boy."

"His name is Dylan, and he and Sophia get along great."

Sophia was a long-haired, strikingly colored calico cat Caprice had found not long after she'd moved in. When she'd designed her living room in sixties-chic bright colors and geometric shapes, she'd worked a floor-to-ceiling cat tree into the plan and had it specially carpeted in turquoise. Sophia loved it. She sharpened her claws on it and left the rest of the furniture alone. A second scratching post upstairs, rubbed with catnip once a week, also helped.

In greeting, Sophia yawned, stood, meowed twice, and jumped down from her perch, her white ruff fluffing more with the motion. Dylan kept up his almost bouncing exuberance.

After tossing her purse onto a high-backed hall

bench, Caprice caught the little dog and hugged him. "Did you have a good afternoon?"

"You really think he's going to answer you?"

Dylan barked twice and Caprice laughed. "He just did." Taking him through the dining room to the kitchen, she opened the back door to let him run onto the covered porch, then down the steps.

"It's a good thing you have a fenced-in yard."

After checking Dylan's progress, Caprice went to the coffeemaker and pulled out a lime-green, yellow-flowered canister. She and Bella both enjoyed flavored coffees. "Chocolate hazelnut? I made a batch of lemon biscotti yesterday." She and her sisters liked to cook. They'd learned by watching both their grandmother and their mom. Caprice's buttercup-colored 1950s vintage-styled stove that matched her retro refrigerator reminded her of the appliances in her grandmother's kitchen long ago. Only these had high-tech features.

"Just one cup of coffee," Bella said. "I really can't stay much longer."

When Bella had arrived earlier, she'd told Caprice that Joe had taken Megan and Timmy to the movies. Joe was every bit as traditional as Bella. Until Megan went to kindergarten in the fall, he'd wanted Bella at home, insisting he liked her there when his workday as an accountant was done. Both Caprice and Nikki felt he expected too much of Bella because he rarely helped with the kids. But if Bella was happy, that was all that mattered.

"Pull out a chair. I'll make half a pot."

The antique maple kitchen table, surrounded by chairs with yellow braided seat cushions, had been a spectacular find. She and her sisters had already had many long conversations around it.

Caprice had just opened the screened door to let Dylan back in when her cell phone played "She Loves You," her latest Beatles ringtone. Pulling it from the pocket of her violet vintage skirt, she checked the screen. "It's Roz," she told Bella. "I should take this."

Bella just waved her hand in agreement and grabbed two mugs from a birch cupboard.

"Hi, Roz."

Dylan ran around Caprice's ankles, his tail brushing her calves. After she slipped off one of her espadrilles and petted him with her toes, he flopped down beside her foot.

"I know you're probably busy, but I need to see you," Roz said, sounding stressed.

Caprice glanced at Bella. "Right now?"

Roz lowered her voice. "Ted and I have been arguing all day about his sword room. He won't do what you suggested and clear most of it. On top of that, he just told me he's going out of town again later today. Can you come over and talk to him?"

Besides a theme, besides bringing in furniture and enhancing the very best features of a house, Caprice warned her clients to de-clutter. Apparently this was a problem for Ted Winslow. Clutter aside, there were also too many valuables in his "sword room" for open-house guests to wander off with.

Sensing Caprice's indecision, Bella checked her watch. "I really have to go. Take care of Roz. I'll phone you next week."

"Caprice?" Roz called, making sure she was there. "I really need help with Ted. He won't listen to me . . . about anything."

Now just what did *that* mean?

As Caprice drove into Reservoir Heights, an exclusive community west of Kismet, she was amazed again at the size of the mansions. That was really the only word for them. The neighborhood had been designed around Kismet's reservoir, a sumptuous, blue-green lake that was a backdrop for many of the homes. When the community had been developed about ten years ago, the planners hadn't planted seedlings and young trees but had moved in full-grown ones. Some of the lots had been wooded to start with, but others soon became exactly what their designers envisioned them to be. The neighborhood was definitely a showcase of homes. Word had it that someone famous had toured one of the recently listed estates.

Someone famous in Kismet, Pennsylvania. Now *that* could be exciting news that would make the *Kismet Crier.*

Caprice wound along the newly repaved road.

The home association in this neighborhood made sure everything was up to par. She couldn't help but admire a log home with its six-foot overhang and gables, which were supposed to convey country living at its finest. The luxury broker who was handling Roz and Ted's listing, a successful one in Caprice's ever-growing network of contacts, had filled Caprice in on many of the properties in the area, including this one. She'd described the massive stone fireplace inside. Several of these houses had adopted a country manor look, with coffered ceilings and Palladian windows. The neighborhood, with homes ranging from four thousand square feet to as many as ten thousand, was a sampling of architectural delights.

In another quarter of a mile, Caprice spotted the towers on Roz and Ted's mansion. The word *mansion* usually brought pictures to mind of a Southern estate with stately pillars and pristine white trim. No, that wasn't Roz and Ted's house. Theirs looked more like a castle.

Roz called it her storybook dream house when Ted had it designed for her. It was unique, stunning, and chock full of lavish conveniences. Roz and Ted had scoured pictures in books and, on their honeymoon, even visited castles in France, Scotland, and Spain for inspiration. The structure had an Old World flavor and had been built with two circular towers capped by cone-shaped roofs. The windows were long, practically floor to ceiling, and symmetrically placed. Double doors and huge columns invited visitors into an impressive entranceway. The walls weren't created with mortar and rocks but rather with faux-stone panels. Inside, a labor-intensive painting process had been used on some of the walls and brick facing on others to make them appear castle-like.

The house was an intriguing mixture of old and new. Because of that, however, the price as well as the style made it difficult to sell even in a healthy market.

So Caprice's philosophy, and her Nana Celia's, had been to play to the house's strengths and intrigue anyone who walked inside . . . intrigue them and make them feel comfortable to boot. Curb appeal wasn't a problem. The mansion sat on a hill with the lake as a backdrop. Creeping phlox in dark pink, purple, and white carpeted the incline. The blue spruce and shrubs surrounding it gave it a calm, sturdy, peaceful air.

Caprice drove into the driveway, which angled from the west side of the edifice, and proceeded around an oval circle with a garden in its center near the front entrance. Parking, she pocketed her keys and climbed the steps. Standing under the portico, she rang the bell, which bonged deep inside the house.

When Roz opened one side of the immense, polished walnut doors, Caprice saw strain on her friend's pretty face. On a bad day, Roz could enter a beauty pageant. Today she was dressed smartly in a spring-green, two-piece suit, beige pumps, and gold cuff bracelets. Her shoulder-length blond hair didn't have a wave that misbehaved. As usual, her makeup enhanced her green eyes and covered any flaws. But there were blue smudges under her eyes no concealer could hide. And was that a tear stain on her cheek?

"I'm glad you're here," Roz said with a forced smile.

Caprice stepped into the foyer, practically the size of her own first floor. Gray, stone-paneled curved walls surrounded her. "Are you okay?"

"Better now, because you can help convince Ted he's being ridiculous. He insists he wants to show off the room and his swords, not hide what's in it."

When decorating the interior of their "castle," Roz and Ted had opted for an Old World look with heavy velvet draperies, giant gold tassels, and thick decorative rods with upholstered valances. Iron-framed chandeliers, some immense, were supposed to add rusticity. On top of that, they'd filled too much space with monstrous sofas, gigantic black armoires, and curio units as if they would run out of seating or surfaces on which to position sculptures and collectibles. It might have been a look they enjoyed, but the decor was one of the reasons the house hadn't sold in the past six months.

After de-cluttering, Caprice had brought in furniture crafted from lavishly grained wood and draperies fashioned of pastel damasks, silks, and gentle wools. The overall feel of the interior now was warm, rich, bright and welcoming. But the de-cluttering process had occasioned a battle royal between her and Ted. His philosophy was that he'd paid an exorbitant amount of cash for the furnishings, sculptures, and paintings, and he wanted to show them off. But finally Roz, along with Caprice, had convinced him to put much of it in storage.

"I've hired the same security firm I always use out of York," Caprice assured Roz. "They'll mingle with the guests and not stand out. If I have to put a security guard just on Ted's sword room, I can. You *are* putting your jewelry in your safe deposit box, right?"

When it came to her clients, Caprice would always rather be safe than sorry. She had a reputation to protect. One mistake, one robbery, one instance of vandalism could ruin the good name she'd developed over the past few years.

"I already took most of it to the bank. But Ted still has gold coins and silver ingots in the bedroom safe. He says no one will ever find it or be able to break into the triple-locking mechanism. He's just so mule-headed sometimes . . ."

To Caprice's surprise and dismay, Roz teared up. She clasped her friend's arm. "What's going on?"

Shaking her head, Roz murmured, "Nothing, really. I'm just—" She shook her head again. "I think Ted's having problems at work and he's grumpy all the time. On top of that, he's been out of town so much this month. I feel like my thoughts echo off the walls here. Do you know what I mean?"

A bigwig in Pennsylvania Pharmaceuticals Incorporated, located just outside the Kismet town limits, Ted had high-pressure responsibilities in his position as senior vice president. Roz had told her that many times. But Roz hadn't told her exactly why they were selling their dream home. Was it because Ted traveled so much and Roz felt lonely here? Or had Ted decided to sell it for some other reason?

Thinking about Roz's question, Caprice realized she never felt as if her thoughts were bouncing off the walls. She had people she loved and pets around her most of the time. There was always someone to talk to, human or four-footed.

But she could empathize with her friend. "Staying here alone must be difficult."

"A security system doesn't make me feel secure," Roz admitted. "Maybe if we have kids, I wouldn't feel . . . abandoned," she confessed, but then looked as if she was sorry she had.

"Is that Caprice?" Ted called from the cavernous interior.

"Yes," Roz called back.

As she and Roz started for the great room, Ted emerged from the hall that led to his home office. "We need walkie-talkies," he muttered. "That blasted intercom doesn't function half of the time. Of course, if we had walkie-talkies, you'd probably forget to turn yours on," he complained.

Ted was a least six feet tall and sharp-featured, and his heavy, dark brows were laced with some gray. He was ten years older than Roz, and Caprice had never seen him wearing anything but a custom-tailored suit, a dress shirt, and a designer tie. Today, however, he looked a little rumpled. Maybe it was just his fierce expression. He looked ready to growl or spit or take a good bite out of someone.

Often Caprice found herself in volatile situations. But she had two sisters and a brother—a family where Italian tempers sometimes flared. She could handle a disgruntled client.

"Roz relayed your concerns about your sword room," she began diplomatically. "And I know about the gold and silver you want to leave in your safe. I'll make sure a guard keeps a significant eye on the master suite. But do you really want your antique weapons available to be handled by strangers? Maybe no one will steal anything. But someone could damage a valuable collectible."

They'd gone over this before, but sometimes she had to repeat common sense like a broken record to clients until it sunk in.

"You sound like Roz, talking as if these are toys that might break." He waved his arm toward the east wing of the house. "Come with me."

Keeping her temper in check—Caprice didn't

take dictatorial orders very well—she followed with Roz behind her. But they'd no sooner reached the sword room when Ted's cell phone buzzed.

He grabbed it from the holster on his belt under his pin-striped suit jacket. "Winslow," he barked.

Caprice stepped into the room. These walls had been treated to the specialty paint effect. The painter had used a gray base coat and added highlights and shadows with differing degrees of gray. The mortar lines must have been tedious to draw.

Caprice's gaze had just settled on a foot-long dagger with a decorated scabbard when she heard Ted's raised voice.

"If he does that, Thompson, I'll kill him."

Chapter Two

Caprice watched the color drain from Roz's face. Had Ted ever turned his anger on her?

Caprice might have appeared to be listening to more of the conversation out of sheer curiosity, so Ted shot an annoyed glance at her and moved out of the room and down the hall, his voice still growly.

Roz laid her hand on Caprice's arm and drew her farther into the sword room, away from her husband's voice.

"I don't know what to do." Roz look defeated. "He won't tell me what's going on."

"At work?" Caprice wanted some clarification on what was happening between the couple. This tension could affect plans for the open house the following weekend and potentially the sale.

"I don't know if it's just at work. Ever since we decided to sell the house, he's been . . . different."

"Maybe he doesn't really want to sell it. The two

of you designed it together. Or maybe he thought it would sell much sooner."

"I just don't know." Roz's breathy sigh let out a wealth of frustration.

Heavy footfalls tapped the tan terrazzo, and Caprice steeled herself for another confrontation with Ted.

He strode into the room, glanced around, and concluded, "I don't have time to deal with this now. I have to get to the office. Put an extra guard on the room if you must. I'm not packing any of this away. It took me too long to collect it."

To Roz, he said, "I have my travel bag in my car. I'll be driving to the airport from the office."

"Did you leave me the info for where you're staying?"

"You have my cell number. That's all you need."

"Don't want me checking up on you?" Roz asked, straightening her shoulders as if she'd had enough of all of it.

Ted's anger seemed to deflate. "No. That's not the reason. Truthfully, I just don't remember which hotel it is. I've stayed in so many over the past few weeks that I can't keep them straight. I'm flying to Cleveland, but the hotel reservation is in my briefcase."

Roz's face lost its sad look with his change in tone. "You will be back in time for the open house next Sunday?"

"I'll be home by Friday, in plenty of time to get

ready for the open house. I won't leave you and Caprice stranded. Now I've really got to run." He dropped a quick kiss on his wife's lips and disappeared again down the hall.

Feeling awkward about everything she'd just witnessed, Caprice drifted toward the locked glass case and wondered how much everything in this room was worth. The monster swords on the walls were daunting. Some rested on brackets; others were mounted directly on the wall. There were also a few stone pedestals that held single specimens. Caprice didn't know the real ones from replicas, but they all looked forbidding—especially the dagger that stood by the burled wood credenza. Sheathed in a leather scabbard, its home was a four-foot wrought-iron stand.

A moment later, Roz stood by the glass case with her. "Sorry about that."

"Marriage is complicated," Caprice acknowledged with a shrug. She'd witnessed Bella's struggles. And she understood that even though her parents were devoted to each other and their marriage was rock-solid, raising four children hadn't been easy, and they hadn't always agreed on how to do it.

"I guess the honeymoon can't last forever," Roz mused, her disappointment evident.

Maybe that was what most people thought—that the honeymoon couldn't last forever. That was a realistic and practical way of thinking. Yet Caprice did remember her paternal grandparents' marriage and still witnessed firsthand her parents' marriage. There was real affection and, yes, passion. If she ever did get married—and that was a very big if—she wanted a marriage like theirs . . . binding, faithful, and true. Yep, she was a dreamer in that area of her life.

She also knew it was a good reason she was still single.

Changing the subject, because she suspected Roz would be more comfortable if she did, she commented on the collectibles in the glass case. "Tell me about these so I know what we're dealing with."

"I think these are what Ted cherishes most."

Does he cherish you? Caprice wondered. Yet his fond farewell said he still might.

Moving to the side of the tall curio case with a key-lock that didn't appear that difficult to jimmy, Roz gestured to a thin-bladed knife inside. "That's a seventeenth-century Italian stiletto dagger. It has a bull-horn handle."

"Seventeenth century," Caprice repeated, actually thinking about it.

"And that—" Roz pointed to a piece resting in a dark green velvet box. "That's a Chinese carved jade dagger pendant dating back to the Ming dynasty."

"Ming," Caprice murmured, totally impressed. "I don't suppose you wear it," she joked.

"I wore it once. We went to a costume party at one of our neighbors' houses. It's insured, of course, as are all of his artifacts. I imagine that's why he's not so worried about the open house."

Roz's husband might not be worried, but Caprice was. Her gaze slid to another unusual-looking knife. "What's that one?"

"Fantastic, isn't it? That one's a late-seventeenth-century or early-eighteenth-century Indian Mughal Khanjar dagger with rubies, diamonds, and emeralds set in a gold-covered hilt. I really can see why Ted enjoys collecting these and the history behind each one. I just know the labels. He's an authority on each piece. That particular one he gave me for my birthday two years ago." She got a faraway look, as if her relationship with her husband had been good then.

Caprice had never really gotten to know Ted. Obviously, he was a complicated man with many layers. Maybe she could make a point of having a conversation with him at the open house.

"C'mon," Roz said. "Let's have a cup of coffee. Do you have time?"

She did. She didn't have an event this weekend. Several were in the works, but they would come together within the next week or so as she and her clients chose themes and she shopped and rented everything she needed for the stagings.

"Coffee is good. I don't have anywhere I have to be for the next couple of hours." Though she did want to get home to spend some playtime with

Dylan. She didn't want him to feel lost again or abandoned.

As they crossed the hall and entered the main portion of the house, Caprice was satisfied with the choices she'd made to brighten up and maximize the highlights of the kitchen. Staying with the Camelot theme, she'd displayed wooden bowls on the counter and replaced the abstract art, which had seemed incongruous in their type of decor, with a softer, medieval-styled still life. She'd also removed a heavy draw drape that had concealed the merits of the back of the property with filmy panels topped by a navy and mauve brocade valance.

"I found a tapestry for the wall in the breakfast nook. I think you'll like it. I'm going to have it cleaned before hanging it."

Roz opened the freezer and removed a sealed bag with a packet of coffee. "Blackberry brandy?" she asked with a wiggle of her brow.

Caprice laughed. "It really tastes like that?"

"I think it does. I don't have any lemon biscotti like you and your family bake, but I stopped at the Cupcake House. Red velvet was the special."

"I'll skip supper and go for it."

It was funny that a woman in Roz's Manolo Blahnik shoes would still take advantage of a special. But then she'd had very few advantages growing up. Her mom had raised her on her own. In their senior year of high school, Roz's mom had been diagnosed with breast cancer. The summer after their graduation, putting flight attendant training on hold, Roz had waitressed while she'd taken care of her mother. When her mom was on her deathbed, she had made Roz promise to follow her dreams. After Joan Hulsey had passed away, Roz had left for the training, happily flown wherever the airline scheduled her, then had met Ted about six years ago. They'd been married for five.

"I guess there's no way of knowing how many house buyers will come to look." Roz took milk from the refrigerator and poured it into a stoneware creamer.

"Some will come just for Nikki's catering." Her sister Nicoletta, Nikki for short, always created inventive dishes to go along with Caprice's themes.

"That's just it. How many people will come to gawk, and how many are serious about buying?"

Caprice transferred the stoneware sugar bowl from the counter to the eat-at island in the center of the kitchen. "We'll find out. You have to remember, this is just the beginning. It's as if you put the house on the market all over again. Maybe even clients who came through before will look at it with fresh eyes because of the changes we've made."

"I'm tired of thinking about it. Let's talk about something fun. I saw Sherry Raddison last week." Another of their classmates, Sherry had been living in Lancaster.

Caprice sat on one of the high island chairs. "She's a dental hygienist, right?"

"Yep. We dated some of the same guys in high school. I guess you could say we were rivals back then."

Unlike her own high school dating history—she'd hooked up with one guy and dated him for two years—Roz had dated a different guy almost every month.

"I wouldn't be able to name all the boys you dated."

"But I can name yours—Craig Davenport. Whatever happened to him?"

"Don't know. That's why we broke up. He didn't keep in touch."

"But you were high school sweethearts!"

"Yes, we were. But I couldn't compete with Stanford and a life in California."

"Would you have been willing to follow him anywhere?"

Caprice had often asked herself that same question, and she always came up with the same answer. "Probably not. I don't think I could have left my family."

The state-of-the-art coffeemaker hissed just like any other coffeemaker. The aroma of the blackberry brandy coffee was temptingly delicious.

"Do you ever see Travis Bigelow?"

Although Roz's travels and then her marriage to Ted had put a damper on the friendship she and

Caprice had shared in high school, they'd still kept in touch. So Roz had known about Travis, who had been one of Caprice's biggest mistakes. At times, she still felt the pain of their breakup two years ago.

"Since he and Alicia moved to Harrisburg, I don't have to worry about running into him," Caprice admitted. "But I often wish I could see Kristi. Just curious." The truth was, as Nana more than once had pointed out, Caprice probably missed Travis's daughter, Kristi, more than she missed Travis.

"You would have made a great mom. It's a shame he went back to his ex-wife. I guess divorced men are forever on your no-no list."

"You've got that right." Talking about the past wasn't something Caprice liked to do. She'd much rather move ahead. "Let's break out those cupcakes."

Roz gave her a conspiratorial wink and went to the pantry to get them.

After spending a madcap week scheduling two new clients, shopping for staging accessories, and perfecting plans for the Winslows' open house, Caprice stood under the mansion's portico Sunday afternoon, peering out at the circular drive. Three valets took the keys of the house hunters who parked in the drive, then moved their cars to a grassy area to the rear of the house. Whether this unique house was the draw or the Winslow name associated with it, the event was attracting quite a crowd. Roz and Ted's real estate broker, along with an associate agent, were busy mingling, showing interested guests every design advantage and unique feature inside and out.

Certifying that all was well outside, Caprice toured the first floor, passing a wandering minstrel strumming a lyre. Smiling, she gave him a thumbs-up sign. As she passed through the immense dining room, she found clients and guests seated around the long, rectangular table with a tapestry runner trailing down its center. They were enjoying wine or ale in pewter goblets and hors d'oeuvres—crusty bread filled with roast beef and venison. Another dish that sat between pillar candleholders was dauce egre—fish in a sweet and sour onion sauce. That was accompanied by a platter of meatballs spiced with fennel and marjoram. To top off the medieval delights, Nikki had created something called a chiresaye, an elegant dessert made with fresh cherries. Her sister had really outdone herself.

In the kitchen, Nikki was supervising waiters—wearing blousy shirts, leather vests, and buckskin pants as they carried trays and refilled goblets and mugs—and generally made sure the serving of food went smoothly.

Noticing the carving board holding crusty rolls

and wedges of cheese, Caprice snitched a slice of Gruyère.

"I saw that," Nikki said, coming up behind her. "Did you fast all day again?"

"I don't fast. I just can't eat the day of an open house. You know that."

"One of these times, you're going to pass out," her sister warned her.

Nikki looked like their mom. She had Francesca De Luca's wide smile and golden-brown eyes. Her hair was golden brown too, helped along by professionally applied highlights. Nikki was two years older than Caprice, and she felt that gave her all the authority she needed to give her advice—all the time . . . any time . . . no matter where they were.

"I won't pass out," she protested. "I don't eat, but I had a protein shake for breakfast and I've been drinking to stay hydrated. I'll try some of your food after everyone leaves. You're getting rave reviews. Where did you find these recipes?"

"Don't be so surprised about my research skills. After all, Vince taught me how to use a computer before they were a necessity." She nodded toward the real estate agent, who was pulling a bunch of grapes from the giant wooden fruit bowl. "Any bites yet?"

"Not that I know of. But everyone looks interested and they're asking lots of buyers' questions. Have you seen Roz or Ted?"

"Not lately. Roz was circulating. She should have been a PR consultant. She can make conversation with anyone. By the way, did you notice Mr. Tall, Dark, and Handsome in the sword room? I wonder if he'd be interested in an after-hours bite of venison."

"You can't hit on the security guard."

"Just why not? Are *you* planning to?"

"No!" Caprice blurted the negative so loudly that a couple of the guests noticed.

"Think about it," Nikki teased. "I'll hold off if you want to ask him out. How long has it been since you went on a date?"

"We're not having this conversation here," Caprice hissed, lowering her voice.

"Then just where are we going to have it?" Nikki demanded. "You spend your free time with cats and dogs."

"Enough! I have to put up with this abuse when we have dinner at Mom's. I don't need it while I'm working. If you don't watch your step, I might have to hire a new caterer."

"You wouldn't dare. You'd have the whole family to answer to."

Nikki's sly grin made Caprice want to pull her sister's hair as she'd done when they were kids. But instead of reverting to ten-year-old behavior, she agreed, "You're right. I wouldn't dare. You're too good . . . even though you can be terribly annoying." She took another slice of cheese. "I'm going to see if I can find Roz or Ted. And really, Nikki, you did a terrific job on the food."

Caprice leaned close to her sister and whispered,

"Stay away from that guard. At least until he's off duty and sheds his weapon."

Nikki's eyes grew very big. "He's armed?"

"He's guarding a *sword* room. It only makes sense, don't you think?"

Glad she'd had the last word, Caprice hurried away before Nikki could think of a comeback.

She did spot Roz. But she was at the center of a group of people. They hadn't had time to talk before setup for the open house began. But her friend had been smiling earlier. That was a good sign. Maybe Ted's trip had taken some of the pressure off him, and he and Roz were finding their footing again. She'd catch up with her later.

The second floor of the house wasn't as expansive as the first. On both the east and west sides, winding circular staircases led from the first floor to the tower rooms on the second. Those small, octagonal spaces were more for show than utility. Caprice had staged one with shelved leather-bound books. The other looked more like a feminine alcove for two friends who wanted to have a chat. Brocade-covered wing chairs were delicately lit from above by a porcelain chandelier on a dimmer switch. A bowl of lavender sachets trimmed in lace gave off a lovely scent.

Caprice spotted guests exploring both towers, so she took the main staircase that led to the bedrooms and Roz's exercise room. No one seemed to be touring this area, though another guard was stationed in the master suite. If anyone came in, he had orders to act as if he was merely taking a tour too.

Caprice was about to head downstairs once more when she heard murmured voices coming from down the hall . . . from Roz's exercise room. Thinking she should explain that the equipment could easily be removed to create a child's play area or even a media room, Caprice started toward the voices.

Outside the door, however, the timbre of their tone changed. She thought she heard the endearment "darling."

Who would be up here? She'd spotted Roz downstairs.

Stepping a little closer to the partially open door, Caprice realized there were no sounds coming from the room now—until she heard a soft moan. Really curious, she peeked inside . . . and wished she hadn't.

Ted Winslow had his arms wrapped around a woman who was not his wife and was kissing her as if the end of the world might befall him at any minute.

Chapter Three

Oh, my gosh! Ted was actually kissing . . . really, really kissing . . .

Stunned, Caprice watched with horrified interest. The woman was Valerie Swanson, a hairstylist at Curls R Us. Bella had pointed out the hairdresser once when they were shopping at Grocery Fresh Market. Valerie owned the hair salon where Bella set up an appointment like clockwork every six weeks. The business had taken off with a flourish when Valerie had bought it about five years ago after being a stylist there for approximately as long. Ten stylists besides Valerie cared for the clients at Curls. Caprice herself preferred the one-woman shop where her mom and Nana had their hair trimmed and cut.

Realizing she was going to get caught gawking if she didn't step back and silently disappear, Caprice tried to stem her amazement, disappointment, and sense of outrage on Roz's behalf. How dare Ted kiss another woman? And in their home! If he was kissing her like that here, Caprice suspected he was doing more than kissing elsewhere.

But what should she do about it? Tell Roz?

Slowly inhaling a very deep breath—those yoga classes had been good for something—she was thankful for the plush carpet runner in the hall that muffled her footsteps. Her mind raced faster than usual. Maybe Roz already knew Ted was fooling around. Maybe that's why there was so much tension between them. Perhaps Ted's grumpiness had nothing to do with work and everything to do with Valerie.

On the heels of that thought, however, Caprice remembered his phone call. *If he does that, Thompson, I'll kill him.* Hyperbole?

Caprice had passed two guest bedrooms when she spotted Denise Langford exiting the master suite with a middle-aged couple. The real estate broker said, "Of course, you can forgo the four-poster bed or even take down the canopy. But it *is* very romantic, isn't it? As you saw, the crystal chandelier is on a dimmer switch. The sound system is magnificent. It can be turned on or off in each room. Really a nice touch."

Attempting to clear her head of what she'd seen, Caprice knew she needed to put on her PR hat and do it quickly. This was *her* show as much as the real estate broker's.

After she introduced herself to the couple, Agnes

and Jeffrey Buckhold seemed to wear pleased smiles. Agnes said, "This is really a unique house. I love the sconces and chandeliers."

That comment pleased Caprice. She had replaced some of the giant, heavier, iron lighting fixtures with antique porcelain bases and candlelight bulbs, shimmering crystal fixtures on dimmers, and copper-finished metal replicas.

"And that bedroom suite. I wonder if the Winslows would consider letting that go along with the house?" Agnes wondered aloud.

At this moment, Caprice didn't want to think about Roz and Ted's bedroom. She didn't want to believe vows had been broken, maybe even *there*. But she'd seen for herself that might be the case.

"If you make an offer, any furniture could be written into the contract," Denise assured her.

Suddenly, Valerie strolled down the hall, looking completely put-together and pleased. But Caprice saw the telltale smudge of lipstick on the right side of her bottom lip that she hadn't been able to repair. She was almost too dressed up for an open house in a red, one-shoulder sheath that was much too low for an occasion like this. The dress was also much shorter than anything Roz would wear. Her red beads were big and bold and shouted "Look at me." Her wavy, swingy hair was platinum, with at least three different shades of darker highlights, so unlike Nikki's, which appeared natural. Why would Ted turn to a woman like this?

Caprice suddenly heard her mother's voice in her head when they had met yet another woman her brother was dating. He seemed to find someone new more often than Caprice went grocery shopping. Okay, that was an exaggeration. But not by much. Her mom often just shook her head and murmured, "There's no explaining the choices some men make. Thank goodness your father had more sense than your brother and chose someone like me!" Then she'd smile.

If Valerie was Ted's "type," then why had he ever married Roz?

But some questions had no answers. Why had Travis Bigelow divorced his wife and then two years later reunited with Alicia? No point asking that question again. Maybe men and women really were from different planets and would never understand each other.

Yet her mom and dad did.

Hope? Was there hope for Ted and Roz? Should she tell her friend what she'd seen?

All smiles and singsong sweet voice, Valerie joined in the conversation. "This house has so many unique features. That master suite is something. I don't think I've ever seen a whirlpool tub that big. And there's even a sauna. What more could you want?"

Seeing a brighter shade of red than Valerie's dress, Caprice wondered if the woman had used the tub or sauna—or had thoughts of using it with Ted in the future. Caprice forced her voice into a pleasant timbre, ignoring Valerie and addressing the interested couple. "Make sure you enjoy the hors d'oeuvres downstairs while you're looking around. And don't forget the game room on the lower level."

Before she gave away the fact she'd seen something she shouldn't have, she excused herself without another glance at Valerie and headed for the stairs.

What to do? She didn't want to hurt Roz. But being loyal and truthful was important to her.

Worrying about what she was going to say and do, Caprice barely heard her name being called a few minutes later until she was walking down a hall, passing Ted's office. Suddenly she felt a hand on her shoulder. It was a gentle grip.

She turned to find an older woman about her mother's age. "Mrs. Arcuri! What are you doing here?" Teresa Arcuri was the choir director at St. Francis of Assisi, the local Catholic church, which Caprice's family had attended for all of their lives. In her lavender knit pantsuit, with her silver-gray hair wrapped in a top bun, she seemed out of place in this mansion.

"I was curious to see what you could do with this place. Your mother told me I should stop in. That's all right, isn't it?"

"Of course, it is. It's an open house. Everyone is welcome. What do you think of it?"

"Oh, I was here for a charity function last year.

Mrs. Winslow had a tea to raise money for a literacy campaign."

"I remember. I couldn't come because I had a meeting with a client in Harrisburg."

"You've made such a difference in the interior! It almost feels like a home. When I was here before, the place felt so . . . cold. Your mother told me you were good at what you do, but I wanted to see for myself. The thing is—" She hesitated. "Do you still redo ordinary folks' homes? I need a change. After John died, I wanted to keep everything the same. But my daughter suggested that maybe it's time for me to make a few changes."

"Do you feel you're ready?" Teresa's daughter could suggest all she wanted, but until the widow wanted to move forward, her heart wouldn't really be in it. Her husband had been gone a few years, but they'd been married for thirty-five.

"Yes, I'm ready. Oh, I'm not going to change everything, mind you. I'd like to start with the kitchen and dining room. Do you have time?"

In her line of work, Caprice had to "read" people very well. If she didn't, they'd sink in over their heads or she'd sink in over hers. Mrs. Arcuri was looking for a way to keep her memories alive yet put her grief in the past. This was the type of work Caprice had always loved doing. Starting with the kitchen or living room was common.

"I have the time. Call me next week and we'll set up a meeting." She dug in the pocket of her skirt and handed a business card to Teresa. "In the meantime, can you make me a list of your favorite colors, hobbies, and styles? That will give me a head start."

"This is going to be such fun." For a moment, Teresa looked a little worried. "I do have a budget. I can't go hog wild." Leaning in a little closer, she lowered her voice. "I don't have a lot to spare like the Winslows."

"I work within budgets with all my clients."

After assuring Caprice she'd call her next week, Teresa headed to the front of the house.

Once again, as Caprice ventured down the hall, she thought about the layout of the Winslow house and how it could be warmed up so much more. If a contractor tore down a few walls and gave it a more open design, each room wouldn't seem so isolated. But it also wouldn't feel like a castle.

She was approaching a small parlor when she heard Roz's voice, then a burst of laughter that sounded totally genuine. In the doorway, Caprice saw who she was talking to. Dave Harding had been one of their classmates. Caprice remembered he and Roz had dated their senior year of high school before Roz's mom had needed almost full-time care.

Dave spotted Caprice first. Standing, he smiled. "We were catching up. How are you, Caprice?"

Now and then she saw Dave around town at the Koffee Klatch or at a community event. Also a business owner he sold garage doors. His store was located on the edge of the downtown area. Actually, Caprice had been meaning to stop in to talk to him about a new garage door. But the errand never rose to the top of her to-do list.

She motioned him to be seated again, though she appreciated the chivalry. "I'm . . . good." Actually she was good for the most part. If it hadn't been for what she'd encountered upstairs—

"Dave and I were just remembering the homecoming dance senior year," Roz remarked, bringing her up to speed.

Now Caprice recalled the wayward fact that the dance had been Roz and Dave's first date. A video played in her mind of that day more than fifteen years ago. "Craig and I started with the football game that afternoon and our date was a bust. He complained about everything the team did wrong all during the dance."

"He has his doctorate now, I hear." Dave sat again and adjusted his tie. "Maybe he'll come east again for next year's reunion."

"Fifteen years," Roz murmured. "That's hard to believe."

Yes, it was.

"Besides catching up, I was just telling Roz I saw Charlie Flannigan at a comedy club in Harrisburg last month," Dave said. "He was actually funny."

Charlie had been their class clown. His chosen career made sense. When Roz smiled, Caprice could tell she was enjoying this catch-up conversation. Maybe Caprice was simply a coward, but she wasn't going to drag her friend away from chatting about old times to inform her that her husband might be having an affair. That could wait until they had quiet time to really discuss it.

"Did you need me for something?" Roz asked her, ready to hop up.

Quickly, Caprice shook her head and motioned her to relax. "No. We're good. I even passed a couple upstairs who seem interested in the house. Everything's under control."

After a "It was good seeing you" to Dave and a re-assuring smile for Roz, Caprice headed for the kitchen, her heart heavy for her friend and anxious about what she had to tell her.

Did she really have to spill what she'd seen?

When Caprice left the Winslows two hours later, Ted had his arm around Roz's waist. And they were conferencing with Denise. What was Caprice supposed to do? Stick around, pull Roz aside, and tell her about that kiss?

Maybe it was simply none of her business. Maybe she should stay out of it. Maybe she needed some time and space to think about it. Roz and Ted certainly might want to pretend they were living in Camelot, but they weren't. Perhaps it had been the case once. But if Ted was the type of man to kiss another woman when his own wife was downstairs, had he done the same thing before?

Once a scoundrel, always a scoundrel, her nana would say. Nana was probably right.

Pulling into her driveway, Caprice pressed the button on the remote control on her visor, and the garage door squeaked up. She should really visit Dave Harding's store and choose a new garage door.

By the time she climbed the step from her garage to the back porch and unlocked the kitchen door, Dylan was barking, voicing his disapproval that she'd been gone so long.

After she switched on the kitchen light, she let her purse fall to the counter. Stooping, she gathered him up for his usual welcome hug. Ruffling the fur behind his ears and leaning her cheek against his neck, she felt his little heart beating overtime.

"Calm down," she soothed. "Did Sophia watch over you like she was supposed to?"

At that moment, Sophia answered her by moseying into the kitchen and meowing in indignation that Caprice would think she'd shirk her duties.

"You didn't let Dylan get into my closet, did you? I don't want to find another of my favorite shoes with chew marks on the toe."

Sophia just gave her one of those slanted-eye

looks a cat gives her mistress when said mistress is being absurd. Reaching her front paws forward, she stretched into a perfect yoga position. Well, perfect for a cat. Caprice wished she could do that stretch so well. She liked yoga and had faithfully taken a class last year. But her time now was just too limited.

Opening the door, she lowered Dylan to the porch and watched him scamper down the steps to the patio and lawn. After church tomorrow, she needed to clean up the yard and mow the grass. With the schedule she'd been keeping, she might have to find someone to help with mowing and pruning this year. She would still plant her own flowers. The forsythia as well as the double-ruffled daffodils were fading now, and soon the pink and purple tulips would be too. The weather was supposed to turn cloudy and gray tomorrow afternoon, but beginning-of-May showers would add vibrancy and lushness to her yard.

Deciding to give Dylan a bit of freedom to run and let off steam, she opened a can of Sophia's favorite good-for-cats food. She snacked on a specialty dry food, but she enjoyed canned for her main course. Dylan, on the other hand, often gobbled up some of last night's leftovers in a healthy mix. Whenever Bella was around to witness their eating habits, she often groused that Caprice cared about what her animals ate as much as Bella cared about what her children ate. That was probably true.

For the next half hour, Caprice's pets kept her

mind off Roz as she fed them and sat at the kitchen table while they ate.

"Nikki did a great job on the medieval-themed food," she relayed to Dylan and Sophia, quite seriously. "I can always count on her to make an open house a success."

She hadn't had a chance to thank Nikki before she'd left. Tearing down was as strenuous as setting up. But she'd call her in a few days. After all, next weekend was their monthly dinner at their parents' house, as well as Mother's Day, and they'd have to coordinate what they were bringing. They all cooked except Vince. He usually opted to bring the wine.

After both Dylan and Sophia had finished—it didn't take long—Caprice picked up their dishes, did a preliminary wash, and tucked them into the dishwasher. She was on her way upstairs to change clothes when her cell phone played the early Beatles' tune. Taking if from her skirt pocket, she checked the screen and smiled. She must have conjured up her brother.

"How was the open house?" he asked without a preliminary greeting.

Vince liked to give the impression he was a devil-may-care bachelor whose mind, when he wasn't handling real estate settlements or divorces or writing wills, was on nothing heavier than having a good time. However, underneath that attitude was a guy who cared.

"Did Mom tell you about it?"

"Nope. I saw it in the paper. How was the turnout?"

"Hefty. But we needed people who came for more than the food."

"That house is a monstrosity."

"You've never been inside!"

"Just from the description in the *Kismet Crier* I could tell. I'd never want to live that far out of town, either."

Vince lived in one of the oldest buildings in Kismet, in the center of town. A vintage school had been reconstructed into modern condos. He was a stone's throw from his law office, a corner deli, and a theater that ran old movies. "If you had a family, you might change your mind."

"I have a family. They're enough to handle. How about you? Did you pick up anyone to date at the shindig?"

"I don't pick up men." She knew her voice held an edge because Vince was always hinting she was too insecure to ask a guy out. The truth was, she didn't want to ask a guy out. She wanted him to ask her.

"One of these days, Caprice, you're going to realize romance is a dream, and reality means you have to settle."

Settle? She'd never just settle.

Yet when she thought about Roz and how happy she'd been before and right after she'd married Ted, Caprice wondered how a woman did make sure she was choosing the right guy. How did she make sure a man shared the same values and loyalties? Again she remembered Travis and their painful breakup. Painful for her, anyway.

"You're too quiet. What's wrong? Usually when I say something like that you're all over me with protests."

"Then why do you say it?"

"Just to get you riled up."

She could hear the smile in his voice. "I have something on my mind."

Since Vince was a lawyer and knew how to listen, he waited in case she wanted to talk about it. But she couldn't talk about it. She had to figure out the right thing to do on her own.

"I did have a reason for calling," he said after a long silence.

She'd guessed as much. Whereas she and Nikki and Bella called each other just to hear the sound of a sister's voice, Vince—like many men she'd come in contact with—was goal-oriented. The old "hunter" versus "gatherer" mentality. Vince was definitely a "hunter." Now she waited.

"So what are you giving Mom for her birthday? She always says she likes my flowers, but I ought to step up for a change and make some kind of effort."

"I'm sure she'll appreciate whatever you give her. Bella and I found a Fostoria bowl to go with the set Nana handed down to Mom. I asked Isaac to keep a lookout for other pieces in the set. Mom could probably use a few of the plates. If he finds more, are you interested?"

"Sure. But if he doesn't find anything—"

"You don't want to go back to flowers. I get it. I've also been considering throwing a surprise party. I don't think she's ever had one. But that's a lot of work. We'll all have to pitch in. Can you commit?"

"You think I can't commit?"

"Can you?"

"You bet I can. If you need me to help, I'll make the time."

"Not if but when."

"When you need me to help, I'll make the time."

"You'll have to pinkie-swear the next time I see you."

"Caprice—" His exasperation was evident.

"This will mean a lot to Mom."

"I know."

Caprice was well aware she had a trust issue. She expected men not to keep their word. Ever since Craig had left Kismet without looking back, after just an e-mail from California informing her they were through, she'd doubted any man's sensitivity, let alone his ability to commit. Ever since she and Travis had become engaged and then he'd decided to reunite with his ex-wife, ever since Vince had forgotten her birthday year after year, been late for Bella and Joe's wedding, and even missed Megan's christening, Caprice simply didn't depend on men.

The only exception was her dad.

"We can have a meeting to figure out exactly what we want to do," she suggested.

"Sounds good. Finding a convenient time to meet will be the challenge. Caprice, did I ever tell you you're a great little sister?"

"Once or twice," she admitted with a laugh. "What kind of wine are you bringing to dinner next Sunday? Something special for Mother's Day?"

"I haven't decided yet. But it will be good."

She knew it would be.

After she clicked off her phone, she realized Vince had taken her mind off Roz and Ted. For a few minutes.

Making a decision, Caprice knew she and Roz needed to talk face to face.

That talk was postponed a few days. After the open house, Ted had decided to take Roz with him to New York City. He had a meeting, but he'd bought tickets for a show she'd wanted to see. So it was Wednesday evening when Caprice drove to Roz's, still unsure what she was going to say. What if Ted had been charming and loving on the trip? Would Roz believe her?

Gray clouds hung low in the sky as Caprice arrived, around five P.M. She was really hoping Ted would not be home. She couldn't very well ask Roz if Ted would be around because her friend would ask questions. Caprice was prepared to answer them face to face—but not over the phone. Of course, the house was big enough that she and Roz could find a private spot and then Caprice could fade away if Roz wanted to have a confrontation with her husband.

Parking to the side of the garage since she might be there for a while, Caprice made her way across the driveway to the circular drive and front door. However, when she rang the doorbell and the melodious bongs reverberated through the house, no one answered.

After waiting at least two minutes, she pushed the button again. More bongs. No one came.

So she tried the knob and the door opened. She might have imagined it, but it felt as if cold air rushed out. Shivering, she wondered if the late-day dampness had caused the eerie sensation.

"Caprice!"

Hearing her name and recognizing Roz's voice, she turned toward the extended driveway and saw her friend jogging up the brick-patterned asphalt. She'd always admired Roz's dedication to running. It surely kept her in shape. But just the thought of sweat and sore legs, knees, and feet made Caprice cringe. She hated to sweat. If anything, she liked to swim the best. But that was in summer. She supposed she could join the Kismet health club, Shape Up, because they had a pool. But she was always too busy to check it out and decide if she wanted to belong.

As she watched Roz run up the driveway, her slim legs in shorts all curvy and muscled, her T-shirt molding to her breasts like every woman might want a T-shirt to cling, Caprice knew she should give serious consideration to joining that club.

"Sorry, I'm late. My timing isn't as good as it usually is. I got distracted and went a little farther than usual, trying to work off those meals we enjoyed in New York. We had such a good time. It was almost like . . . when we were first married."

Just what Caprice had feared. Ted had romanced his wife on this trip. Instead of responding to Roz's restored outlook on her marriage, Caprice said, "You're not late. I'm a bit early." And she was. She wanted to get this over with. She hadn't slept well since the open house, thinking about the exact words she was going to use.

Roz went to the door. "You should have gone in."

"I rang the bell, but Ted didn't answer. Is he home?" She held her breath, hoping Roz would say "no."

To Caprice's dismay, Roz responded, "He should be. We're going to the Murphys' for cocktails. Sean Murphy is an important business contact. His financial firm holds PA Pharm's retirement accounts."

After Roz pushed open the heavy door, Caprice stepped inside.

"Ted," Roz called, her voice seeming to ricochet off the walls.

There was no answer.

"Maybe he's in his office or upstairs. I'll try the intercom."

Caprice's sweater coat swayed along her calves, and her lime-green bell-bottoms swished around her ankles as she walked with Roz, readying herself for the conversation she was about to have. The right words were still eluding her. Not "right" words, but less destructive words.

Roz turned to the left, leading Caprice down the hall. "I want to check his office first."

They stopped in the doorway of a very masculine room, all leather, with stubby carpet and a hardwood hutch with geode bookends holding what looked to be volumes of pharmaceutical guides. Caprice hadn't done much to this room since it was sparsely furnished to start with. She'd added a plaid throw over the back of the burgundy leather love seat, a ficus plant in one corner, and two needlepoint proverbs above a credenza.

Crossing to the intercom on the wall, Roz spoke into it. "Ted, if you're in the house, Caprice is here. Can you let me know where you are?"

Silence met Roz's suggestion.

With a shake of her head, she left her husband's office and continued down the hall that led to a sunroom. The door to both the sunroom and the door leading outside were standing open.

"I don't know why he left it open. I guess he went for a walk around the lake. If he doesn't return soon, he's going to get wet," Roz said with a smile. "But he needs the exercise to work off some of his stress. Come on. Let's get a glass of wine. Denise called while we were away and said there are two couples who seemed most interested in the house."

Anxiety knotting her stomach, Caprice resolved that once they were seated in the kitchen, wine glasses in hand, she would broach the subject of Valerie Swanson.

Returning to the foyer, Roz stopped. "I had two messages on the house phone about Nikki's food. I gave the women her number."

"She'll appreciate the business."

"Is she still cooking out of her condo?"

"She sure is. Although she's doing well, she doesn't want to add on more overhead at this stage. I can't blame her."

As Caprice and Roz headed for the kitchen, they had to pass the sword room. Caprice didn't give it much notice . . . just kept walking. But Roz suddenly stopped.

Caprice turned around.

Roz stood in the doorway, looking puzzled.

"Is something wrong?"

"The curio case is open and—"

Roz took a step inside and . . . screamed. It was a blood-curdling scream that shook Caprice to her core.

Hurrying to her friend, she stepped into the room and saw—

She couldn't believe what she saw. Ted Winslow lay on the floor, one of his prized daggers protruding from his back.

Chapter Four

Caprice's knees shook in her bell-bottom slacks as red, blue, and white streams from light bars atop patrol cars flashed across the Winslows' yard. She stood near one of those patrol cars almost at the entrance to the driveway, aware of the yards and yards of yellow crime-scene tape. She couldn't shake the vision of Ted, blood staining the back of his white oxford shirt, the tall dagger from the wrought-iron stand next to the desk plunged deeply into his body.

Roz had crumpled to the floor beside her husband as Caprice had dialed 911.

Emergency vans and other law enforcement vehicles had zoomed onto the property at intervals. An officer from the Kismet P.D. had guided them outside and down the driveway, needing to clear the crime scene. He'd also separated Caprice from Roz and fingerprinted her. After the paramedics left—they'd pronounced Ted dead—a detective had questioned Caprice while another questioned Roz. Now Roz was leaning against the forensic team's van as if it was holding her up in the May night, which was turning cooler, damper, and drearier.

Spotting the Kismet P.D.'s chief of police, Mack Powalski, Caprice felt somewhat reassured. Her dad had gone to school with him. He had even attended their family gatherings now and then and was often around when she was growing up. She'd seen him briefly after he'd arrived.

Maybe she should call her brother. Did she and Roz need a lawyer?

No. She'd watched too many crime shows . . . read too many suspense-filled novels.

Yet this was real life. She was standing outside a house where a murder had been committed. A man she'd known was dead.

Checking her watch, she noticed Roz's questioning had gone on for more than an hour. She was standing too far away to overhear. The chief had suggested she could sit in the patrol car—warrants were being obtained to search her and Roz's cars— but she'd decided to stay as close to Roz as she could.

What were the chief and the detective talking to Roz about? It didn't take that long to describe what had happened.

Finally, the detective put his small notebook into his pocket and the chief walked with Roz toward

Caprice. Her friend looked as if she was going to collapse.

Caprice wrapped her arm around Roz's shoulders. "Are you okay?"

Roz shook her head, and Caprice knew she'd asked a stupid question. Of course Roz wasn't okay. She was shivering. Her lips even appeared a little blue, and her face was as pale as the white marble in the Winslow foyer.

"Mrs. Winslow isn't feeling well," the chief explained. "She says she's light-headed. We'll continue this discussion later. I can call the paramedics and have them come back, or you could take her to the ER at the hospital—"

"I . . . can't . . ." Her friend's gaze slid up the drive to the house.

"You can't what?" Caprice asked gently.

"I can't leave. Ted's—" Roz just pointed to the front of the house, and Caprice felt so sorry for her.

"There's nothing you can do."

Roz's eyes were huge. "He's—"

Caprice suspected Roz was in shock. She couldn't even string a sentence together. Is that why her interview had taken so long?

Roz's shivering grew worse, and Caprice saw, as the chief had, that she needed medical attention. "I'll take her to the urgent care center. We shouldn't have to wait as long as at the hospital. However . . . I can't drive my car," she murmured.

"No, you can't," he agreed.

"I can call Nikki to pick us up." Caprice was already pulling her phone from her pocket. Hitting speed dial, she called her sister. She would be here in ten minutes . . . if she was home.

Nikki's small, cobalt-blue sedan had racked up 80,000 miles in fewer than five years but was still reliable.

"Heat," Caprice ordered as she tucked Roz into the passenger side and climbed in the back, out of the fine drizzle that had just started.

Nikki didn't say a word as she carefully made a K-turn in front of the crime scene. The police had blocked off an area in front of the Winslow property so reporters and news vans would keep their distance. She mumbled, "I can't believe this."

"Neither can we," Caprice assured her, watching Roz closely.

After a quarter of a mile, Caprice noticed a vehicle following them. A reporter? She moved forward on her seat. With the heater fan blowing and windshield wipers swiping the glass, she whispered to Nikki, "Lose the car on your tail."

After glancing in the rearview mirror, Nikki nodded.

On the road leading away from Reservoir Heights, obviously mindful of a winding side road, Nikki made a sharp turn onto it, sped up, and swiftly made another turn onto a hard-to-see gravel access road that led to the rear of one of the properties. She shut off her lights.

"You know this area?" Caprice asked her sister.

"I've had catering jobs out here. Besides, I like to explore back roads in case traffic gets tied up. You know me. I try to always have Plan B."

The car that had been following sped by. Nikki waited until the vehicle was out of sight, then took the same road more slowly.

Roz didn't seem to notice as Nikki took another detour and emerged again beside one of the huge houses. Quickly she pulled out onto the road to town, checking her rearview mirror. Caprice could see no one followed them.

Roz was too still, staring straight ahead, and Caprice felt she had to make contact. Maybe if she could get her talking . . . "Roz, are you still light-headed?"

Her friend didn't respond, so she tried something different. Maybe they should talk about what happened. "What did they ask you?"

"Jones." Roz said the name, still staring ahead.

At first Caprice didn't understand, then she did. She must be in a state of shock herself because she hadn't recognized the name of the detective immediately. They'd introduced themselves when they'd arrived. Detective Carstead, the friendlier one, had interviewed her. Detective Jones had interviewed Roz. "What did Detective Jones ask you?"

Roz just shook her head.

Chafing at her friend's inability to express herself—a condition so unlike Roz—Caprice tapped Nikki's shoulder to speed up. With that sisterly communication they'd always enjoyed, she did.

"Did you tell him what we saw?"

Roz wrapped her arms around herself.

Maybe she was still cold, a cold the car heat couldn't penetrate.

At the town limits, when Nikki waited at a red light, Caprice had a flash again of Ted's dead body, the smell of blood and—

She closed her eyes. All of it was so stark . . . so awful. If she was this rattled, she could hardly imagine how Roz was feeling, with grief settling in on top of the horror of finding her husband dead. Not just dead—murdered.

Murdered.

Caprice couldn't quite wrap her mind around it—not only Ted's death but the fact that Roz's house was now a crime scene. She wanted to ask Roz a bunch of questions. After all, that was Caprice's nature. She especially wanted to know what questions the chief and the detective had asked. But Roz didn't appear to be in a condition to discuss anything. That's exactly why they'd let her postpone more questioning.

The urgent care center was located on the north side of Kismet. To Caprice's relief, Nikki took a few side streets to bypass traffic lights and zipped over

to Hickory Boulevard. Most of the streets in the
north end were named after trees.

Yes, both she and Nikki had a tendency to drive
too fast through town. They were both on the road
a lot to and from appointments, meeting with
wholesalers and suppliers, scouting out sales and
good deals. Usually staying within five miles of the
speed limit, Caprice hadn't been ticketed in years.
Tonight, just let a patrol car try to stop them. From
the looks of Roz, this was an emergency.

The front parking lot at the urgent care center
was practically empty, though a few cars were
parked in front of the pharmacy next door. If she
remembered correctly, the staff parked in the back.

"Go around back," she directed Nikki. Just in
case someone had managed to trail them, Nikki's
car wouldn't be visible out back.

The building, with its white siding and peaked
roof, was only about a year old. The pharmacy
beside it was the only one in Kismet that was open
until ten P.M. More emergency care companies were
moving into the area as real competition to hospital ER services. This one was almost full-service,
with a lab, X-ray equipment, a doctor and nurse on
staff 24/7, and a physician's assistant who filled in
when needed. Bella brought her kids here when
they fell or got sick in the middle of the night.
She'd always been pleased with the care and service
she'd received.

While Caprice had been waiting for Roz's statement to be taken, she'd thought about texting
her sisters, maybe even Vince. But she hadn't
wanted to shock them. Now Nikki knew. There
would be plenty of time to tell everyone else what
had happened. Or at least some of it. The detective had warned her not to give away details, and
she guessed Detective Jones had done the same
with Roz.

Parking between a red Honda and a white Ford
Focus, Nikki didn't switch off her wipers and
heater. "I'll wait here. If anyone finds me who
shouldn't, I'll drive off, then text you."

Roz still looked shell-shocked, and Caprice
squeezed Nikki's shoulder in appreciation before
she climbed out.

Thank goodness Caprice hadn't told Roz about
Ted and Valerie. She'd have that weighing on her
along with everything else. With a sense of ur-
gency, she rounded the car's hood and opened
Roz's door.

Her friend just sat there.

Ducking inside the car, Caprice unfastened Roz's
seat belt, then rubbed her arm. "We're going to see
the doctor to make sure you're okay. Can you come
with me?"

Finally, reacting to Caprice's voice, Roz looked
up at her. "Ted is . . . dead."

"Yes," Caprice responded because Roz's voice

held a hint of uncertainty, as if it had all been a dream.

Roz's gaze met hers, and tears welled up in her eyes.

Caprice was glad they were here because she wasn't exactly sure what to do next. After she took Roz's elbow, she helped her out of the car. Roz let Caprice guide her, and she was thankful for that as she pulled open the heavy rear door that led into a hallway and the waiting room. She thought she heard a bell ring inside.

Security measure?

In the waiting room, Caprice noticed the green and tan tile, the cream wallpaper with its green splashes in abstract designs. The color combination was probably supposed to be welcoming, but it still projected "clinical." Two reception windows opened on opposite sides of the waiting area, where upholstered chairs with tan and green tweed fabric offered a little comfort. The glass window to the left was topped by a sign in thick black letters— LAB. The sign on the window across from it read PHYSICIAN SERVICES.

Taking Roz's arm, Caprice led her to the clipboard and sign-in sheet for a physician's services.

The receptionist shoved the window open. "I can register you now. Name?"

After Caprice gave Roz's name, the older woman with frizzy gray hair asked, "Do you have your insurance card?"

Caprice hadn't thought about that. Roz didn't even have her purse.

But Roz seemed to rouse herself as she reached into the pocket of her running pants and pulled out a slim card keeper/change purse. "I carry this and my phone. I once fell . . ." Her voice trailed off.

What was she remembering? Caprice wondered. Did the memory involve Ted?

While the receptionist waited, Roz's fingers fumbled. She couldn't seem to pluck out the right card.

Caprice took the wallet and found Roz's insurance card between her driver's license and credit card.

After the receptionist put information into the computer and printed out a terms-of-service agreement for Roz to sign, she motioned for them to have a seat.

A few minutes later, an LPN showed them to the cubicle with the requisite exam table, taupe counter, and sink, where she asked why they were there and jotted down notes. She'd just asked Roz if she was taking any medication when there was a sharp rap on the door. When it opened, Caprice's nervous system seemed to go on overdrive.

Adrenaline was already speeding through her body because of finding a dead man, outmaneuvering someone who might be following them, and worrying about Roz as they'd rushed here.

Now as she gazed up into very blue eyes, she had a weird feeling in her tummy. As she canvassed the handsome, square-jawed face and rumpled blond hair, she guessed maybe she was in shock like Roz.

"I'm Seth Randolph—doctor on call tonight."

His smile was friendly rather than practiced, and Caprice liked him right away. She wasn't swayed by good looks, was she? It was his medical skills that mattered.

Since Caprice got around—from stores to professionals to her many clients—she'd heard there was a handsome new doctor working here. The tidbit that had burned up the Kismet gossip grapevine was memorable because he was supposedly single.

Recovering her good sense if not her equilibrium, Caprice stretched out her hand. "Caprice De Luca. This is my friend Rosalind Winslow. She's had a . . . shock."

Seth Randolph's grip was strong as he shook her hand. His blue eyes held hers for a heartbeat before he turned to Roz. "It's good to meet you—" He checked the form. "Mrs. Winslow. Were you in an accident?"

Roz shook her head but didn't say any more. Rather, she stared at the floor as if she didn't want to think about why she was here or recall any of it.

The physician glanced at Caprice for an explanation.

There was no way to sugarcoat this, so Caprice blurted out, "We found Roz's husband. He was dead. Murdered. She gave a statement to the police, but the longer it went . . . She didn't feel well . . . was light-headed . . . couldn't seem to answer questions. So I brought her here."

The compassion in Dr. Randolph's eyes was genuine as he pulled his stethoscope from his lab coat pocket and hung it around his neck. "I'm so sorry for your loss." After a respectful silence, he said, "Let's draw some blood, do a little exam, and make sure everything is working as it should be."

As Caprice watched them, Dr. Randolph moved efficiently and quickly. He put data into the computer while the tech drew a blood sample. Then he took Roz's blood pressure and pulse and listened to her heart. As he moved around the table, Caprice was aware of his lean, basketball player–like physique, his broad shoulders.

He spoke to Roz as he shone a penlight into her eyes. "How long were you married?"

"Almost five years," Roz murmured. "We were going to fly to Cannes next month for our anniversary."

The doctor must have had magic powers because that was the longest sentence she'd heard from Roz since they'd stepped into Ted's sword room.

"Have you been there before?" the physician asked nonchalantly.

It was apparent he was trying to bring some kind of normalcy back into Roz's world.

She nodded. "Ted always said I was—" She stopped as if maybe she shouldn't mention Ted's name.

"What did he say?" the doctor asked with interest, obviously trying to keep her talking.

"He said I was a celebrity hound."

"Why did he say that?" Picking up the mallet in a stand on the counter, he moved to the foot of the table to check Roz's reflexes.

"I read *Star Spotters*' online blog. It listed where celebrities were staying, if they were on yachts, sailing."

"You tried to spot them?"

"Sometimes."

Obviously observant, he asked, "Are you a jogger?"

She nodded again.

"When did you last eat or drink?"

"Had a protein bar at lunch. Water before I left to run before—"

Going to the door, he opened it and called, "Jenny? Can of juice and crackers in here."

The LPN was there almost instantly.

Caprice was thankful this was apparently a slow night for urgent care. "Quiet night?" she asked as Dr. Randolph popped the juice can tab and handed it to Roz.

"Drink that."

Roz did as she was told without a murmur, which was telling in itself.

As the doctor's gaze met Caprice's, he gave her a half smile. "We're not busy right now. Give it five minutes. Eat the crackers too," he directed. "Do you always have low blood pressure?"

She shrugged as she pulled open the snack. "I haven't been to the doctor for a while."

"You're sure you're not on any medication?"

"None."

"Are you allergic to anything?"

She shook her head, then nibbled on the crackers.

"I think you're dehydrated. Your sugar plummeted because you hadn't eaten. On top of that you had a terrible shock. You need to go home, drink lots of fluids, and eat. You shouldn't be alone."

"I can't go home," Roz said. "The police are there."

Caprice was quick to jump in. "You're coming home with me. You can stay as long as necessary."

"A new Chinese restaurant opened up down the block—the Peking Duck. The takeout is great," he offered as a solution to the food problem. "That is, if you like Chinese."

"I do," Caprice said. "But I cook. I'll make minestrone to ward off the chill."

The look of assessment Dr. Randolph gave Caprice was a bit unnerving. He seemed to be trying to gauge exactly what kind of person she was.

Finally he said, "I'm glad Mrs. Winslow has someone to take care of her tonight. I'm going to give you a prescription for sleeping pills. Just a week's supply." To Roz he said, "If you need more than that, you should see your family doctor."

A commotion suddenly erupted outside the door. A child was crying.

"Quiet spell over," he said.

Roz had finished the snack and juice. Dr. Randolph took the wrapper and can and stowed it in the trash. "If anything sinister shows up on the blood work, someone will call you."

He helped Roz down from the table, then his gaze met Caprice's again. "It was good to meet you, Miss De Luca."

He'd remembered her name. And maybe he was trying out the "Miss" to see if she'd correct him.

There was nothing to correct.

The next minute he was gone, moving on to another medical problem. They'd be the proverbial ships passing in the night.

Such was life.

"Let's get your prescription filled and go home," she said to Roz, dropping her arm around her friend's shoulders again. Maybe they could help each other recover from what they'd seen. Maybe she could somehow comfort Roz and help her start the grieving process.

"Do you want to come in?" Caprice asked as Nikki pulled into her driveway.

"No, it's probably better if I don't. You and Roz can talk. I'll call you tomorrow."

After a quick hug for her sister, Caprice led Roz to her front door.

As always, Dylan was ecstatic at anyone's arrival.

The main thing Caprice loved about dogs was their unconditional friendship and love. Cats expressed those same qualities in a quieter, more independent way.

Now as Dylan yipped, then took time to sniff at Roz's sneakers, Caprice saw her friend was distracted by him, and that was a good thing. Roz bent down to him and ruffled his fur in such a way that Dylan looked up at her with adoring eyes.

"He's cute," she said. "I know you told me he was. I guess I just didn't imagine what he actually looked like."

"I'll let him out. Why don't you curl up on the couch while I start the minestrone."

After a quick glance around, Roz sighed. "Your house invites anyone to come right in. I know you changed ours so it would have more of that . . ."

The word "ours" seemed to stand out. Roz and Ted. There was no couple anymore. Roz's expression changed and became so sad. But she didn't cry. As she took a few steps toward the sofa, Dylan started to follow her.

Caprice snapped her fingers—a signal he knew now—and he stopped, turned toward her and wagged his tail. "C'mon," she said. "You can sit with her after you come back in."

As Roz sagged onto the sofa, Dylan followed Caprice to the kitchen.

Nana's recipe for minestrone soup was vegetable soup at its finest. Like her mom and grandmother,

Caprice kept produce in her fridge. She tried to visit Kismet's Grocery Fresh Market at least once a week.

Waiting patiently, she watched Dylan hurriedly do what he had to do. Afterward, he scampered inside as if he knew Roz needed him. Caprice suspected that Sophia was curled on the office chair, waiting for her owner's nightly check of e-mail. She'd fed them both before she'd left.

Dylan ran to the living room, where Caprice saw him jump up on the sofa, yip once, then sit beside Roz.

Caprice couldn't help thinking about everything that had happened as she washed up, then pulled out a pack of ground beef she'd bought, expecting to make burgers. Along with that, she picked up endive, a pack of grated carrots, and a bag of shredded cabbage. She found a zucchini in her produce drawer and yanked frozen green beans from the freezer. As she set everything on the counter, she ran over the murder scene in her mind.

The glass case where Ted had kept his most valuable collectibles had been standing open. Did that mean the murderer had robbery on his mind? From what she could recall, the case hadn't been emptied. How many pieces had been taken? Any? Maybe the murderer had just surprised Ted in that room. But that meant he or she would have had to have broken in. Could a woman have done this?

Caprice moved to the pantry, where she grabbed

an onion from a basket and wiggled a clove of garlic from a cheesecloth bag. There were so many questions about what had happened to Ted. Would they ever have the answers? Another trip to the pantry closet produced beef and chicken broth, and cans of beans, diced tomatoes, and tomato juice. Then she began washing and chopping.

A few minutes later, she poured two tablespoons of olive oil into the bottom of the soup pot and added the ground beef. With satisfaction, she noted its sizzle. When it was almost browned, she added the chopped onion, grated the garlic, pinched in the red pepper, and added the other spices, tomatoes, and all the liquid. The aroma wafted through the kitchen. A hearty soup was just what Roz needed to ward off the damp chill and brace her for whatever came next.

No, food couldn't solve problems, but its preparation could show caring and love.

After the soup came to a boil, Caprice added the cut endive, plopped the lid on the pot and set the burner on simmer.

When she went to the living room, Roz was staring into space, petting Dylan, who had sprawled across her lap. Caprice sank into the dark-fuchsia upholstered chair nearest the multicolored, narrowly striped sofa.

"It's okay to cry," she said. "You can't keep holding everything in."

"I can't cry," Roz said as if she were confessing the worst sin. "I just feel numb."

Curling her legs under her, Caprice asked, "Do you have any idea who might have done this?"

For some reason, the face of Valerie Swanson flashed in her head. She couldn't tell Roz about Ted and Valerie kissing. Definitely not tonight.

"Ted could be abrasive," Roz admitted. "Sometimes even mean. But usually he was charming and considerate."

"You mean with you?"

"Yes," Roz answered quickly.

"Roz, he wasn't charming and considerate when I was there before his business trip. Remember?" Imagining wives could have a selective memory, she was pointing out the truth.

Roz looked as if she was going to protest, but then she murmured, "We were going through a rough patch. All couples have rough patches. And in New York, everything was almost perfect again."

Almost perfect, Caprice thought. Could that even be possible?

Before she could delve deeper, her cell phone played "She Loves You." Pulling it from her pocket, Caprice intended to let the call go to voice mail. But then she saw her assistant's number on the screen. Juan Hidalgo handled her moving crews and painting contracts.

"Excuse me a minute," she said to Roz. This late on Sunday night there must be a problem.

"Hi, Juan. What's up?"

"I have good news and I have bad news. The good news is that Denise did a walk-through of the Koontz's house this morning and priced it twenty thousand higher than we expected."

The Koontz's house, which was located in York, was vacant. That had made staging it relatively easy. The fact that Caprice's staging expertise had added that much value pleased her immensely.

"But . . ." Juan continued. "I was in an ATV accident this afternoon and broke my ankle."

"Oh, Juan. Your ankle? How bad is it?"

"The doc mentioned putting in a pin or two. Surgery is Friday."

"Do you have help so you don't have to be on it?" She knew Juan. He'd still try to do everything himself.

"My sister is here. You of all people know how sisters like to help."

She could hear the smile in his voice and wondered how much pain he was in. "Are you on painkillers?"

"Yep." He paused. "Caprice, I'm sorry about this. I won't be able to move furniture around for a while."

"Of course, you won't. You tell your sister if you don't behave or if she needs help, she should call me."

"She's going to stay with me after surgery too, to make sure I can get around. Don't worry. I'll be fine. The bigger question is—who's going to take my place?"

Without her right-hand man, what *was* she going to do? "I'll figure out something. You just take care of yourself. And ask your sister to call me to let me know the surgery went okay. Got it?"

"Got it."

As Caprice ended the call, she hoped Juan would take care of himself. If she had to call a temp agency to hire help, that's what she'd do.

Chapter Five

"What's wrong?" Roz asked.

"I lost my assistant who helps move furniture, lay rugs, hang paintings. He broke his ankle."

"My gardener can probably help you. He's sort of an all-around handyman. He's done those things for me." She fished her phone out of her pocket and stared down at it. "I should call Monty anyway and tell him what happened."

"Are you sure you're up to that?"

"Everybody is going to know soon. Ted's parents are gone, and he was an only child. I should call our neighbors. Sheila and I run together sometimes. And I should probably call Chad Thompson at PA Pharm. I just can't believe—" Roz's voice caught.

"Come with me to the kitchen. We'll see if the soup's ready for the pasta. The calls can wait a little longer."

"No," Roz responded. "I have to make them.

Monty probably won't be too upset. He and Ted didn't get along very well. In fact, they had an argument right before the open house."

Caprice's curious antennae seemed to zoom up. "Do you know what about?"

"Ted was going to cut Monty's hours."

Thinking about Ted's supposed problems at work, his affair—or whatever it was—with Valerie, his decision to sell the house, Caprice asked, "Were you having financial problems?"

Roz sighed. "The truth is—I don't know. Ted handled the bills and investments. But last month he did deposit less in my checking account than he usually does."

"Without discussing it with you?"

"We hadn't been discussing much. And when he returned from his business trip before the open house and seemed in a better mood, I didn't want to rock an already unsteady boat. The same was true when we went to New York."

To tell her about Valerie or not to tell her? Caprice just couldn't make herself do it. Not tonight. Not when Roz was dealing with so much else.

"Do you want privacy to make your calls?"

As if the dog gave her comfort, Roz kept her hand on Dylan's furry little body. "That probably would be best."

"I'll warm up some of Nana's bread to go with the soup. Take your time. If you need me, yell."

Caprice left Roz in the living room, wondering if

Roz would hold up or collapse under the weight of all that had happened tonight.

Roz looked as if a stiff wind had blown her around and weakened her as she came into the kitchen.

"Eat," Caprice encouraged, setting a bowl of steaming minestrone and a thick slice of home-made bread at her place.

"I'm really not hungry—"

Caprice just gave her a look.

Dylan squatted next to Roz's chair as she sat and picked up her spoon.

Silence reigned until Caprice broke it. "How did Monty react?"

After a bite of bread Roz answered, "I'm not sure."

"I don't understand."

"He didn't seem shocked. He was very pragmatic. Just asked if I was going to keep him on. I told him I don't know what's going to happen. I'll need him to work on the grounds if I can't sell the house. But for now, he said he'd be glad to help you. You can give him a call."

"I will. When we're finished. Then we're going to my closet and find you some clothes—something to sleep in and something for tomorrow. You're taller and thinner than I am, but that won't matter with a nightshirt. And I have a couple of no-waist dresses that might work."

"I wonder when I'll be able to go home."

Caprice wished she knew. But she guessed Roz's nightmare was just beginning.

The following morning, a potential client said to Caprice, "Patty Colinstead told me to contract with you before I called a real estate agent." Marge Gentry seemed to want Caprice's reassurance that she'd done the right thing.

Patty had been one of Caprice's first staging clients, and her house had sold within a month. Marge looked to be about the same age, in her late forties, though her husband Grover was more than a dozen years older. "I believe that's the best strategy. Often an agent can see more potential after I've staged."

"You're known as a fluffer," Marge said as if she was proud she knew the term.

"A *house* fluffer," Caprice confirmed with a smile.

As she examined Marge's house in York, taking notes, she had trouble concentrating. Roz had looked pale this morning. Although she'd slept after taking the medication Dr. Randolph had prescribed for her, she still seemed tired and drawn. Yet she'd told Caprice she needed some alone time and she should keep her appointment. Nevertheless, Caprice was worried about her. She herself couldn't get the murder scene out of her head. The story on the news had been sensational but short—Ted Winslow had been stabbed in his home. There had been long camera shots of Roz's house. Caprice's car hadn't been visible tucked beside the garage.

Marge interrupted her introspection. "Grover said we should redo the kitchen before we sell. But all that money and mess. Is it necessary?"

Bringing her focus back to the task at hand, Caprice considered her initial assessment of the Gentry house. She always targeted the main areas that needed the most change. After considering those, the client chose a theme. This home, which was five thousand square feet and about twenty years old, didn't need to be brought up to date as much as it needed some polish.

"I'll write up a proposal and plan, which will include the most time spent on the kitchen and family room and overall de-cluttering. Are you prepared to sell or put into storage everything that isn't absolutely necessary?"

"I guess we are."

"That means furniture as well as personal belongings. We want a prospective buyer to see his or her family living here as soon as he or she steps inside. We'll do a virtual tour for the agent's Web site as well as choosing ten or twelve more exceptional photos to use for the MLS."

"Multiple Listing Service."

"Right," Caprice said approvingly. She glanced around the living room where they'd ended up. "You seem to like French country furniture. How about a theme like Country with Panache?"

"I think Grover would approve of that. He was afraid you'd want to do something more . . . unusual . . . like that Camelot house in Kismet. You know, the one where Ted Winslow was murdered. Can you imagine a killer in Kismet?"

"Every house has a distinctive character," Caprice explained to Marge, hoping to put the conversation back on the home-staging track rather than on murder. "I try to emphasize that."

"Grover and I went through the Winslow house on Sunday because we wanted to see what you could do. Mr. Winslow explained to Grover the history behind some of his . . . weapons. You know, all those swords and knives. I wasn't interested, so I looked around. Grover knew Ted because he's on the board of directors of PA Pharmaceuticals."

Grover Gentry was CEO of one of the largest air-conditioning companies in the state. "I see."

Marge didn't need much incentive to keep going. "He was shocked when he learned Ted Winslow was killed. Though he did say there had been dissension on the board last month. Something about expansion. Apparently Ted didn't want any part of it."

Why wouldn't Ted want to expand? The economic climate? Something more serious happening to the company?

"Did your husband say why?"

"I think Ted was concerned with pleasing shareholders and keeping their dividends stable."

That made sense. But why wouldn't the rest of the board want that too? Unless they thought even higher dividends were possible.

"Did you get the feeling Ted was respected and well liked?"

"I don't know about that. Grover once mentioned that Ted Winslow had a ruthless side."

"In business," Caprice said just to clarify.

"Well, I think he was known to fudge his golf score too. Didn't like landing in the rough."

Kismet's Country Squire Golf and Recreation Club had a course bigger communities would envy. They also had an elite clientele, and the members paid a hefty yearly fee to belong.

"Grover plays at Country Squire?"

"As a guest. I've passed Roz Winslow now and then when I've played tennis there. I can't imagine being in her shoes right now, wondering who did this awful thing. What if it was someone she knew?"

"What makes you think it might be?" Caprice was curious, and since the subject had been well and truly opened . . .

"Well, I would imagine a house like that would

have a security system. Not just anybody could get in easily."

Yet Caprice remembered the unlocked front door and the back door standing wide open. A security system couldn't be reliable if it wasn't turned on.

"And to be stabbed . . . I bet it was with one of his own swords. How ironic."

The best tack for Caprice to take was to remain silent, then return to the reason she was here. "I don't want to tie you up any longer than necessary today. Do you think you'll be able to remove yourself from the memories you have in this house so we can make the best changes to sell it? You're going to have to think of your house as a product."

"Grover has been telling me over and over that I need to do that. If we find the type of estate property he wants, where we can have horses, I think I'll be able to leave this behind. We didn't want to start looking until this sold."

"You mentioned not wanting to tear apart your kitchen. You don't have to. We can redesign it with paint, accessories, and an uncluttered look."

"We were impressed with your portfolio and the results you've accomplished," Marge assured her. "You seem to be able to do a lot with whatever budget your client gives you."

"I don't remodel, Marge. I redistribute, redesign, and give a buyer a chance to imagine herself in your home."

"I really do like the idea of Country with Panache."

Caprice could tell Marge was ready to sign on the dotted line. As she opened her briefcase to pull out a contract, her phone vibrated. She always turned off the ringtone when she was with a client.

Considering everything that had happened, she checked the number and said to Marge, "Excuse me for a minute." Since it was Roz's number, she had to take the call.

Extracting a contract from a manila folder, she set it before Marge. "This is my standard contract. If you'd like to look it over, I'll answer any questions you might have."

Then she stood, walked into the hall, and answered her phone. "Roz. Is everything all right?"

"No! It's not. Detective Jones called my cell. The police want a list of everything in the curio cabinet in the sword room, as well as a list of Ted's friends and colleagues. They also want to talk to me, and I don't know what to do. Do you think I should call a lawyer?"

In everyday life, reason told Caprice that innocent people had nothing to hide so they should answer questions freely. But . . . Caprice had read enough suspense novels and watched enough TV— especially the program with the adorably sexy, intuitive investigative consultant—to know even truthful answers could get a person in trouble if they became the target of the investigation. Better to be safe than very sorry.

"Do you have a lawyer in mind?"

"No! And I don't just want to finger someone in the yellow pages. Your brother's a lawyer. Could he help?"

"He's involved in family law, wills, and house settlements."

"That means he's all-purpose. At least I'd know he'd be honest."

"You don't know him."

"I know if he's a De Luca, he's honest."

"When does Detective Jones want you there?"

"Now. He wants me now. I suggested tomorrow, but he just snapped at me and asked if I want to help them catch my husband's killer. He made it sound as if I didn't go in right away, that I'd have a reason for waiting." Roz sounded desperate, and Caprice didn't blame her.

"I'll call Vince. Hold tight." She didn't check with Marge before she did.

First she called Vince's cell. The call went straight to voice mail, which meant he had his phone turned off. Next she called his office. The firm's office manager, Giselle Browning, answered. In her fifties, Giselle was efficient, no nonsense, and indispensable. She was on top of every case and client that passed through the De Luca and Weatherford law firm's door.

"I need to speak to Vince, Giselle. Is he in?"

"Caprice! No, he's in court. He said he'll be tied up all day. Can I help?"

"No. I need his physical presence."

"Grant's in his office. Maybe he could help."

Grant Weatherford.

Automatically, Caprice could see the rugged-looking attorney in her mind's eye, with his thick black hair and intense gray eyes. He'd been her brother's roommate in law school. Once in a while he'd come home with Vince for the weekend. He'd gotten married right out of law school and worked for a large firm in Pittsburgh. But then tragedy had struck. He and his wife had lost their child to a pool accident, and their marriage had broken apart. According to Vince, Grant had wanted a fresh start, and that's why he'd moved to Kismet and teamed up with her brother.

When Caprice had first met Grant, she was attracted to him—he was a few years older, confident, irresolutely masculine—but she'd set aside pulse-racing fantasies when he'd gotten engaged and then married. Since his divorce and his move to Kismet, she'd kept her distance. Grant seemed to be a changed man . . . much more guarded, not as talkative, very introspective. A few times, Vince had brought him along to one of their family dinners. Now when she thought about asking him for help, something in her rebelled.

But Roz's future was at stake.

"All right," Caprice capitulated. "Patch me through."

It was only a few seconds until Grant came on the line. "What do you need, Caprice?"

No small talk. Not even a "How are you?" Just straight to business.

"I'm sorry to bother you, but I can't reach Vince."

"So Giselle said." He waited.

"I have a friend, Roz Winslow. Last night her husband was murdered. She and I found the body."

She thought she heard him blow out a breath. But he didn't say anything. Maybe he was surprised because he'd thought this would be about a family dinner.

Continuing, she explained, "Roz just got a call. Detective Jones wants her to come to the station as soon as possible. We thought maybe she should call a lawyer."

"Vince and I aren't criminal attorneys."

"I know that. But she didn't want to call a stranger. And on short notice . . ." She trailed off.

"Did the police call you?"

The question threw Caprice off balance. "No, Detective Jones called Roz's cell. He didn't call mine, and she didn't say he'd left a message at the house. I told the detective who questioned me everything last night. But Roz got dizzy, so Detective Jones postponed the rest of the interview with her."

Grant had obviously sifted through what she'd just said because he asked, "She's staying with you?"

"She didn't have any place to go. I didn't think she should be alone at a motel."

Again there was silence, but this time it seemed thoughtful on his part. She waited.

"I'm free for a few hours. Tell Mrs. Winslow I'll meet her at the station in half an hour."

"I'm going with her."

"Caprice, if the police didn't specifically direct you to go in, you should stay away."

"We'll meet you there."

After a momentary pause, he said, "On second thought, I'll pick you up. There could be reporters if the word gets out Mrs. Winslow is coming in. Be ready in half an hour."

Although she could get home by then, she really did have a problem with his authoritative tone. "We'll be ready," she said tersely and hung up on him.

Now hadn't that been a childish thing to do?

Caprice had pleaded an emergency and run out after Marge had asked questions about the contract and decided to show it to her husband. Her foot had been heavy on the accelerator on the way home, but now Caprice parked her van in front of her house. If there were going to be reporters at the station, her van was totally recognizable. Painted with swirling psychedelic colors and a few large flowers, with large turquoise lettering that read CAPRICE DE LUCA—REDESIGN AND HOME-STAGING, it was even more noticeable than her yellow

Camaro. Promotion was essential in her business. But in this situation, she really should remain inconspicuous.

Before she could climb out of the van, Grant pulled up to the curb in his silver SUV. It didn't look like a late model. She'd wondered before if it was vestige from his old life. She wondered even more now.

At Grant's SUV, she introduced Roz, who had come outside when she'd heard the vehicles pull up, and they climbed inside. Five minutes later, they stood at the double glass front doors of the Kismet police department's office building and jail.

To keep herself from studying Grant's craggy face too long, Caprice concentrated on the changes the last couple of years had wrought on Kismet's P.D.'s housing. The building had started out as red brick. Over the years the bricks had worn and the mortar had cracked. A few years ago, it had been sandblasted and repointed. The wooden door had been replaced by the double glass. Replacement windows in the front office section were state of the art. The cupola on the peaked roof had been stripped and repainted the brightest white. She'd heard there had been changes inside too. She wouldn't know. She'd never been inside.

Grant held the door for them, murmuring, "At least we don't have the media to deal with."

Inside the building, a police officer at the front

desk asked their business. When they told him they were there to see Detective Jones, he buzzed him.

Jones emerged from a hall office and eyed Grant disapprovingly. Then he turned his attention to Caprice. "No need for you to be here."

"I brought Roz. I'm here for support."

"You can support her out here."

Since Caprice saw Grant's warning glare and took it to heart—she didn't want to get arrested for mouthing off to an officer of the law—she responded, "I'll wait over there," and pointed to a wooden bench that looked about as comfortable as a pile of rocks.

Time slid by at an incrementally slow speed as she tapped her foot. Willing herself to calm down and wait, she took a few deep breaths and tried to visualize each of the projects she had going, her lineup of clients she strove to more than satisfy. With every job she wanted a recommendation and a commendation. Her portfolio was growing along with her reputation, and she'd even begun virtual staging assessments with clients in other states.

Although she glanced frequently at the hallway that Detective Jones, Roz, and Grant had disappeared into, Caprice tried examining every detail of an open house scheduled in a few weeks that would shout a "tropical" theme. A few accent pieces she needed eluded her even from her online suppliers. But experience had taught her all would fall into place eventually. Still, she worried until it did.

Even a pastel color palette, bright airy fabric, and wicker furniture with comfortable cushions couldn't distract her from what might be happening in a back office or an interrogation room. The hands on her watch moved ever so slowly as she posted on social media—a presence there was necessary in her line of work—and checked her messages.

An hour and twenty minutes later, Grant and Roz emerged from the doorway that led into the less-visible area of the police department.

Grant's mouth formed a grim line as he said in a low voice to Caprice, "I'll answer your questions, but let's go someplace more private to talk."

At least he realized she had questions.

"Can we go back to Caprice's?" Roz asked. "I'm feeling a little weak in the knees."

Roz did look as if she could collapse at any moment, and Grant must have realized that. "Sure," he answered quickly. Then he peered outside the double glass doors. "Uh oh. Word must have leaked out that Roz is here. Reporters out there want to talk to the grieving widow."

"I've gotten calls on my cell, but after the first one, I started screening," Roz said.

"They don't know you're at Caprice's or even that Caprice witnessed anything. Unless they saw Caprice's car being towed away from your house." After peering outside again, he said, "Wait here a minute."

Grant crossed to the desk and spoke to the officer. Returning to them, he said, "There's a back entrance. I'm going to pull up smack against it and you two are going to jump in. Caprice, it's better if you remain anonymous as long as possible. Take that sash thing from around your waist and use it like a scarf over your head. And as soon as you're in the backseat, duck down."

"Grant—"

"Do you want a news van camped outside your house?"

Of course, she didn't. She untied the wide sash at her waist.

A few minutes later, she was hunched down in the backseat as Grant sped out of the parking lot.

"Stay down," he ordered her.

Caprice's shoulder hit the door as he made a fast turn. From her position practically on the floor, she asked, "What happened in there?"

"I'm a suspect! They think *I* killed Ted," Roz answered her.

"Did they *say* that?"

Maybe Roz was overreacting. Maybe Grant's take on the interview session was altogether different. Yet she remembered the way his jaw was set when he'd emerged from the back of the building.

"They didn't have to say so. It was the way they looked at me."

"Grant?"

"Hold your questions until I lose the car and the van following us."

Fifteen minutes later, they did. After Grant gave her the all clear, she sat up in the backseat.

Grant had never been inside her house before. She hadn't had time to straighten up this morning before she'd left. She'd removed clothes from the dryer in the basement and the laundry basket still sat on a kitchen chair. Dylan and Sophia had made messes around their food dishes when they ate—Sophia sometimes pawed her dry food onto the floor—and she hadn't bothered to sweep the kitchen last evening.

Why was she even worrying about this now when she should be focused on Roz?

A little voice in her head whispered, *Because maybe you care about what Grant thinks?*

She ignored the voice as they exited his car and hurried to the door. Barking began inside as Dylan heard their steps on the porch. After unlocking her door, Roz and Grant followed her inside.

Dylan yipped at Roz and Caprice.

"Easy," Caprice directed firmly, not knowing how Dylan would react to Grant. She was a great believer in the theory that dogs and cats were a good judge of character.

After a glance up at Grant, Dylan's barking stopped so he could sniff at Grant's trousers and loafers. Finally, he sat at Grant's feet, looking up at him as if he expected a pat on the head.

Grant didn't hesitate to crouch down and ruffle the dog's fur. "What's your name?" he asked as if he expected the dog to tell him.

"Dylan," Caprice filled in. "After the singer."

As Grant rose to his feet, he appeared to assess her house. His gaze canvassed the colorful living room, the cat tree where Sophia was curled into a sleeping ball of fur, the early-seventies pop art psychedelic print framed and hung on one wall. After a glance into her dining room with its 1950s mahogany hutch, table, and buffet sideboard, he gave her a curious look.

Then he asked matter-of-factly, "Where would you like to settle?"

She gestured toward the living room. "I'll make a pot of coffee."

Roz picked up Dylan, and the dog quieted in her arms. "I let him out before I left, so he's good."

It was easy to see Dylan and Roz were forming quite a bond. Maybe he'd found a home.

Within minutes they were all seated in the living room, and questions had stacked up in Caprice's head. She started with, "So tell me exactly what happened."

Grant nodded to Roz. "Why don't you tell her."

"I did! They think I killed Ted."

"They didn't say that," Grant assured her. "They're just questioning your alibi."

"Why would they question that?" Caprice wanted to know.

Explaining, Grant leaned forward in his chair. "An alibi only works if someone can corroborate it. No one saw Roz."

"I saw Roz."

"You saw her at the end of her run, not where she might have been a half hour or an hour before."

"So what does that mean? That they're going to charge her with Ted's murder?" Caprice held her breath as she waited for Grant's answer.

Chapter Six

"They're not going to charge her with Ted's murder . . . yet," Grant answered, the nerve along his jaw working. "They brought her in to see if they could poke holes in her statement. She's a person of interest."

"She was in shock last night!" Caprice reminded him.

"Yes, she was. I reminded them of that. The fact that you were worried enough about her and took her to urgent care helps. A lot of facts are working in her favor." He checked with Roz to see if he should go on.

"What's working in my favor?" Roz asked.

"Because of the open house, your place was overrun with fingerprints. Except . . . The curio cabinet's door was wiped clean and the key is gone. It wasn't on Ted. It's missing. That's why the police asked for the list of what was in the cabinet." His gaze met Caprice's. "They showed her a photo of the cabinet after she gave them a list. Roz saw that a valuable antique dagger is missing."

"It's the one Ted gave me with the rubies, diamonds, and emeralds embedded in the handle," Roz explained. "The key is usually in the cabinet unless we have guests. Then Ted pockets it. At least, he . . . used to."

"With the back door hanging open as it was, the murder could have been about theft," Caprice mused.

"That's a possibility," Grant agreed. "Maybe it had just happened, and when you rang the bell, the killer grabbed a valuable piece and took off. The rain could have already washed away valuable evidence. There's another problem too. Roz gave her prints for elimination purposes just as you did. They might be on the dagger that killed her husband. Also, several people might have touched it at the open house—anyone who passed through that sword room."

"So the murderer wiped the door on the glass case?"

"Perhaps. I don't know why he or she took the key. Didn't want to take the time to wipe it clean? A memento?"

"A memento?" Roz asked with astonishment.

"You never know what's in the mind of a killer," Grant said.

"And why do the police think Roz did it when the motive points to theft?"

"They believe she could have staged it."

Grant made the statement so flatly it really shook Caprice. Because the police might be looking at Roz as their prime suspect, she knew she had to tell both Roz and Grant about Valerie Swanson.

"I have something I need to tell you both. But let me get the coffee first. I think we're going to need it."

The rattle of colorful mugs being collected and the refrigerator door being opened and closed brought Sophia into the kitchen. Seated by the refrigerator door, she meowed.

Grateful that she could postpone hurtful information for a few minutes longer, Caprice said, "One tablespoon of cream. Two a day, your vet said. We need some for our coffee, and I'm planning to make cannoli filling, so I'll need the rest."

Sophia blinked as if she understood.

Against popular folklore, Caprice knew many felines couldn't digest cream. But she purchased hers along with other milk products from a local dairy. It was thick and rich, and Sophia loved it.

After she set the royal blue dish with a spoonful of cream in its center on the floor, Caprice arranged turquoise, yellow, and lime-green mugs on a tray with a crystal creamer and sugar bowl. She poured cinnamon-hazelnut coffee into the mugs, then carried the antique tray with its picture of pink peonies under the glass into the living room.

Grant rose immediately to take the tray from her.

But she shook her head because it seemed important to show him she didn't need his help. "Just move the silent butler."

The brass container with its wooden handle had been unearthed at Isaac's shop. About once a month, Caprice slipped a note inside it—an affirmation she wanted to concentrate on for a few weeks. Anything from—*I will be patient with Bella's attitude toward strays* to *I will do my part to clean up the environment.*

With a look that seemed a bit puzzled, Grant moved the silent butler, and she set the tray on the square coffee table, whose top was inset with colorful ceramic tiles. She had found the quaint piece of furniture online when styling a client's house.

Grant took his coffee black. Roz added cream as well as sugar. Caprice added a drip of cream. She didn't want to drown out the flavor of the coffee.

After everyone took a sip, Caprice set down her mug. "I saw something at the open house that I was going to tell Roz about the night Ted was murdered."

"At our open house? What could you have seen?" Roz asked.

There was no further way to postpone the inevitable. "I was checking where everyone was and if we had any interested lookers. I thought I heard voices coming from the upstairs exercise room. When I peeked in the door—" She stopped, then looked directly at Roz. "Ted was kissing Valerie Swanson."

Roz's green eyes grew wide with surprise, her mouth rounded, and then she dropped her head, concentrating on petting Dylan who was still settled in her lap.

Finally, she said, "I sensed something was terribly wrong between us. I mean, a woman knows when her husband comes home late every night and doesn't seem interested in . . ." She trailed off and just waved a hand at them as if they should get her drift. "But then he asked if I wanted to go to New York, and we had a honeymoon all over again! What was *that* about if he was having an affair?"

Caprice glanced at Grant, and he looked terrifically uncomfortable.

"Roz, I'm sorry," Caprice apologized. "I didn't know if I should tell you or not. But I had decided to do it and then—" She didn't have to finish.

Grant leaned forward in his chair. "If anyone gets hold of this information, that won't be good for you," he insisted, addressing Roz. "Because you now have a motive."

"Oh my gosh," Roz said, dropping her head into her hands. "Maybe the police already know. Even if Ted was discreet, someone always sees. And gossip runs rampant in this town. If Ted kissed her in my house, God knows where else he kissed her!"

"My thoughts exactly. You know, Mrs. Winslow, I'm not a criminal lawyer, but I can recommend one."

After seriously considering his comment, she shook her head. "I don't want someone else. I feel comfortable with you. Everything's so strange and uncomfortable right now. I want you, Mr. Weatherford."

Although Grant looked troubled, he said, "There's nothing more we can do for now." Standing, he was obviously ready to end their meeting.

"Don't you want a retainer or something?" Roz asked.

"Let's just see what happens next. I gave Jones my card. They should contact me—not you—if they decide to question you again. If they do, then we'll discuss my fee. I have to get back to my office."

"I'll walk you out," Caprice offered.

She closed the door behind her as she and Grant stood on the small porch practically toe to toe. "Tell me what you really think. Do the police believe Roz did this?"

"They're examining her closely."

Caprice's mind was racing, had been ever since Ted was murdered. "Yes, Roz has a motive. But Valerie does too."

"How do you figure that?"

"What if Ted broke off with Valerie? What if he got tired of her?"

"That's not what you saw," Grant pointed out.

"No, it wasn't. But Ted rekindled romance with Roz in New York the next day. Men are fickle. They want one woman one day and someone different the next. That's what could have happened."

"You have no facts."

"Maybe I can find some," she returned almost rebelliously. "And maybe if I call all of Roz's neighbors, I'll find one who saw her jogging."

Grant was already shaking his head. "No. Don't even think about it. You should stay out of it."

"Would you stay out of it if your friend was accused of murder?"

"She hasn't been accused of murder," he replied blandly in that lawyer tone her brother used that always irked her.

Apparently he could see her annoyance and relented. "If my friend were involved, I'd want to do something. And you are. Letting her stay here with you is the support she needs."

"I could help."

"You could get in the way of the investigation and make everything worse."

Is that what would happen? Or would she find answers the police couldn't?

Grant scowled at her. "From what Vince has said, trying to change your mind is like buying a one-way ticket to frustration. So really think and consider the consequences before you do anything. While you're at it, try to convince your friend to consult a criminal defense attorney."

"She's not a criminal."

"Fine," he said with obvious frustration and turned to go.

But she couldn't keep from calling his name. "Grant?"

He faced her again.

"Thank you."

For the first time that morning, he gave her a half smile. "You're welcome. And thank you for a good cup of coffee. Giselle's tastes like dishwater."

Before she could comment, he started down the walk.

Although she was smiling when she went back inside, her smile dropped away when she saw Roz with Dylan on the sofa. Her friend had sustained many blows, and Caprice didn't know how Roz was maintaining her composure.

Sitting beside her, brushing her hand over Dylan's head, she asked Roz, "How can I help you?"

Roz stared at her as if deciding what to say. Finally she requested, "Tell me exactly what you saw when Ted and that hairstylist were kissing."

That took her aback. "Roz, you shouldn't think about—"

"I have to know. Apparently there was so much I didn't know."

"Have you ever had your hair done at Curls R Us?" Caprice asked, trying to sidetrack her a bit.

"Before I married Ted. But afterward the women I associated with moved in a different circle. I have a standing appointment now with Roberto at Rapunzel's Locks."

Rapunzel's Locks was Kismet's elite salon. Patrons were served glasses of wine, as well as imported tea and coffee, and offered pedicures and manicures. Supposedly clients came from York and Harrisburg, and Roberto's roster was often closed to new clients.

"Do you know Valerie?"

"No. I mean I know who she is. The way she dresses, everyone notices her. She sashays into the Koffee Klatch as if she owns the place."

Valerie's short skirts and low-cut necklines, along with her piled-on makeup, caused many heads to turn—women who disapproved and men who wanted a better glimpse of the many-times bleached blonde.

"She doesn't seem to be Ted's type," Caprice ventured.

Roz gave a snort. "What *is* a man's type? I want to know if Ted invited her to our open house or if she barged in on her own."

"What I saw won't help you."

"Tell me anyway."

Caprice reran the film in her mind. "It's really no more than what I've already said. I heard voices and saw them."

"Who was more involved? Ted or . . . that woman?"

"Roz—"

"Please tell me."

Closing her eyes, Caprice thought about it. Valerie had had her arms wrapped around Ted's neck and had been clinging to him like a vine that hadn't wanted to let go. But he hadn't been tearing himself away, either.

"They were kissing, Roz. They were both involved. He didn't have his hands all over her—"

"He didn't?"

"They were kissing. And it didn't look like it was the first time. Afterward Valerie was acting like a primping peacock. She said—"

"Go on," Roz demanded.

At that moment Caprice was sorry any of it had come out. "She was telling prospective buyers how large the whirlpool tub was."

Roz looked horrified.

Changing the train of Roz's thoughts, Caprice said, "I think Bella goes to Curls R Us. I'll talk to her about Valerie. But is there anyone else who might hate Ted or want to hurt him?"

"Lots of people didn't like Ted. He told everyone what he thought. He had strong opinions. As I told you, he and Monty had words. He and one of our neighbors, Jack Fielding, actually stopped speaking. Jack believes pharmaceutical companies have no interest in relieving human suffering, that they're just out to make money. He cited a new pain reliever that could foster more addiction."

"I don't understand. All sorts of patients could benefit."

"They could. But the medicine has to be carefully controlled, which means more doctor's office visits. Jack believes it's all a conspiracy to make a profit."

"That's complicated," Caprice acknowledged. Then with her mind clicking away, she said, "When I talked to the two of you a few days before the open house, Ted was on the phone with someone and seemed angry. Do you know who Thompson is?"

"Chad Thompson is another vice president at PA Pharmaceuticals."

"Do you know if he and Ted got along?"

"I never heard Ted say anything negative about him."

"But Ted said, 'If he does that, Thompson, I'll kill him.' Do you know who they were discussing?"

Dylan wiggled off Roz's lap, got his bearings on the sofa, and then jumped down. He trotted through the dining room to the kitchen and back again.

Caprice knew what that meant and held up her hand. "Give us a minute."

He sank down onto the floor but continued to watch them.

Rising to her feet, Roz shook her head. "I have no idea. Or what that conversation was about. For the most part, Ted didn't talk to me about work."

"I might go over to Ted's office and ask a few questions."

"You'd do that for me?"

"Maybe I watch too much TV, but I don't want to

sit around while law enforcement concentrates on you and doesn't cast a wider net."

Caprice stood too, and Roz gave her a hug. "Thank you. You're the best friend."

"If I were in your shoes, I'd want someone to help me."

Now that both women were standing, Dylan came to attention and ran in a circle around them.

"Do you mind if I take him to the yard for a while?" Roz asked. "With all the trees between the houses, no one should get a glimpse of me. Playing with Dylan might take my mind off everything for a while."

"I wonder when you'll be able to get back into your house."

"I don't know if I want to get back in. Though I do need clothes."

The dress Roz had pulled from Caprice's closet looked good on her. It was a copper-colored, high-waisted shift with embroidery across the bodice. It attractively molded to Roz's body when she moved and fit her in a way it didn't fit Caprice. But then Roz looked like a fashion model in anything.

Dylan yipped.

Stooping down, Caprice asked, "Would you like to go out with Roz while I make lunch?"

Dylan barked again.

"One of his balls is on the back porch. If you throw it, he'll bring it back to you until he gets tired. Then he'll just plop down."

Roz smiled. "Don't go to any trouble for lunch."

"I won't. I'll find something to go with the soup."

After Roz took Dylan outside, Caprice started toward the pantry but stopped at the kitchen window. Roz had thrown the orange ball. Dylan scampered after it. It was a shame Roz couldn't take Dylan for a walk down the street. One of the reasons Caprice liked this neighborhood so much was the decades-old trees that shaded the sidewalk and the front yards of many of the properties. This time of year dogwoods were blooming, and shrubs were greening and filling out. In a few weeks she'd be planting zinnias. They'd add lush color wherever she planted them. Zinnias were one of those dependable summer flower varieties that didn't take a lot of care.

In the pantry, she pulled a can of tuna from the shelf. If she remembered correctly, she had a hard-boiled egg in the refrigerator. With pickle relish and mayo, she could make tuna cups that would go well with the soup. She set the oven for 350 degrees.

She was about to open the can with her grape-colored electric can opener when the counter phone rang. She smiled when she saw her mom's number on caller ID.

"Hi, Mom."

"How are you?" Her mother's voice was filled with concern. "And how is Roz?"

She'd called her mother last night and told her

what had happened, swearing her to secrecy with everyone but her dad and Nana. "I'm fine. Roz seems to be coping. She just took Dylan outside."

"That will be good for her. I know you believe animals can help anyone through anything. Do you still take Sophia to the retirement center?"

"When I can."

There was a pause. "I called because I heard a rumor that there was a commotion at the police station this morning. I wondered if you were involved."

"I was there." She sighed. She might as well tell her mom what was going on. Vince would find out from Grant, and he'd have questions. Vince never let anything slip by. Besides, very few secrets kept well in Kismet.

"Why were you there? You said you already gave a statement."

How much to say. As a high school English teacher, her mom was plugged in to the community in a way Caprice wasn't. She taught kids from families living in Reservoir Heights and would hear a variety of tidbits, some true, some not.

"Roz and I both gave statements last night. But they wanted to talk with her some more."

"I hope she had a lawyer with her. She shouldn't say a word without one present. The spouse is always the first suspect."

So her mother watched the same TV shows or read the same books that she had. "I tried to call

Vince," Caprice admitted, "but he was in court. So Grant stood in."

"What did they ask her?"

There wasn't much she could do but give her mom a little more detail. "I couldn't sit in on the interview. I tried to go in with Roz for moral support, but Grant gave her that instead."

"How did you feel about that?"

"I didn't feel anything. I was glad he could help when Vince couldn't."

"Oh, really. You and Grant got along well?"

"We weren't together long enough. Getting along wasn't a priority. Helping Roz was."

"Caprice—" Her mother's voice had that motherly, singsong quality that all daughters knew meant trouble. She tried to brace herself for what was coming.

"Honey . . ."

That endearment meant even more trouble.

Then it came. "The past few years you and Grant have had a sort of tension between you. Wouldn't you agree?"

She had to extricate herself from this conversation quickly. "Grant and I have hardly seen each other the past few years. I don't know why you think you see tension."

"I see something when the two of you go out of your way to avoid each other."

"Your imagination—"

"Is *not* working overtime. I'm just calling a spade

a spade. You've always liked him. Since his daughter drowned and he got divorced, you think you have to treat him with kid gloves. You don't."

"I don't treat him that way at all," she protested hotly.

"Then how do you treat him? Don't you think your dad and I could see how much you once liked him?"

Oh, Lord. If they had seen it, who else had?

"I was a kid."

"Maybe. Now you're not. Don't just sit back, Caprice, and let a possibility pass you by. If you're both going to be helping Roz, anything could happen."

Oh, yes, anything could happen. Roz could end up in jail, and Caprice could regret ever calling Grant. "You don't usually interfere in my life."

"No, I don't. Because I learned long ago if I tell you not to do something, you will do it just to prove you can."

"I do not!"

"You do. You take advice from Nana much better than from me."

"She just gives me decorating advice."

"With a little life advice thrown in. You just don't notice it."

Was that really true? She'd have to think about that later. "So what have you heard about Ted's murder?" If she managed to coax her mother back to the original subject, maybe she'd forget about Grant.

"I don't gossip."

Caprice sighed. "I know you don't, Mom. But didn't you have a parent-teachers' organization meeting last night?"

"It was a committee meeting for the last fund-raiser of the year. We're selling submarine sandwiches again."

"And?"

After a long pause, her mother finally dropped her bombshell. "I think I know who killed Roz's husband."

Chapter Seven

"You know who might have killed him?" Caprice was shocked, surprised, and mystified.

"One of the parents, Mr. Waxman, blew up at Tracey Torriman."

"Tracey's the sweetest teacher in your building!"

"I know what you mean. She's young, perky, bubbly, and nice to everyone to a fault, if you ask me."

Her mother didn't believe in tiptoeing around a subject, even with parents. But Tracey hated to hurt anyone's feelings, including telling a parent her child wasn't working up to par. She lavished praise often, sometimes even when it wasn't deserved. Caprice knew Tracey because she'd redesigned a couple of rooms in her parents' house, and Tracey's parents were peers of Caprice's parents.

"So what happened?"

"I'm not betraying any confidences because the

situation happened in the hall in between classes. Tracey's room is right next to the teachers' room."

The teachers' lounge was hardly that. Visiting her mother there on occasion, Caprice knew it consisted of a unisex bathroom, an old couch someone had donated, a cafeteria table with about ten chairs around it, and a large coffeemaker that whoever was first into the room every morning started. However, it was a haven where some teachers ate lunch or did planning, and others stopped in before or after school just to chat. There were classrooms on either side of it and across from it.

Her mother continued, "Tracey's chemistry class sometimes wanders into the discussion of modern medicine and pharmaceutical companies. Apparently she mentioned PA Pharmaceuticals and some of the advances they've made over the years in research and development. Well, Bart Waxman's son is in that class. The next day Bart marched into Tracey's classroom a few minutes before his son's class started and began reaming her out because she was giving PA Pharmaceuticals good press. He'd been let go the week before without much explanation, and his blood pressure was up, that's for sure, because his face was all red. He yelled at her, telling her she shouldn't be advertising anything about that dirty-dealing company in her classroom."

"And you heard all this?"

"All of us heard it. He was loud enough to wake the dead! Everyone was buzzing about it last night."

"What was his position at PA Pharm?"

"I think he was a production manager. At least that's what I heard after his outburst."

"And he didn't know why he was fired?"

"Not according to him. He said they were all crooks who just want to take the money and run."

That sounded like a blanket statement, and Bart Waxman could just have been venting his frustration and anger.

"I didn't tell you the best part," her mom confided with a little bit of slyness that Caprice wasn't sure if she'd ever heard before.

"The best part?"

"The day after Ted Winslow was killed, one of the other teachers told me Ted was Waxman's boss, and the one who fired him."

"Whoa." Caprice blew out the word without thinking.

"Exactly. Whoa."

That was certainly a motive if Caprice ever heard one. In these economic times no one wanted to be fired from anything. Jobs were too hard to find, especially in Kismet. Interviewing in Harrisburg or York would mean a commute. Most people weren't happy with change, not unless they were running toward it.

So the question was: did the police know about

Waxman? "Do Dad and Chief Powalski still have a monthly poker game?"

"Your dad hasn't mentioned Mack recently, but I think he's still one of the guys who antes up."

Caprice chuckled. Her mom thought she knew the language, but she'd never sat at a poker table in her life. On the other hand, Caprice and Vince had filled in once in a while when her dad felt the group was short of players.

"In fact," her mom continued, "one is scheduled for Thursday night."

"Does Dad know this story about Waxman?"

"Sure, he does. I don't keep secrets from him. We talk about everything. Or at least I talk and he pretends to listen."

Her mom and dad had been married for thirty-seven years. Caprice knew their romance very well because, along with her brother and sisters, she'd heard it many times over. Her mom had attended Shippensburg University, about an hour and a half away. She'd been home on summer break, living in York with her parents. She'd spent mornings helping her mom with her gardens, then during the afternoons and evenings worked in a clothing store in one of York's malls. One morning, she'd gone outside to clip a bouquet of flowers to bring indoors. She'd just finished collecting roses and zinnias when she'd heard noise on the roof. When she'd looked up, she'd spotted a man around her age, nineteen, all bronzed and tanned and muscled, with black hair tousled by the wind. Their gazes locked, and the rest, as they say, was history.

Nicolas De Luca was a brick mason who had come to fix the flashing around the chimney. Today, at age fifty-seven, he was still a brick mason, though he had a crew of men working under him now. But he went out on jobs himself sometimes, and she knew that worried her mother. Her dad had been from Kismet, and they moved here after they married. When Francesca lost her parents—her mother to a heart attack, her father to a stroke—Caprice's mom had found it more than difficult to sell that house. It had held so many memories, including the one where she'd found the love of her life. A few years back, they'd decided to put an addition on their house in Kismet so Nana Celia could move in with them, and that had helped. Bonds and connections were everything to Francesca De Luca, and Caprice found they were important to her too.

"Maybe Dad could say something to the chief about Waxman."

"I imagine he could, but Mack never talks about ongoing investigations."

"Not even after a few glasses of Dad's favorite wine or a shot of Rock and Rye?"

"Mack is pretty tight-lipped, but maybe your dad can find out something. Maybe he can find out if Roz is a real suspect or not. Even if Mack won't talk, your father can tell him about Bart Waxman."

It hadn't taken many detective skills to figure out that Roz was a prime suspect. Changing the subject, because that thought caused chills to run up and down her spine, Caprice asked, "So do you know what everyone is bringing for dinner on Sunday? I wish you would just let Bella, Nikki, and me cook."

"Nonsense. You know your grandmother and I enjoy doing it. We're making ravioli. Some cheese, some sausage. Bella is bringing a vegetable casserole. Nikki's making antipasto salad and the cannoli shells. And you're bringing the cream for the cannoli and baking bread."

"Don't forget Vince's wine."

Her mother laughed. "I could never forget Vince's wine."

The back door opened, and Roz and Dylan came in.

Caprice said to her mother, "Roz just came in with Dylan. We're going to have lunch, then I think I'm going to give Bella a call. I might stop in for a visit."

"You're stopping in for a visit? You'll be seeing her Sunday. What's up?"

"Not a lot. I just wanted to talk to her about her beautician."

Later that afternoon Caprice picked up a basket from the stack just inside the door of Kismet's Grocery Fresh Market. The small store, with its produce, fruits, and deli was her favorite place to shop for ingredients for home-cooked dinners. When she'd called Bella, her sister had invited her to come over anytime, and asked if she could pick up some vine-ripened tomatoes and peppers so Bella could use them for dinner. Her car was on the fritz again.

The vehicle had been giving Bella problems for the past year. But her sister insisted she and Joe just didn't have the funds to buy a new car or the monthly income to sustain higher payments. With two kids and one breadwinner, their budget was stretched to the limit. But just like all the De Luca women, and even their father on occasion, Bella preferred fresh ingredients for cooking. She clipped coupons, watched for sales, and skimped in other ways in order to buy fresh fruits and vegetables. Caprice knew her sister would insist on paying her for whatever she bought, but she didn't have to tell her the real total of the bill. The vine-ripened tomatoes would just happen to be on special today.

For some reason Caprice suddenly compared Bella's scrimping to Roz and Ted Winslow's ability to buy anything their hearts desired. She'd left Roz making phone calls and working on an obituary for her husband. How hard was that going to be, knowing the man had been unfaithful?

For now, all Caprice could do for her friend was provide her with a place to stay, be available to listen, and cook food that would keep Roz healthy during this difficult time. Since it was a warm day, tonight she would whip up Nikki's avocado, tomato, and pasta salad. Strolling past the produce counter, she picked up an avocado to use for that dish.

With that in her basket, she proceeded to the ledge that held the tomatoes. Caprice couldn't wait until the plants her mother raised from seedlings were growing in cages in her own garden and she could pick the tomatoes right off the vines.

But she didn't want to rush summer when there was so much to enjoy about spring.

She'd dropped several tomatoes into her basket and was ready to move on to the poblano peppers when she noticed the man striding through the sliding-glass doors. Dr. Seth Randolph took a basket from the stack and headed toward the produce.

Caprice felt her heart give a little skip. Should she wait for him to catch up and maybe say hello? Would he remember who she was? Or should she just move on and forget about every silly notion that had just entered her head?

But the decision was made for her. Dr. Randolph walked up beside her, picked up a tomato, glanced at her . . . and recognized her. As he mentally placed her, the lines around his eyes crinkled and he smiled.

"Miss De Luca, isn't it?"

"Caprice," she said, pleased much more than she should have been that he'd remembered.

He set a tomato in his basket as his gaze passed

over her flowered and fringed vest, her Beatles T-shirt, her red jeans. "And it is Miss, right?"

"Yes, it is." Was he checking again for a reason? Her heart did that pitty-pat thing, and she wished she could just act like an adult and have a conversation without feeling all . . . giddy.

So she said the first thing that came into her head. "I didn't expect to see you here at this time of day."

"This happens to be my day off. At least it's a day off until my phone buzzes or vibrates."

That was the life of a doctor, she supposed. Mostly on call. That thought was fleeting as she registered the fact that he'd looked good in a lab coat, but he looked ten times better in a green football shirt and blue jeans. His sneakers had been around the block more than a few times. This was the everyday Dr. Seth Randolph, and she had to admit, shallow as it was, she really liked the way he looked—broad shoulders, tousled tawny hair, and all. Not to mention those very blue eyes that looked as if they were studying her now, trying to find an answer to a question.

"How's your friend?"

She knew privacy laws kept her from getting information from him, but there was no reason he couldn't ask her. Especially if he cared and he seemed to. "Physically she's doing better. I encourage her to eat and drink, and mostly she just does it by rote. Emotionally, I'm not sure. She still stares into space a lot."

He lowered his voice. "It's awful imagining the two of you finding her husband's body the way you did. I've come across accident scenes and of course trauma in the ER. It's not easy to forget afterward."

"No, it's not." In fact, she'd awakened last night with visions of the murder scene in her head. "I know how it affected me. I can only imagine the impact it had on Roz. One thing is helping, though. I took in a stray dog about a month ago. He and Roz have taken to each other. He even slept on her bed last night."

"Animals are good therapy. Encourage her to take him for walks and she'll get some exercise too."

"On a walk she's afraid reporters will find her. But she took him outside to play. That could become a habit while she's with me."

"Do you know how long that will be?"

"I have no idea, but I'm worried." Maybe because Seth Randolph was a doctor, it was easy to confide in him. "The police asked her to come in for questioning this morning."

"Because she wasn't coherent last night?"

"I don't think so. They wanted to delve a little more. They're questioning her alibi, so we don't know what to think."

"If she was out running, someone probably saw her."

"You really do have a good memory." Maybe that just went along with being a doctor.

"I hope so."

He checked out her basket. "It looks as if you're going to be doing some real cooking."

"The tomatoes are for my sister. I'm stopping over at her house for a while."

She checked his basket. "One tomato, Dr. Randolph? Endless possibilities for that."

He laughed. "It's Seth. And try bacon, lettuce, and tomato sandwiches. Do not tell me I shouldn't be eating bacon."

"I wouldn't dare. You're the doctor."

"Yes, I am, and on the healthy side I was thinking about picking up a pineapple to slice for dessert. You approve?"

Was he flirting with her? A man was actually flirting with her, Caprice De Luca . . . a man she was interested in too. "I approve."

"I don't want to hold you up," he said.

She suddenly wished she wasn't going to Bella's to ask her about her hairstylist. As he paused, she held her breath.

"Do you like to play miniature golf?"

"I haven't played since high school," she admitted.

"That's good. Then I can beat you. I was thinking maybe next Saturday afternoon. I'm on call this weekend. Unless you're busy?"

He seemed a bit uncertain, and she liked that. She liked that he didn't take for granted she'd fall at his feet. Many women would, and she suddenly wondered why he'd decided to ask her out. "Can I ask you something before I accept?"

"Sure, if it means that you *are* going to accept."

"I am. But I'd like to know if you pick up girls often in a grocery store?"

He chuckled, then checked her expression and saw she was serious. "No, I don't pick up women in grocery stores. Actually I haven't dated at all since moving here a year ago. Experience has taught me that being a doctor and dating don't often go well together."

"Because of your hours?"

"Because of interruptions. My phone and pager often become hated items by women I've dated."

"So why me?"

"I guess the very reason that you asked is why I would like to go out with you. You seem really interesting. You like to cook, which is a plus. I like the way you dress, which is unusual. I mean the way you dress, not that I like it. You like animals, and at the top of the list is the fact that you seem to care about *everything*."

"Wow!" she responded, not knowing what else to say.

"What time is good for you?" Seth asked.

"Around two would be good." Saturday mornings were usually busy with errands and pulling together all the loose ends from the previous week.

"Two, it is. What's your phone number?"

She reached into her purse and pulled out a business card.

"A home-stager," Seth said with another one of those smiles. "Good to know. I'll call you next week to make sure you're still free. Have a good visit with your sister."

"I will." Caprice gathered two peppers, plopped them into her basket, gave Seth another glance, then went to the checkout counter. She was going to play miniature golf with Dr. Seth Randolph.

Should she tell Bella about this date or keep it to herself?

Caprice found herself still smiling as she approached Bella's front door. A date with a man shouldn't make her feel . . . happy. After all, she was a self-sufficient woman who guarded the door to her own happiness. She grabbed it whenever she could. No woman should rely on a man to make her happy. Still, she felt as if she'd won some kind of prize.

Bella's ranch-style house was very much like Bella, all manicured and precisely perfect on the outside. Joe could be as much of a control freak as her sister. He kept the lawn trimmed, the bushes banked, and the weeds to a minimum. He could edge with the best of them. To Caprice's way of thinking, a little color would have been nice, but Joe didn't take time for flowers or care anything about Caprice's suggestions. That was okay. She knew by now when to button her lip around him so as not to create friction between husband and wife, or between him and her family. Though it was hard sometimes.

Caprice never knocked. After all, sisters didn't have to do that. Besides that, Bella was expecting her.

With Seth's smile still turning up the corners of her mouth, she opened the screen door, which was letting the May breeze invade the one-story house.

There wasn't much of a foyer, just a step-in with a door leading to a closet on the left. The living room was to the right, and a hall through another archway led to the three bedrooms. The dining area and kitchen were to the left; the laundry room and garage were that way too. Bella's house was compact and at times seemed to be stretching at its seams as it accommodated the Santinis' daily needs.

Four-year-old Megan came running as soon as she saw Caprice. She practically tied her arms around Caprice's knees, and Caprice burst into a laugh. "Hi there to you too, munchkin. How are you today?"

"My name is *not* munchkin," her niece insisted in a back and forth they had almost every time Caprice saw her. "My name is Megan," she said importantly.

Caprice let the bag of tomatoes and peppers drop to a green and tan plaid arm chair. Everything in Bella's house was coordinated to the nth degree. Green and tan were the only colors in the living room, from the carpeting to the drapes to the furniture. Bella had gone with basic earth tones because Joe liked them. Caprice had her own thoughts about that because she knew her sister would have preferred flowers and a little more color. If Caprice could redesign the room . . . How many times had she thought about that? She'd move the sofa there, a light over here, get rid of the heavy drapes, add box shelves for the kids' toys. But she wasn't redesigning. Heaven forbid that Joe would let Bella do anything like that.

Kind thoughts, she told herself. *Think kinder thoughts about Joe.* He loved Bella. That was the important thing. And he loved their kids, though he didn't shoulder the burden of caring for them very often.

"Wanna play with my American Girl doll?" Megan asked.

Bella called from the kitchen, "In here. If you have those tomatoes, I'll skin them and put them in the Crock-Pot. The sauce will be ready whenever Joe gets home. He's still busy from tax season. I guess clients are amending their returns."

Caprice bent down to Megan again. "Why don't you dress Lanie in the very latest outfit you have for her. Then you can bring her in and show me."

Megan thought about the idea, then agreed, "Okay."

She scampered over to the sofa, where doll clothes were spread from one end to the other. Caprice knew Bella would be gathering all of them up before Joe came home. Everything in its place when the husband entered his domain.

Stop it, Caprice told herself again. Joe was a perfectly nice guy. If you weren't married to him.

Bella was removing a frying pan from a hook in the kitchen closet when Caprice set the grocery sack on her counter.

"Do you need me to do anything?" Caprice asked.

"Sure. You can start the onions and peppers in some olive oil while I skin the tomatoes. Add two cloves of garlic too."

Bella already had a pot of water on the stove, simmering, to plop the tomatoes into. After she did that, she pulled a silicone bowl from a cupboard, scooped ice into it from the freezer, and set it in the sink.

As she added a little water, she asked, "Where did you get that outfit?"

Caprice's clothes were an ongoing abomination to Bella. She hated vintage anything, let alone a tapestry fringed vest that could have been as old as she was.

"You know where I get most of my clothes, Secrets of the Past, downtown. Believe it or not, the T-shirt's new. Lots of retro going on right now."

When Bella didn't respond to that, Caprice wondered why. Her sister usually took every chance to make a jab at Caprice's penchant for Paul McCartney and anything about the Fab Four.

Her sister took a pair of tongs from a drawer. "How much do I owe you?"

"Seven bucks."

When Bella gave her a look, Caprice shrugged. "On special today."

Bella frowned, but again didn't give her usual rejoinder.

Something was up. Caprice could feel it in her bones. Or maybe the telltale sign was the way Bella kept sliding her gaze away from Caprice's. That usually meant she had something to hide.

But jumping into it feet first was never the way she operated with Bella. Nikki, yes. But with Bella, she had to be more subtle, even though Bella never was.

Knowing where her sister kept most things in her kitchen, Caprice slid a cutting board from a shelf in the closet, grabbed an onion from a basket on the counter and one of the peppers that had tumbled out of the bag when Bella upended it to reach the tomatoes.

After washing the pepper and peeling the onion, Caprice took a knife from the wooden block near the sink. That knife brought back pictures she didn't want to remember. *It's not a dagger,* she reminded herself. She was just going to chop some vegetables.

As she sliced the pepper in two and seeded it, she asked Bella, "When did you have your hair done last?"

"Why? Do I need a trim?"

Bella took everything personally. "No, you don't need a trim. Your hair always looks perfect." It was thick and curly, and who could tell when she *did* need a cut? "I wondered who your stylist is."

"My stylist is Rhonda Fitzmore. Aren't you happy with Peggy?"

Peggy Latimore did a fine job with Caprice's long, straight hair—angling it around her face, fringing her bangs, making sure the back blunt cut was just right. "I'm good with Peggy. I just wondered if Rhonda ever talks about her boss?"

"You mean the queen of décolletage?"

Caprice had to laugh. "Yep, she's the one."

Bella's lips finally turned up in a smile. "What do you want to know? Rhonda's mostly discreet, but she does talk about Valerie when she's not there. All the stylists do."

"What do they say about her?"

"I think a lot of it stems from jealousy because Valerie sure knows how to turn heads."

"Do they talk about her clothes or her dating habits?"

"Why all this interest in Valerie?"

Usually Caprice didn't keep anything from Bella.

But if word got out about Ted and Valerie, and the police heard about it, that could be bad news for Roz. So she simply said, "I'm interested, that's all."

Bella's eyes narrowed. "Does this have something to do with Ted Winslow's murder? Mom told me Roz is staying with you."

"I can't say anything else, Bee." She lapsed into her childhood nickname for her sister, so Bella would know she was serious. "I'd really rather you not tell anyone that I was asking questions, okay? Or that Roz is staying with me."

Bella nodded. "Okay." After a pause, she filled Caprice in. "Valerie herself talks about who she dates. It's no secret she's always wanted to marry up."

"Marry someone with money."

"Exactly. In fact, Rhonda told me that Valerie let it slip to a client that the man she was seeing was married. Not only that, but she confided that he was going to leave his wife. Valerie's boyfriend told her *she* knew the meaning of hot sex, where his wife didn't."

Caprice let out a low whistle. "That's nasty."

She sautéed the onion and pepper for a short while, then slid Bella's hand grater from a drawer and shaved the garlic cloves over it into the mixture. She allowed it to cook for a half minute before she turned off the heat. "Do you want this in the slow cooker?"

"Yep, it's ready and waiting."

Bella had transferred the tomatoes from the hot

water to the icy mixture in the sink. In no time she had them skinned, squeezed, and dumped into the slow cooker with the pepper, onion, and garlic. Taking a spice container from the cupboard, she shook some crushed red pepper into the mixture.

Then she said in a low voice, "Don't you wonder sometimes if all a man wants is hot sex?"

Was that a rhetorical question? Caprice wondered. Or was she really supposed to answer it? "What makes you ask?"

"Oh, nothing."

Bella was not an oh-nothing kind of woman.

"Bella?"

Bella turned to her, her eyes glistening, and announced, "I'm pregnant. Joe's not going to like it one little bit."

Chapter Eight

After her surprising announcement, Bella glanced into the living room and took two steps toward it. "I hope Megan didn't hear," she whispered, her hand over her heart.

Caprice could see into the living room, which was a good distance away. Megan sat in the middle of the sofa, looking as if she was struggling with the closures on her doll's clothes. She didn't look up and didn't glance their way.

Caprice moved toward her sister and clasped her arm. "She didn't hear." Caprice lowered her voice though, just in case. "You haven't told Joe?"

Now Bella almost appeared angry as she pulled away. "No, I haven't told Joe. We're living paycheck to paycheck. Every year when Mom and Dad give us money at Christmas, I insist we stow it away for a rainy day and we have that to fall back on. But just one crisis and it will be gone. I was going to find work again as soon as Megan goes to school in the fall. But now—"

When she stopped abruptly, Caprice realized Bella was almost in tears. "Maybe you're wrong about how Joe will react."

Shaking her head vehemently, Bella blurted out, "We've had lots of discussions about kids. I've always wanted more, but he always says we can't afford them."

A thought entered Caprice's mind. After all, her sister was strong-willed.

But before she could even voice it, Bella's brown eyes flashed, and she shook her head again. "No, I did *not* do this on purpose. Joe and I . . . You know Joe and I had to get married. Well, we didn't *have* to, but Joe insisted. I've always wondered if I hadn't gotten pregnant, if Joe would have married me."

Bella had never expressed this fear before. Had it been eating at her all these years?

"Joe loves you."

"Yes, I believe he does. But sometimes I think *he* thinks family life is a burden he'd like to escape. I never would have gone against him to get pregnant. It was an accident. Well, not exactly an accident. I was on an antibiotic and sometimes birth control isn't as effective when you are. And one night Joe wanted to, well, you know—"

No, Caprice didn't know. But she wasn't going to go into that now. "Maybe you could find work until the baby's born. With summer coming, I know

Mom wouldn't mind taking care of Megan and Timmy."

Bella bit her lower lip. "I suppose that is one compromise I could suggest to Joe. But I'm just not ready to tell him yet. I have to prepare a little more. I have to come up with some other ideas. You know how I like to make costumes for kids. I sold a few the past couple of years. Maybe I could sell them online."

"Maybe you could," Caprice agreed. Bella had gone to a fashion-design school and received an associate degree. She'd always liked to sew. But on a weekend visit home, she'd met Joe, so she'd returned to Kismet to be with him and had taken secretarial positions ever since.

"Promise me you won't tell anyone about this," Bella implored.

"You're not going to tell Mom or Nana?"

"No, no one. Not yet. Joe has to be the first one to know . . . I mean after you. I just . . . I just used the third pregnancy test this morning, and I had to tell somebody."

Caprice supposed she was glad that she fell onto Bella's "somebody's" list. But she didn't like the idea of keeping this secret. She didn't like it at all. It was against her better judgment. Keeping this information inside wasn't good for Bella, either. Yet she could see her sister wasn't about to listen to reason, not now and maybe not tomorrow, either.

Bella was like that. When she got something into her head, it stayed.

Throwing her arms around Bella, Caprice gave her a tight hug. Her sister leaned into her for a couple of seconds, and then she pulled away and squared her shoulders. "I have to get this sauce on. Talk to me about something that will get my mind off all this."

Suddenly Megan came racing into the kitchen with her doll. "Lookie, Aunt Caprice. Isn't she pretty?"

Studying the doll that Megan had dressed in slacks, a sweater, and a cute little hat, she answered, "Yes, she's pretty. Almost as pretty as you."

Megan giggled. "She's gonna go shopping."

"What's she going to shop for?"

"Jewelry. I'll get the jewelry Mommy gave me." And Megan was off again as quickly as she'd appeared.

"I had an old purse, and I filled it with costume jewelry that I no longer wear. I swear she can play with that for hours."

Although Caprice didn't know if she wanted to talk about it, she knew there was one subject that would take Bella's mind off her newly discovered pregnancy. At least she hoped it would. "I'm going on a date next Saturday."

Bella practically squealed. "Who is it?"

She knew this was the part that Bella would

probably like. "He's a doctor. He works at the urgent care center."

Bella's eyes grew wide. "Dr. Randolph?"

"How did you—?"

"He's the only single doc who works there. He might be the only single doc in town, for all I know. And he asked you out?"

That made Caprice feel really good. There was a bit of annoyance in her voice when she asked, "Is there a reason he shouldn't have?"

Bella looked chagrined for a few moments. "Sorry. I didn't mean to make it sound—" She lifted her hands. "You know. I've heard talk about him at Curls R Us, and when I went to a PTO meeting a couple of weeks ago. There's a buzz about him. Actually I heard he never dates."

"He said he hasn't since he came here."

"How did you meet him?"

"I took Roz there. Then I ran into him at Grocery Fresh, and he asked me to play miniature golf."

"That's terrific! Don't treat him like you've treated everyone else."

Leave it to Bella to put a damper on things. "I don't know what you're talking about."

"Yes, you do. You don't give men who are interested in you a second chance. You've got to get over Craig dumping you by e-mail. And I know Travis did a number on you. He was such a jerk for not realizing he still had feelings for his ex-wife. Men are so clueless."

Maybe Joe was clueless, but Caprice didn't lump all men into that category. She liked men. She liked dating. She just had trouble trusting the men she dated.

"There's always an impediment," Caprice almost said to herself, as she thought about Seth's profession, the interruptions he'd cited.

"For once, don't think about the future, just think about the time you're with a man. You're at a great place in your life, and it's not going to come around again. Enjoy yourself and just let things happen."

Even though Bella was younger, in some ways she sounded world-weary. Did she regret marrying Joe in her early twenties? Had she settled into having a family too quickly? Had she really known the man Joe was when she married him?

"Don't tell anyone," Caprice said. "I don't want anyone to know about the date until after it's over. If it doesn't go well, I'm not going to breathe a word."

Bella looked dubious.

"I mean it, Bella. I'm keeping a secret for you. You keep this one for me."

When Caprice stopped at the security gate at the storage-locker center after her visit with Bella and entered her pass code, the gate slid open. After driving down one row, she made a left, drove up that row and down another. She'd rented two storage compartments, both the largest ones the company had to offer. If she wasn't careful, she'd soon need a third. She didn't like to pack them to the ceiling like some renters. That would make shifting out furniture, carpets, and artwork much more difficult. When she first entered the home-staging business, her parents had let her use one of their garages. But she hadn't wanted them to leave one of their cars out in the weather for long. Within a few months, she'd rented a storage compartment, and then, soon after, another.

After she parked to the side of the asphalt so another car could pass if it had to, she dug into her purse for her key ring. Finding it, she turned it until she grasped the small key for the padlock. In a matter of seconds, she unlocked the first storage compartment.

Grasping the handle on the door, she began to lift it. The door rumbled, stuck for an instant, then raised the rest of the way. Her gaze took a quick inventory of everything inside.

Her compartments were ten feet deep, fifteen feet wide. They were stacked high, but not so high that she couldn't reach everything. Rolled rugs stood in the corners, and labeled boxes lined the edges of the compartment. She kept a path open to walk through. Now she headed to the back, searching for the items she wanted to use for Marge and Grover Gentry's house. She had a meeting with them tomorrow morning to go over the proposal. She could begin staging on Monday. She'd alerted Bob Preston, whose painting crews she often used and a former classmate of Bella's, that she might need him on short notice.

As she was reading a list of items in one of the boxes, she heard a car engine outside. She didn't know why, but the sound scared her a little. This place was usually deserted. She wasn't normally skittish, and being alone here usually didn't bother her. But, of course, she'd left her pepper-spray gun in the car.

It was probably Ted's murder that had her spooked. If someone could break into his house and murder him, no place was safe.

Throwing off a fear she wanted no part of, she stepped outside again, just as the car pulled to a stop at her compartment.

She recognized that sedan. It was one of those sporty luxury cars where you talk to the console or something, and it either talked back or called someone on your list. The vehicle braked and the engine shut down. Her brother opened the driver's-side door. He had her personal code to get into the storage-locker center because he'd often helped her lug furniture in and out. Vince worked out, and his muscles had been a godsend. Today he was still dressed in a white shirt with a classy tie and suit trousers.

"What are you doing here?"

"I called Bella about Mom's birthday. She said you were headed over here. We have to pick a time to get together to talk about what we're going to do. My schedule is probably the least flexible, and I was wondering what you were thinking of."

Something about Vince's demeanor told her that wasn't all he had on his mind. "If we have the party at one of our places, we'll only need a few days to pull it together. After all, this is what I do," she said with a sly smile. "But you could have called my cell."

He was silent a moment. "Yes, I could have, but there's something more serious I thought we should talk about face-to-face."

"At my storage compartment?" Her question held curiosity he could obviously hear.

"Roz is at your house."

She didn't like the sound of that. "Is this something she shouldn't hear?"

Vince swiped his dark brown hair over his brow and scowled at her. "How did you get yourself mixed up in this?"

"*This* meaning a friendship with Roz?"

"Of course not. How did you get yourself involved in a murder investigation? You should never have gone down to the police station with her. Jones didn't ask you to come."

Be calm, she told herself. *Stay perfectly calm.* "You

should have seen Roz after the murder. She could hardly put two words together. I didn't want that to happen again."

"You're not her protector."

"Someone has to be. I don't know if Grant wants to be. I tried to call you."

"I was in court. There was nothing I could do about that. There's not much I can do now . . . or Grant, either, for that matter. She needs a criminal attorney, a defense attorney."

"We're hoping it doesn't come to that."

"Hope won't go very far if the district attorney brings charges against her," Vince reminded her with a bit of sarcasm.

"Do you know something I don't?"

"No. I know Grant talked to a contact in the D.A.'s office. That's about it. But they're not going to tip their hand in this. I just came here to talk some sense into you. Stay away from this. Stay far away from it."

"I found the body. I saw what someone did to Ted. No, he wasn't my favorite person, but nobody should die like that."

Although Vince's brows still furrowed, his expression softened somewhat. "You care too much." That was a criticism, but the way her brother's voice gentled, it didn't sting like it might have.

"Vince, isn't that the Italian way?"

He gave her a cockeyed smile. "I won't even go

there. Just promise me you'll call me if you get called in for questioning."

"Grant is handling it."

"No. Roz is his client. You're not. I doubt if the cops will even look your way. But I'm serious. Don't you say anything to them unless you have me with you."

"I'm sure it won't come to that." She wasn't about to tell Vince she was going to Curls R Us and the pharmaceutical company to check around. He wouldn't like that idea one little bit. But a girl had to do what a girl had to do.

"Did you pick up the wine yet for Sunday?" she teased.

"One of these times I'm going to bring a bottle of the cheapest Chianti, then we'll see how much everybody appreciates me."

She laughed. Her brother could be a bear sometimes and a real pain at others. Yet he could be charming too, and they loved him. "Seriously, what did you find for Sunday?"

"I'm going to drive up to Adam's County Winery on Saturday. I'll find something good."

Adams County Winery, north of Gettysburg, had a variety of wines to choose from, and she knew Vince would find something terrific. Since this Sunday was Mother's Day, it was a little more special than most. Her mom and Nana still insisted on cooking, but the kids had a tradition too, one they'd started when they'd gotten their first cameras. Every year she, Nikki, Vince, and Bella pooled photographs they'd taken over the year and created albums for their mom and Nana. They rotated the responsibility. This year Nikki was doing their mom's, and Vince was supposed to put together Nana's.

"Is Nana's album ready?"

"I finished it last night. I know I sometimes wait until the last minute, but not this year." Vince motioned to the storage compartment. "Do you need help with anything?"

"No. I'm good."

He focused on the contents of the shed, then turned his attention back to her. "I'm glad you're doing so well. Then Mom and Pop don't have to worry about you."

"And you never worry about me?"

He just gave her one of those big brother looks and walked to his car.

She waved as he drove off and then went back to taking inventory. She'd make a list. That way she wouldn't waste time if the Gentrys signed the contract. She hated wasting time. Right now, she didn't have any to spare.

Roz looked a combination of flustered, sad, and angry when Caprice returned home. The first thing she said was, "The police won't even let me get Ted's suit out of the house."

For a moment Caprice wondered why Roz needed Ted's suit, and then the fact hit her—Roz needed it for the funeral.

Dylan was winding in and out of Roz's feet as she paced across the living room. They looked as if they were doing some kind of odd dance, but Roz didn't seem to be bothered by the little dog almost tripping her.

"I called Grant, and he said he would see what he could do. But the police wouldn't budge. They won't tell me when they are going to release his body, either, but Grant seems to think that will be by Monday. He did say you can pick up your car at the police station. Mine might be available tomorrow."

Roz had so much to think about and so much to feel. Caprice saw Sophia had been keeping her friend company too. She was stretched out on Nana's afghan on the back of the sofa. Nana had crocheted the zigzag-pattern in the colors of Caprice's room. In the winter, she loved having a fire going in the fireplace while she curled up in the afghan with Sophia beside her.

Sophia's golden eyes seemed to follow Roz on her trips back and forth across the room.

"Now what are you going to do?" Caprice asked.

"I called the men's store, Just for Him. They do custom work. I told them I wanted a nice blue tweed and gave Ted's measurements. They're supposed to have the suit ready for me tomorrow afternoon."

She sighed and brought troubled eyes to Caprice's. "What worries me is that I can't seem to control my reactions. When Grant told me what the police said, I wanted to just yell and scream. Logically, I know that would do no good. Not only that, it would be totally out of character for me. I don't know what's happening. I feel a little bit crazy."

Her voice caught when she said it.

Caprice understood that Roz had lost her future. She'd not only lost the man she loved but the man she thought she'd have forever with. Add to that the news about Valerie Swanson and she'd lost her dream. The proverbial rug had been pulled out from under her feet. She was uncertain about what each day would bring and absolutely resented not being able to access everything she needed for her life.

Caprice knew exactly how *she'd* feel if she couldn't get back into her home. She wasn't sure anybody could keep her out.

"I'm going to do a little shopping for myself tomorrow afternoon too," Roz said. "I can't keep wearing your clothes. If I disguise myself a bit, no one will know I'm out and about. I just can't stay cooped up."

"Do you want some company? I'd like to stop

at the vintage shop." She was thinking about her date with Seth and what she wanted to wear. Sprucing up something she already had might be a good idea.

"That would be good. Then I don't have to worry about getting my car yet if you drive."

Roz suddenly stopped pacing and Dylan stopped too, gazing up at her as if he wanted to jump up into her arms. She opened them and he did. "I know I shouldn't let him do that. Bad habit."

Roz carried the dog to the sofa and sat with him. Dylan stood on his hind paws on her lap and licked her face.

"He's such a cutie. I'd like to take him for a real walk." She sighed. "Maybe I shouldn't go shopping."

"Because of reporters or because you're supposed to be in mourning?"

"Both. Especially because I'm in mourning. All of a sudden, I just want to break into tears. Sometimes I do. But then other times I'm worried about everything that happened and wonder what I should do. Dylan has been a great help. He licks my face when I cry, and he makes me feel like I'm not so alone."

"Maybe you should consider keeping him when this is all over." When Roz didn't respond, Caprice thought maybe she didn't want a dog after all.

But then Roz said, "If I don't go to prison."

"You can't think that way. I won't think that way."

After long moments when the only sound was

Dylan's contented sounds as Roz scratched his ears, Roz said, "I really have to look for an apartment, so I don't keep imposing on you. Even when the police release the house, I don't know if I can go back there. When I think about how cold it has felt lately, what you saw upstairs, what happened in the sword room, how can I possibly go back there?"

"Have you thought about what's going to happen when this is all over?"

"Not really."

"Would you consider going back to work again?"

Roz concentrated on Dylan and solely on Dylan for a long while. Finally she met Caprice's gaze. "I never have to work a day again in my life. Ted was heavily insured, and now I am, of course, the beneficiary."

Roz said it as if she was signing her arrest warrant.

Caprice jumped up so fast from her chair that even Sophia seem startled. She meowed, tilted her head, and looked at Caprice, asking why she'd disrupted her very nice nap.

Ignoring Sophia's meow of protest—or maybe it was just a yawn—Caprice asked, "You didn't tell anybody about this, did you?"

"No, but I'm sure it's one of the first things the police check."

"Did you tell Grant?"

"We didn't get into anything like that."

Caprice's stomach felt like it had sunk to the soles of her espadrilles. Roz was in deep doo-doo. Her motive for killing her husband was getting stronger and stronger. That didn't sway Caprice's belief in her, but it sure could sway everybody else's.

When her cell phone played its tune, Caprice was glad. She wasn't sure what to say to Roz about this new development. No wonder her cheeks looked a little sunken and the blue smudges under her eyes seemed darker. Caprice had to do something to help her feel better.

Checking the screen on her phone, she said to Roz, "It's Nikki. Do you want me to let it go to voice mail?"

"No, take it. I'll let Dylan out."

Roz was still standing in the kitchen, opening the storm door, when the first thing Nikki said to Caprice was, "So you have a date next Saturday."

"I can't believe Bella told you! She was supposed to keep it a secret. My date isn't anyone else's business."

"You know Bella can't keep secrets, certainly not from me. I used to torture her when we were kids, remember? Either she told me what she knew, or I hid all her barrettes where she'd never find them."

That made Caprice smile. Bella had cared as much about her hair when she was in grade school as she did as a teenager and an adult. Those barrettes had been prized possessions, and Nikki had known it and taken advantage of it. "So he's a doctor?"

"Do I really want to tell you any of this?"

"If I promise *I* can keep a secret, you will."

That was probably true. Nikki was much better at keeping secrets than Bella. "I'd just like to keep this under wraps for a while. At least through the first date. There might not be a second."

"If there isn't, it will be *your* doing, Miss One-Date-Wonder."

That's what they called her, and it always riled her. "Nikki . . ."

"You go out with a guy once and you decide he's not worth the risk. You put up lots of walls, and that's the end of it. Don't make this the end of it. You're going miniature golfing. That should be light, easy, teasing. Just let it be a lead in."

"A lead in to—"

"A lead in to another date, and then another, and then another. I know women who'd like to date Dr. Seth Randolph."

"*I* want to date him."

"Then give him something so he wants to see you again."

"Like . . ." The word was part question, part warning.

"Like a fun time with good conversation, not worrying about how much you're telling him, or how much you're not. For once in your life, don't think about what comes next. It's not like a room to be staged, Caprice, with this piece of furniture here and that piece of furniture there, and this color of paint on the wall, and that rug on the floor. Do *not* plan it. Just let something natural happen."

"This is what *you* do?"

There was a moment of silence when Nikki obviously felt caught. "It's what I *try* to do. Granted, it doesn't always work."

"I haven't seen it work at all."

"Last year I dated a guy for six weeks, remember? The one who was going to open his own restaurant?"

"But he didn't open it."

"No, his financing here fell through, and he decided to open it in a town in New Jersey!"

Suddenly they both burst into laughter. "So don't use me as your guru," Nikki advised her. "But go have some fun."

Roz opened the door and Dylan came in.

"I intend to have fun with Seth. I just don't want anyone to know about it." She'd intended to tell Roz, though, at the right time.

"Vince would get a big kick out of it and tease you unmercifully. Especially since you'd be dating a doctor. How cool is that?"

"*Not* all that cool, from what I understand. You know what a doctor's schedule is like. Or maybe you don't. Even Seth admits it's constant interruptions."

"So you just have to be the kind of woman who can handle them."

Maybe she was and maybe she wasn't. "We'll see. We have a lot of holes to clatter over before we get to that point. Speaking of holes to clatter over, we have to call a family meeting. When do you want to do it? I don't know what your schedule's like."

"Packed. It will have to be late one night after my jobs. Like nine o'clock."

"That would probably work better. Maybe we can meet at Bella's so she can put the kids to bed."

"That sounds good. Do you want me to call Vince to see when he's free?"

"Fine. Just don't tell him about my date. Please."

"I'll even pinkie-swear."

Caprice was still smiling when she hung up the phone.

"So you've got a date?" Roz asked with a hint of a smile. "I approve."

Caprice felt her cheeks flush a little. "I saw him at Grocery Fresh and he actually seems interested."

"Well, of course, he does. Why wouldn't he be interested?"

"Because I don't look like you," she said simply. "On top of that, I don't dress like you."

"So that's why you want to stop into the vintage shop and see what you can find for your date. I can spot a motive as well as you can." Roz was trying hard to force a lightness she didn't feel, but Caprice would help her in that. They'd go shopping tomorrow afternoon, and she might even let Roz pick out what she should wear. But for now . . .

"Come along with me to my parents' dinner on Sunday."

"I don't want to intrude."

"You won't be intruding. It's always confined chaos. It might help you forget for a little bit, and you can even help me get ready. I'm going to make bread on Saturday and the cream for the cannoli. Do you want to help?"

"I'm not good in the kitchen."

"Anybody can knead dough, and you can pretend you're a kid again, playing in the flour. What do you think?"

After a moment to consider it, Roz said, "I think I'm game for almost anything, except being questioned again about Ted's murder."

"We'll come up with a plan after we go clothes shopping."

"You're trying to keep me busy."

"You bet I am."

"Thank you."

Caprice knew even *busy* wasn't going to help Roz when she had to plan Ted's service. Yet Caprice understood a service could help with the grieving process. If friends and family were supportive.

Her family could help her support Roz, but would the police be at the funeral?

Caprice had the feeling Detective Jones and his partner would cover all the bases they could while keeping their focus on Roz, who was their prime suspect.

Chapter Nine

Caprice and Roz passed Cherry on the Top, Kismet's favorite ice cream shop, where almost as many passersby gathered as they did at the Koffee Klatch. Gossip ran rampant at both.

Roz didn't even glance at Cherry on the Top. Wearing a baseball cap, a ponytail, sunglasses, and a pair of Caprice's embroidered jeans that were too big at the waist and too short, she'd been silent during most of this errand, which had been more practical than enjoyable.

Early this morning, Nikki had taken Caprice to the police station to pick up her car. Afterward, Caprice had met with the Gentrys, who'd signed on the dotted line. This afternoon, before she and Roz had left the house to shop, Caprice had received a call from Juan's sister, who'd explained his surgery had gone well. Relieved, Caprice had driven Roz to the back entrance of the mall. Within a half hour of selecting from the racks, they'd paid and come downtown, stopping at Just for Him on the way.

Now spotting Secrets of the Past, the vintage shop Caprice favored most, only a few storefronts away, Caprice touched Roz's elbow. "We don't have to shop. I'm sure I can find something in my closet for my date."

Immediately, Roz rallied. "Nonsense! We came to find you something special, and we will."

Caprice tried again. "I understand if your mind is elsewhere. Mine would be too."

"It's everywhere. And I don't know *how* I'm supposed to feel. I learned Ted betrayed me. Yet he's dead and I can't even yell at him!"

"You never yell," Caprice reminded her reasonably.

It was true. Roz was one of the most even-tempered women she knew. Or else her friend merely held everything in. Because she'd practiced holding everything in as a child who'd missed her deceased father? Because the whole time she'd taken care of her mom, she was feeling the pain too? Because a good wife supported her husband no matter what she suspected?

Caprice knew she could never be that kind of "good" wife. Not ever.

"I feel like yelling now," Roz said. "I feel like screaming at the top of my lungs. Then the next minute I want to close all the blinds and hide. But

I can't do either. Grieving for my husband is just going to have to get in line with everything else I'm feeling. In the meantime, we're buying you an outfit. The last time I spoke with Suzanne, she was adding a new designer to her inventory."

Customers shopped at Secrets for many reasons. All of the clothes were retro in design, fabric, or age. Merchandise that Suzanne Dumas, the owner of the boutique, didn't find at auctions, yard sales, or online, she took on consignment from designers trying to establish a brand. Roz bought designer clothes, but Caprice looked at true vintage whenever she could.

Mannequins posed in the front window dressed in a fifties-style sleeveless dress in a flowered pattern, a seventies tunic with coordinating plaid slacks, and a cardigan sweater with pearl buttons paired with a skirt fashioned with embroidery around the hem. Purses from past decades decorated the front window dais. The most special element of this shop was the fact that each and every item for sale was unique. That was the main reason Caprice bought most of her clothes here.

When Roz pulled the door open, a chime tinkled, announcing their arrival.

At one of the circular racks where coats and jackets hung on a chrome bar, Suzanne stood with a customer and waved. "I haven't seen either of you for a while."

So much for Roz's "disguise." She'd removed her sunglasses and Suzanne had recognized her immediately.

A thought registered then on the shopkeeper's face—probably one of the many news accounts that had been broadcast since the murder—and her demeanor changed. She approached Roz. "I'm so sorry for your loss."

"Thank you," Roz murmured.

Suzanne wore vintage clothes herself. Today she was dressed in a long, fitted, black-and-white tunic with a mandarin collar and a slim black skirt. Her jet-black hair was curled back from her face in a forties style. In her late forties, she was always impeccably dressed and groomed. Her long nails were painted red and matched her lipstick.

Caprice stepped away from Roz to allow her to speak privately with the shop owner. She needed the condolences of friends and acquaintances to move forward in the grieving process.

But other customers in the store had heard Suzanne and glanced toward Roz. A brunette trying on hats at a corner mirror registered Roz's presence, then adjusted her felt fedora, paying no more mind. Two women in sportswear, as if they'd been out for a walk and decided on the spur of the moment to see what Secrets had to offer, were suddenly conversing head-to-head in low tones. They looked to be around her mom's age. At the front window, a blonde who might have been in her late twenties fingered a black patent-leather purse.

Since Suzanne and Roz seemed involved in conversation, Caprice moseyed over to a display of tunics and blouses. Since she owned an array of slacks, she could mix and match almost any style or color of blouse. She didn't wear suits for appointments and was glad her clients didn't expect her to. If they did, she disabused them quickly of that notion. She'd made a name for herself because her style was different. The fact that her clients recommended her to their friends and coworkers confirmed the fact that they liked "unique" and appreciated Caprice's results.

A bright tunic in purple and blue with crocheted bell sleeves quickly captured her interest. Removing it from the hook, she studied the ticket. Vintage, all right. She fingered the fabric, which would be comfortable as summer moved in. This part of Pennsylvania could remain warm and balmy until mid-June or turn incredibly hot overnight.

Moments later, her decision made, Caprice carried the blouse over to the cashier's desk, knowing it would fit. It was flowing and a little loose. With lilac capri pants it would look terrific for a game of miniature golf. She would look terrific. Now she just needed Seth to think so. *And what if he thinks you look terrific? Then what?*

According to Nikki, she shouldn't be thinking of "then what." But she always did.

Automatically her thoughts flew back in time to Craig. A long-distance relationship just hadn't worked. They'd been young, and she'd obviously been more in love than he had.

Suddenly she realized that same condition had plagued her with Travis. She'd loved him. They'd talked about buying an engagement ring and planning a future. She'd gotten attached to his little girl and looked forward to becoming her stepmom— someone important in her life. But then Travis and his ex-wife had attended an interview for Kristi's preschool. And they hadn't just gone to the interview. Travis had fixed a leaky faucet at his old house and then . . .

A month later he'd broken off his relationship with Caprice.

Yep, she'd cared too much, a lot more than he had. Was he happy now? Had the problems that had caused his divorce reared their heads again? She was a terrible person if she wished that. So time after time, she'd willed herself to wish him nothing but happiness.

Lost in ghosts of relationships past, Caprice didn't realize the two women in sportswear outfits had moved. They were approaching Roz fast, and their expressions didn't project an intention to give her condolences.

They looked angry!

The woman in green stretch slacks and a zippered top marched up to Roz and asked combatively,

"Are you Ted Winslow's wife?" The woman's friend was right beside her, and both of them were in Roz's face.

"Yes, I am," Roz responded with dignity, casting a questioning look at them both.

"Your husband got what he deserved!"

There was so much venom in the woman's tone that an audible hush blanketed the shop.

Suzanne tried to step in. "Mrs. Benson. This isn't the place or the time—"

But Mrs. Benson cut her off. "This is exactly the time and place. I don't run in the same circles she does." She turned her wrath on Roz again. "Your husband let fifteen workers go, some who only needed a year or two before they could retire . . . like my husband. Where is he supposed to get a decent job at age sixty? With no pension, what are we supposed to do? We're not old enough for Social Security. I can't get more hours where I work. Ted Winslow destroyed people's lives. And for what? All because he wanted to take PA Pharm overseas and make more profit. Despicable! That's what that whole company is. Maybe now that he's dead, some of us can sleep better at night."

Caprice had had enough. She hurried to Roz's side and pushed in between Roz and Mrs. Benson. "No matter what Ted Winslow did or didn't do, you have no right to attack his wife. She lost her husband."

"Yeah, and he probably left her well off too," the

other woman muttered. Then she grabbed Mrs. Benson's arm. "C'mon, June. I'm sorry I brought you in here with me. Let's go."

As soon as the two women left, Suzanne's face flushed with embarrassment. She said to Roz, "I can't believe she went after you like that. I'm sorry."

Roz looked shaken but managed to say, "That wasn't your fault. I just wish I had known everything that was going on at PA Pharm." She shook her head. "I just wish I had known what was going on in my life. Was I absolutely blind?" she asked Caprice.

"Not blind. The company probably wanted to keep layoffs and firings quiet until they shaved down their workforce . . ." She trailed off, remembering what her mother had told her about the parent-teacher meeting.

"What?" Roz asked, watching her expression.

Vince always told her she made a lousy poker player because too much showed on her face. No point hiding from Roz a confrontation that had been so public. She related her mom's story.

"My gosh! Ted had so many people mad at him. Anyone could have done this."

But Suzanne shook her head and lowered her voice. "Not just anyone, Roz. Someone with more to lose than anyone else."

Smart woman, thought Caprice. Just who did have the most to lose?

One thing Caprice knew for sure. She was definitely going to fish around at the drug company and see what damaging information might be hidden behind closed doors.

On Sunday evening, Caprice and Roz approached her parents' house. It was the house where Caprice had grown up, and its architecture seemed out of place in Pennsylvania. In fact, it might have been better suited for California.

When her parents had bought the corner property, with its golden stucco exterior, red-tiled roof, casement windows, and balconies, they'd known it would probably be a fixer-upper for the rest of their lives. They'd made improvements over the years that had made maintenance easier. They'd also designed an addition so Nana could have her own apartment. Her father had always maintained they'd gotten a great deal on a house they might never have been able to afford as a young, married couple because buyers didn't want upkeep or to pour sweat into a project that could take years. But her dad had been used to working hard, and some of his construction-wise buddies had helped along the way.

As Caprice opened the side porch door that led into the foyer—another door on the same porch led into the kitchen—she glanced over her shoulder at Roz. If anything could help her feel better, it was a dinner with the De Luca family. Roz had none of her own family to rally around her at a time like this. She didn't have the comfort of anyone else who missed Ted . . . anyone else she could share stories with and bring back the good memories.

Especially on Mother's Day, she knew Roz could use some mothering. The past few days had been rough, to say the least. After their shopping trip, she'd learned her house had been released, but she was in hibernation mode and hadn't wanted to face reclaiming it after the York County forensic team had done their job. Persuading her to come along tonight had been a monumental task. Caprice had finally enlisted her mother's help. After a phone conversation with her mom, Roz had agreed to join them today.

Caprice had parked along the curb behind Vince's sporty sedan. The Santini family's red van, as well as Nikki's cobalt-blue sedan, lined the curb around the side of the house. Also parked there was a silver SUV that looked like Grant's. Had her brother asked his partner to come along? Lots of drivers owned silver SUVs.

Standing in the foyer, Caprice could see the empty living room through the high archway to the left. Voices carried to the foyer from the dining room straight ahead. A cuckoo emerging from an antique cuckoo clock on the dining room wall announced five o'clock.

Roz said, "I remember being fascinated with that clock when I was a teenager."

Suddenly, Bella's children zoomed from the dining room into the foyer. Timmy, Bella's eight-year-old, was never still for long. Four-year-old Megan followed wherever he went. Caprice could remember trailing Vince around in the same way.

"Where are you headed?" Caprice asked, when they would have run by her.

Timmy motioned to the stairway that led to the second floor. "Gran needs her sweater. It's on her bed upstairs. We're gettin' it."

Then they were gone, clomping up the stairs.

"Mom probably has all the windows open in the dining room. She can't wait to let warmer weather in. C'mon. I have to drop my cards on the table, stow this cream in the fridge until we're ready for dessert, and slip this bread into the oven to warm it."

"I can smell onion and garlic and tomatoes. This house always smells so good."

When she, Bella, Nikki, and Vince were kids, the family had a hectic schedule. While Vince played basketball, Bella took dance. Nikki had been involved in soccer, and Caprice had taken music lessons. But their mom had urged them to sit down to dinner as a family as often as they could. She and Nana both agreed that a good meal was the one great event that could draw people together. That's why on Mother's Day, they insisted on cooking too.

The dining room was bedlam, and Caprice spotted the vase of pink roses her dad always sent to her mom on this day. She knew a vase of tulips would be gracing her grandmother's suite of rooms. Everyone stopped to hug each other. Another De Luca tradition. Amid "Happy Mother's Days" for both her mom and Nana, Caprice noticed that her family enthusiastically welcomed Roz into the fold. Everyone was enthusiastic except for Grant, who stood to one side of the room looking uncomfortable. Caprice didn't know whether she should just stay away from him and get involved in the rest of the commotion or acknowledge him. Long-ingrained manners took over after extra-long hugs for her mother and grandmother.

"This is a surprise." Probably not the best opener she ever thought of.

As soon as she said it, Grant had a defensive tilt to his chin.

"I mean—" she quickly went on.

But Grant held his hand up to stop her. "Vince and I played one-on-one this afternoon. I said something about catching a game on TV and ordering a pizza, and he said I should forget the pizza, eat ravioli, and watch the game here with him, your dad, and Joe."

"You're welcome to come anytime." Again the

words were out of her mouth before she had time
to filter them. All she could think about was that
once Grant had been part of a family too, and now
he wasn't. Dinners in front of the TV were probably
the norm.

"That's what your mom said," he admitted.

"She and I think alike *some* of the time," she
joked.

Then the air between them went silent even
though conversations swirled around them.

Caprice had the strangest sensation that she
needed to step away before—

Before what?

She didn't know. She lifted the container she'd
set on the table during the hugging fest. "I have to
put the cannoli cream in the fridge and warm up
the bread. I'll talk to you later."

When he nodded, she suddenly felt as if there
was a gulf as wide as the continental United States
between them.

After a quick trip to the kitchen, she entered the
dining room again and, to her surprise, saw that
Vince was the one talking to Roz. Caprice watched
from across the room as her brother said something and Roz smiled. Good for Vince. He could
use his "charm" gene for once today. She looked
from her brother, who was usually grinning, to
Grant, whose expression gave nothing away. Both
men were dressed in jeans and T-shirts. Both were
tall enough to make a game of one-on-one really

interesting. Both could easily get weekend dates with a casual invitation. Vince did every weekend. Grant didn't. Two very different men.

She thought about her date with Seth next weekend. He seemed like the type of man who knew how to have fun. Did Grant? Or would someone have to teach him how to have fun all over again?

That question was unsettling.

A half hour later, Caprice's father sat at the head of the table and asked for a quiet moment of thanks for the food before them and for mothers everywhere, particularly their own. Afterward Caprice passed the ravioli mounded high on the platter, the antipasto, broccoli casserole, and homemade bread. Conversations chased each other around the table. Nikki had taken the chair on Caprice's right and Bella the one on her left. Grant sat between Joe and Vince on the other side of the table.

To keep her focus from drifting to Grant, Caprice concentrated on Joe, wondering if Bella had told him she was pregnant. He didn't seem bothered by anything and was joking with Vince about sports teams, as he always did. Bella, on the other hand, seemed quieter than usual. After she cut Megan's ravioli into bite-size pieces she could handle, she reached over her daughter to tap Timmy on the shoulder, making sure he had everything he wanted. As Caprice had noticed many times before, Bella was such a good mom. Although acerbic and sometimes impatient with her siblings, she never seemed to mind fulfilling her children's needs.

And Joe? He paid attention when he had to.

Apparently trying to make conversation with everyone around the table, Vince caught Bella's eye and asked, "So what was wrong with your car this time? I heard it was out of commission."

"Heard from whom?" she asked tersely.

Vince looked perplexed at her tone. "From Dad. Or Joe." He glanced at Joe, but he was recapping a baseball game with Grant.

Bella eyed Caprice, then answered her brother's question. "A head gasket."

Vince let out a slow whistle. "You might as well put that money into a down payment on a new car."

Bella rose quickly to her feet and pushed her chair back. "Maybe *you* could do that. But we can't afford that kind of bill every month. I'm going to cut more bread. The basket's almost empty."

Before Caprice even had time to register what *that* was all about, Bella had disappeared into the kitchen with the basket.

Nikki started rising to her feet to go after Bella, but Caprice laid a hand on her sister's shoulder and stood herself. "I'll talk to her." If Bella hadn't told anyone else she was pregnant, she sure wouldn't confide in anyone right now.

In the kitchen, Bella was sawing at the loaf of bread as if her life depended on it.

"What's wrong?" Caprice asked, keeping her tone low.

"Nothing's wrong."

"Bella," Caprice said with some exasperation. "Everyone can see something is. Have you talked to Joe?"

"Not yet. I'm just not ready. I thought *you* told Vince about the car and maybe about my pregnancy." The last was said on almost a whisper.

"I wouldn't do that. I told you I'd keep your secret."

Bella looked guilty for a moment. "I didn't keep yours. But I thought you'd want Nikki to know you were going on a date."

Caprice kept silent but transferred the bread Bella had cut to the basket.

"I'll tell him soon," Bella assured her.

Giving Bella a few more minutes to compose herself, Caprice returned to the rest of her family.

Nikki tossed her a questioning look, but Caprice just shrugged.

To her relief, Nana was asking Vince, "So who did you take out *last* night?"

Nana's dark brown eyes were alight with mischief. She always wore her long, gray-brown hair in a knot to one side of her nape, and today tortoiseshell combs decorated with seed pearls held it in place. Although wrinkles across her forehead and around her eyes hinted at her seventy-five years, her voice held the vibrancy of someone much younger.

"How do you know I was out last night?" Vince returned with a grin.

"If it was Saturday, you were out."

He gave up sparring. "I took Janet Grayson to a club in York."

"Where did you meet her?" Nana persisted.

Vince might have shut down the questions with anyone else, but not with Nana. "I met her at the convenience store. There was a long line and we started talking."

Forestalling the next logical question, he added, "She works at the home improvement store." He wiggled his brows. "She can get me a discount if I want to repaint my place."

"So you're going to take her out again?" Nana wanted to know.

"We'll see."

"I'm not ready to give up on you yet, young man. When you bring one of your dates to our dinners, I'll know you're ready to settle down."

Studying everyone at the table, Caprice could see Roz appeared comfortable now, seated between Nana and her mother. They were keeping the focus off her, and that's just what she needed.

After everyone had their fill of the main course, Caprice filled the cannoli, garnishing them with the requisite shaved chocolate, pistachio pieces, and chopped, glazed cherries. Nikki and their mom brought in the coffee, and then all of them presented their mom and grandmother their photo albums. After comparing the pictures, which were different in each album, Caprice served dessert while her mom and Nana opened their cards. Conversations eventually dwindled. The kids had already been excused, and the grown-ups began clearing the table.

Vince, Joe, and her father migrated to the living room and the large, flat-screened TV. Caprice, Bella, and Nikki urged their mom and Nana to sit and talk while the sisters rinsed dishes, stowed away food, and loaded the dishwasher. When Caprice returned to the dining room to remove the tablecloth so she could dump it into the washing machine, she found Grant standing at the triple set of casement windows overlooking the tiered backyard. Bushes and flowers adorned the upper level, while the vegetable and herb gardens spread across the lower level.

"Not watching the game?" she asked lightly, wondering if he was going to leave because all of her family was too much for him.

"I was hoping to catch you. Roz has given me permission to talk openly with you about her case."

"Has something happened?"

"Not specifically. Not substantially. But I spoke with a friend in the D.A.'s office and he's reliable. Apparently Roz seems to be the main person of interest."

"But there *are* others." She hurriedly told him about the parent in her mother's school who'd been laid off as well as the confrontation in Secrets of the Past.

Grant rubbed his chin. "Maybe Detective Jones discovered her husband's affair."

Caprice thought of something else he might have discovered. She moved a step closer to Grant and caught the scent of soap rather than cologne. "Did Roz tell you Ted's life insurance policy would keep her comfortable for life?"

"No, she didn't." Grant stuffed his hands into his jeans' pockets. "She's in trouble. They have more than enough motive."

"That's why I'm going to PA Pharm and fish around."

Surprised dismay on his face, Grant took her arm. "No, you are *not.*"

She stared him squarely in the eyes and stated firmly, "Yes, I am."

He must have heard the you-can't-tell-me-what-to-do determination in her voice because he said with just as much determination, "Then I'm going with you."

Chapter Ten

When Caprice and Monty Culp pushed the rust and blue sofa into place facing the fireplace at the Gentrys' house on Monday, Caprice finally admitted the room was almost ready. Monty had been a huge help and was a good worker.

So why had he and Ted argued? Simply about cutting hours?

Monty was in his late twenties, with limp, sandy hair that was usually falling over his eyes. He was wiry, but strong, and had hefted furniture like a mover. When she'd called him, he'd jumped at the chance to help her. They'd met at the storage locker, where they'd loaded everything they'd need into her van. Over the weekend, the couple had put into storage everything Caprice had suggested.

Before she'd arrived today, Bob had finished painting the kitchen the palest blue, a backdrop for the rental company's distressed white baker's rack. Marge's dining set was perfect the way it was. By evening the house would be ready for sale. Caprice had scheduled the open house for Sunday of the Memorial Day weekend. They'd moved fast because Grover and Marge were anxious to find their dream estate and move. Denise Langford was an expert at publicity for these open houses. Tomorrow, she'd have a crew shoot photos and video for her Web site.

Monty wiped his brow and glanced up at the high ceiling and the wall of windows, which let in magnificent sunlight. "Nice place," he said as if seeing it for the first time.

"Yes, it is. Not as uniquely different as the Winslows', but beautiful in its own right." She was hoping to encourage Monty to talk about Ted. She hadn't wanted to just jump into the conversation earlier, but now with everybody else gone, the timing seemed right.

"You were a friend of theirs, weren't you?" Monty asked, eyeing her curiously.

"I'm a friend of Roz's."

"Mrs. Winslow's nice. She gives a guy an even break."

Monty had possibly seen her around when she'd visited Roz, but he probably didn't know she'd been with Roz when they'd found the body. That information hadn't been released. And Caprice was glad because that meant no reporters were hounding her. Yet Roz had gotten call after call on her cell phone that she hadn't answered. Thank goodness, the journalists hadn't found her. After the funeral, that might be a different story. Roz wanted to keep the service at the funeral home and the cemetery private, but everybody noticed when a hearse traveled through Kismet.

"So Mr. Winslow wasn't fair?" she asked Monty after he moved a library table in place behind the sofa.

"He didn't know the meaning of fair. After I worked for him for four years, he was cutting me loose."

Now that surprised Caprice. "Altogether?"

"He said they'd be selling the house soon, and he didn't need somebody full-time. I pointed out he'd still need somebody to cut the grass every week, but he was hiring some kid to do it. He was going to pay him under the table, probably less than minimum wage."

Caprice wondered if that would be news to Roz too.

"Was that the first you'd . . . disagreed about something?"

"Hell, no! Usually he wasn't around, and that was fine with me. Mrs. Winslow knew what she wanted, and when I did it, she was happy. But Mr. Winslow . . . He would come home from one of his trips, ask why I didn't do this or how come I didn't do that differently. He was a pain in the . . ." Monty stopped.

"I get it," Caprice said with a smile to show she understood. After all, sometimes she'd had overly critical clients who could be more than a thorn in her side.

There was no easy way to ask her next question delicately, so she just asked it. "Were you on the property at all the day Ted was murdered?"

Monty gave her a long, studying look. "Why do you want to know?"

How much to say? How much not to say? But since Monty liked Roz, and since most people knew the spouse was suspect number one, she responded, "Mrs. Winslow needs someone to help account for her whereabouts that day. I was just wondering if you saw her."

His body stance seemed to relax a bit. To her dismay, he shook his head. "No, I didn't see her. I was there that morning early, to dump some mulch in a couple of the flower beds. But I was gone before anybody was up."

Of course, she couldn't tell for sure, but he seemed to be telling the truth.

Until he offered nonchalantly, "I did come by the next morning, though. I hadn't heard about what happened. When I got there, there were police cars and that yellow tape all around. They wouldn't let me on the property."

"You mean they wouldn't let you near the house."

"No, that's not what I mean. I came up the back road to the place, and I guess they weren't expecting that. So I was in the backyard before I realized

I shouldn't be. They were doing stuff around the back of the house."

Caprice suspected that "they" were York County's forensic team. "Did you see anything different that morning? Different from when you were there the last time?"

"Yeah, I did. It was a break in the side hedge where it looked like someone had pushed through. I know those bushes. I trim them every couple of weeks."

A break in the hedge. She remembered the evening of the murder and the open back door. Studying Monty now, looking him over from his lank hair to his oversize T-shirt to his baggy jeans, she had to wonder if he could've been angry enough with Ted to stab him.

Caprice was attaching a curtain tie-back into place two hours later when her cell phone rang. She pulled it from her pocket, hearing Monty moving around in the kitchen. He was emptying the cartons of place settings, the cookie jar for the counter, and some woven place mats.

When she saw Grant's number she pressed TALK. "Hi! Are you ready to do some sleuthing with me?" she asked.

Grant's answer was quick. "No, I'm still trying to talk you out of it, remember?"

"What if I told you I don't need you to go along to PA Pharm?"

There was a beat of silence. "If you're determined, we can set up a time. I have my schedule for the week in front of me. But I think it should wait until after the funeral."

"The funeral? Was Ted's body released?"

"Roz hasn't told you?"

"I'm working, Grant. I'm on site. I wasn't with her this morning. But she hasn't called me and that worries me."

"Give her some space, Caprice. She has arrangements to make and a hundred and one things to do. I just wanted to give you a heads-up. I can't go with you out to PA Pharm until later in the week. Roz has asked me to accompany her to the services. I don't want Jones or anyone the chief might have called in to assist to catch her in a weak moment."

"She didn't do it, Grant."

"I don't make that determination. I'm just protecting her rights."

Was he really that cold? Or was this a tough-guy act that he put on for the world so they wouldn't see what was really inside?

He didn't wait for a response from her, but added, "My guess is the funeral will be on Wednesday. Giselle is going to rearrange my schedule. If it is, I'll have about an hour or so Thursday afternoon around three if you insist on going to PA Pharm."

"I insist."

"I thought you might. It will probably be easier if I meet you there. I should be able to spot your car in the parking lot."

Was that sarcasm or a bit of humor? It was hard to tell.

"Three o'clock Thursday is okay with me. You've got ten minutes leeway. Beyond that I won't wait." She could be as tough as nails if she had to be too.

"Have you always been this . . . strong-willed?" he asked with some irritation.

"I've developed that very good quality over the years."

He made some kind of a noise, but she wasn't sure what it was supposed to mean. Then he said, "Once funeral arrangements are made, I might have to act as chauffeur to make the situation easier. Roz and I will figure it out. She'll probably want you with us. Try to stay out of trouble until then." He hung up.

It was probably good he didn't know she was going to go to Curls R Us tomorrow to do some questioning. If he knew, he might want to go along there too.

But she doubted it.

The following afternoon, Caprice dropped off a casserole at Juan's apartment, checking in on him. He was doing as well as could be expected, learning to use his crutches. Afterward, on the way over to

Curls R Us, she'd decided to be a walk-in appointment. Curls R Us was one of those salons where a
client could call for an appointment or walk in and
take the next stylist who wasn't busy.

Ted's memorial at the funeral home and his
graveside service was scheduled for tomorrow.
Fitting in this visit today had seemed to be the best
idea. Hairstylists liked to talk. They talked more
freely in the course of a hairstyling than they did if
someone came in off the street and asked them
questions.

Bella had told her about the sign-in sheet as well
as some of the stylists who worked there. Their
shifts varied, and sometimes they covered for each
other.

As Caprice parked in the small side lot and approached the salon, she hoped this was Valerie's
day off. Bella had told her Valerie usually didn't
work on Tuesday.

The salon wasn't fancy. The hours on the door
were painted in black block lettering under
CURLS R US. The heavy glass door pulled hard.

As soon as she walked in, she could see the
whole shop. There were about ten black vinyl
and chrome chairs. Two of the stations were special cubicles for washing hair. To the right, a wall
holder held books with all different kinds of
hairdos for both men and women. There were
magazines too, scattered on a low table under the
front plate-glass window. To the left were shelves

of styling products—mousses, gels, shampoos, and conditioners from at least two different suppliers. Bella had told her there wasn't a receptionist per se. Each stylist checked her own customers in and out. Whoever was free and nearest the phone picked it up. It was definitely a low-overhead shop.

Caprice spotted the clipboard on the black Formica desk with its pencil attached by a string. No one waited in the reception area. Seven out of the eight stations—four along each wall—were occupied. One client was having her hair frosted or highlights added, however you wanted to look at it. The tinfoil wrapped in her hair made her head look as if she were going to receive signals from outer space. Another woman was having a full color treatment. One was getting a perm. The others were in various stages of the wash, dry, and style process.

Caprice didn't particularly want a strange stylist cutting her hair. Yet just a wash and dry wouldn't take enough time. And with a hairdryer blasting, they couldn't talk. If she asked for just a slight trim, she should be safe enough. The bottom line was that Bella had her hair trimmed here, so they must do a good job. Bella was a perfectionist, and she wouldn't keep returning if she didn't like the service.

The stylists all wore black smocks. The patrons

were covered in pink aprons. She could certainly tell who was who. She just wished—

In some ways she wished she didn't have to do this investigating. She wished she could just comfort Roz, support her through this ordeal, and not have to deal with more. However, Roz herself couldn't figure out what had happened. She was too deep into lies and betrayal and love and memories and grief. Now that she had to plan the funeral too, Caprice could see that. When she'd come home to check on Roz yesterday, the first thing Roz had said to her was, "I played with Dylan outside and I fed Sophia. You don't have to worry about them."

Caprice had said, "I'm worried about *you.* Grant called me. Are you okay?"

"As okay as I'm going to be. I spoke with the representative of the funeral home. And the minister came over while you were gone. I hope that was all right?"

"Of course it was."

"I have to spend some time today deciding on readings for the service. I just have such mixed feelings about all of it."

"But you did love Ted."

"Yes, I did." Roz's voice had trembled and tears had come quickly.

"Do you want me to stay here with you? I can finish up at the Gentrys in the morning. Afterward

I'm going to Curls R Us and question a couple of the stylists."

"I can't believe you're doing this for me."

"If I were in the bind you're in, I'd want someone to look out for me. I'm just trying to find the answers, Roz. That's all."

And now Caprice wondered what those answers might be as she studied the clipboard and the form there. She could probably get more information out of everyone who had worked around Valerie, rather than Valerie herself, whom she didn't see anywhere. She could be in a back office. Or she could be off. Caprice wanted to hear the buzz, the rumors, and the facts as Valerie's employees saw them. She guessed those would be very different than what came out of Valerie's mouth.

A young stylist who had to be younger than twenty-five, her blunt-cut, chin-length hair swaying against her cheeks when she walked, came toward the desk and smiled at her. Caprice knew where she was going to start. "Hi! A friend told me I could just walk in, get a trim, shampoo, and style. Is that true?" The name tag on the stylist said YVONNE.

"Yes, that's true. Did you have anyone in mind?" In a lowered voice, she confided, "If you did, you'll have to wait."

"My friend said I should try to get Valerie. She owns the place, right? My friend said she's very good."

Yvonne gave a little sniff. "Valerie's good because

she owns the shop. Her rep gets gossiped about more than ours. But the rest of us are talented too."

"So Valerie isn't here today?"

"She hasn't been in since last week."

"Vacation?" Caprice asked innocently.

"We're not sure."

Thinking she better dial it back a notch, Caprice asked, "So you'll be my stylist?"

"If you're okay with that and don't want someone else."

"Let's give it a try. I just want the barest trim, wash, and blow-dry."

"Then come on," Yvonne said with a smile. "I'm your girl."

At the other stations, hair dryers blasted and women gossiped about whatever the hottest topic of the week was. Many of the conversations were personal. It seemed like these stylists took an interest in their clients' lives. She heard one stylist ask, "So Cindy has decided what college she wants to go to?" At another station Caprice overheard, "Now he wants our kids every other weekend. I don't know if I'm ready for that."

Yvonne led Caprice to one of the two sinks designated for hair washing and motioned for her to sit in the chair. She attached the pink apron.

"Have you worked here long?" Caprice asked, seemingly making small talk.

"Two years now. Usually I work evening hours. I

have a two-year-old at home. But we were short-staffed this week, so here I am."

"Easier to get a babysitter in the evenings?" Caprice asked.

"My husband watches Linda then. More economical if we don't have to pay for day care . . . or night care."

Caprice was glad that Yvonne seemed forthcoming. It would be much easier to elicit information.

For the next few minutes, Caprice gave herself up to the lovely sensation of having her hair washed, her scalp massaged a bit with the shampoo, and then a nice-smelling conditioner smoothed through her hair. She loved the idea of being pampered. She didn't indulge herself often. When she thought about Bella and how she liked having her hair trimmed every six weeks, Caprice realized a gift certificate from here could be a great present.

As soon as Yvonne was finished with the washing and conditioning process, she squeezed the excess water out of Caprice's hair. After she expertly wrapped a towel around it, she directed, "Come on over to my station."

Once Caprice was settled, Yvonne removed the towel and pulled a wide-tooth comb through her hair. "You have beautiful hair. It's in great condition. Ever think of adding a few red highlights?"

Caprice had thought about it, but she just didn't want to process her hair. To Yvonne she said, "I've considered it, but I really like it to look natural."

"Oh, it would look natural. I wouldn't put in streaks or anything like that. I'd just bring out your hair's natural color."

Caprice's natural color was dark brown, and she intended to keep it that way. Yvonne was probably working, in part, on commission. The more processes she did, the more she made.

"I'll think about it," Caprice assured her. She would think about it. She just wouldn't have it done.

After Yvonne sectioned off her hair with clips, she began snipping.

"I suppose this is your busiest time of year."

"It's busy. Everyone wants summer cuts," Yvonne responded.

"It's a shame you're short-handed. Do you know when Miss Swanson will be back?"

"She hasn't called in, which is unusual for her. She's constantly watching over our shoulders." Yvonne looked a bit sheepish. "Please don't tell anybody I said that."

"Of course, I won't. Other than that, is she a good boss?"

Yvonne shrugged. "Mostly she just wants to make sure her clients are satisfied so they come back. I guess in the long run, she's really looking out for all of us."

"I guess," Caprice agreed, giving the nod for Yvonne to tell her more.

"The thing is—" Yvonne looked around and saw everyone was busy. She trimmed a little more, then went on, "Valerie doesn't seem to care about us as women. She doesn't really want to hear what's going on in our lives. Probably because hers is too full."

Caprice could see Yvonne was making excuses for an employer who might be a little cold.

"You mean if you're late because your little girl is sick, she doesn't really care?"

"Something like that. Really, I think it's just because she's in love."

"Love can do funny things," Caprice murmured. "A girl could lose her good sense."

Yvonne laughed. "That's for sure. I know I did. And Valerie, well . . ." Yvonne leaned a little closer to Caprice. "She's dating a married man."

"Really?" Caprice didn't want to seem too shocked or Yvonne wouldn't go on.

"Lots of sneaking around," Yvonne said. "She often leaves work early, leaves her car in the parking lot, and gets into this big, black one with tinted windows."

Caprice could feel her temper rising on Roz's behalf. But Yvonne was just repeating what she knew. "So all of you know about this?"

"We talk when Valerie's not here. We don't know who the guy is, though. She's kept that part a secret. My guess is she's on vacation with him right now on some island."

Or not, Caprice thought. Valerie might be holed up with the blinds drawn. She could be hiding, hoping nobody found her out. *If* she'd killed Ted. Or she could be curled up in a ball, crying because he was dead.

"About how long has Valerie been dating this guy?"

"At least the past six months. That's when she got that extra spring in her step. Not so long ago, she told us he was going to divorce his wife and marry her."

When Caprice had walked into the salon and passed by the other clients, a gray-haired woman in the stylist's chair directly across the room from her had given her the once-over and was staring now. Every time the stylist turned her chair around toward Caprice, the woman studied her more closely. It was making Caprice vaguely uncomfortable.

The hairstylist put the finishing touches on the older woman's hair and gave it a last coating of hair spray. Then the woman stood and, instead of going to the cashier's desk, came toward Caprice. "Aren't you that home-stager who takes in animals?"

A couple of months before, the *Kismet Crier* had printed a story on her and her occupation as home-stager and had mentioned that she took in stray animals. It had been a well-written article. A few Kismet residents had even stopped Caprice on the street when they saw her. She'd also gotten a couple of calls for jobs and had been pleased with the splash the article had made. She'd sent a thank-you e-mail to Marianne Brisbane, the reporter who'd interviewed her.

"Yes, I do home-staging, and I take in strays now and then when I find them . . . or they find me."

The woman thrust out her hand. "I'm Ruth Pennington."

Caprice shook it. "It's good to meet you." At least she hoped it was.

"I'm so glad I saw you here today. There are three kittens in my backyard that are too small to fend for themselves. They need a home. I've already taken them to a vet and they're healthy. They're staying in our garage. My husband insists we can keep only one. Can you take the other two?"

The woman, who was staring at her with imploring eyes, added for good measure, "They're really adorable. Three yellow tigers."

She could easily picture them. Just how would Sophia and Dylan react to two kittens? She'd figure something out if she had to because she couldn't refuse this woman. That's what taking in stray animals was all about. "I'd be glad to take them."

Ruth said, "I live at 423 Maple. I'll be running errands today, and my husband and I have plans for tonight. Do you think you can pick them up tomorrow?"

Caprice thought about the funeral and her schedule. "How about tomorrow evening? Around seven?"

Ruth nodded happily. After a "See you tomorrow," she went to the desk and paid her bill.

Yvonne began trimming Caprice's bangs. She'd almost finished when the door to the salon flew open and a redhead in a short skirt and a tight T-shirt rushed in.

"You guys!" she called, apparently to all the stylists. "You won't believe what I just found out. I went over to Valerie's and she's a mess. You know that guy she was dating? It was Ted Winslow!"

The shop went absolutely silent. The news was out. Just what would it mean for Roz?

Chapter Eleven

Caprice felt jittery late Wednesday morning with Grant standing to one side of her at the cemetery and Nikki on the other. Since her sister never made her nervous, it must have been her proximity to Grant.

Or else the antsy feeling originated in the circumstances—Ted Winslow's memorial service at the funeral home and now the burial here at Peaceful Path Cemetery. There were two security guards from PA Pharm stationed at the cars to prevent reporters from intruding. How hard this had to be for Roz. But throughout the morning she'd been nothing but gracious to anyone who'd approached her.

Most of the people who'd come to the cemetery were now offering Roz final condolences under the canopy. She and Nikki and Grant had stepped aside. But Grant was watching Roz closely since Detective Jones and his partner were still part of the crowd.

Nikki laid her hand on Caprice's arm. "I'm going to go too. I have to set up this afternoon for an engagement party."

"Very different from this," Grant muttered. "How can she act like a grieving widow with Winslow's associates?"

Caprice automatically bristled. "What do you mean *act*?" In a much lower voice, she insisted, "Roz loved Ted in spite of his infidelity. This day is tearing her up inside. Maybe you need to search deep down for your compassionate side for the next hour or so. Then you can be as cynical as you want."

After Nikki murmured, "Caprice, go easy," and Grant cut a glance at her, then remained silent, Caprice couldn't believe she had let her words fly out like that. On the other hand, hadn't her mother advised her not to treat Grant with kid gloves?

More reasonably, Caprice asked, "What would you have Roz do? She said a private good-bye, then had a closed casket for the service. She kept the service short and sweet with the readings and then the minister listing Ted's accomplishments before he said a prayer. The other prayers that he said here, Ted will probably need in the hereafter."

"Maybe she shouldn't have had a funeral at all," Grant muttered.

Maybe Grant's problem wasn't with Roz at all,

but with being at a funeral. Had today brought back raw memories?

"Ted Winslow was a prominent man in Kismet. She really had no choice."

Grant tossed her a skeptical look.

"Okay, she had a choice. But I think she needed to do this for—"

"Don't you dare say closure," Grant directed her. "Burying someone does *not* bring closure."

Now they *were* talking about Grant, and they both knew it.

Nikki broke the tension by pointing to Detective Jones and his colleague, who were standing by a tall sycamore, watching Roz say good-bye to men in custom-made suits. "So why are they still hanging around?"

"Maybe they know something we don't. I heard through the grapevine that everyone who signed the guest list for the Winslows' open house is being interviewed."

Suddenly, there was movement near the lineup of cars that stretched along the well-tended burial plots.

"Uh oh," Nikki said. "Isn't that—"

Uh oh, indeed! Caprice practically groaned. She was pretty sure the woman dressed in the short, black, sleeveless dress, high heels, and veiled, large-brimmed hat was Valerie Swanson.

"Trouble with a capital T," Grant said without moving a muscle.

"We have to do something." Caprice started forward.

But Grant caught her arm. "You stay put. You're not getting in the middle of a catfight."

"Then you do something."

"If you stay here with your sister."

"Caprice, listen to him," Nikki advised her.

"I'm going with you," she stubbornly told Grant. "I'll stay out of it, but I'm going to let Roz know she has my backing."

Shaking his head, stepping out ahead of her, Grant headed for the canopy and an unsuspecting Roz.

It was practically impossible to intercept Valerie. There were at least fifty funeral-goers still milling about, grouped between the canopy and the gravel lane. Roz was standing near the casket at the end of the row of folding chairs. Tall flower arrangements from gladioli to chrysanthemums to carnations and roses had been positioned in a broken circle around the casket.

Even though Valerie's heels sank into the grass, she moved fast, winding her way in and out of mourners and flowers like a soccer player intent on a goal. Caprice knew condolences weren't on this "other" woman's mind. She and Grant, however, couldn't reach Roz before Valerie did.

Ted's mistress zoomed in on Roz and stepped into her personal space. Her vitriol spat out in a torrent. "You're standing there like a queen as if Ted belonged only to you. He didn't belong to you at all! He was going to be *mine*. He was going to leave you behind like an old shoe and marry *me*. As soon as your monstrosity of a house sold, we were going away together."

Roz was stunned and speechless. So was everyone else.

Except for Grant.

He moved quickly and took Valerie's elbow firmly in his grip. "Ms. Swanson, you're making a scene. Surely, you don't want Mr. Winslow's funeral to be remembered for your outburst."

She yanked away from him. "Yes, I do. He loved *me*, not her. I want the world to know that."

Grant's expression grew grim. "It's too late for that. Ted Winslow is dead. Rosalind is his lawful wife. That's what matters."

Caprice suspected Grant wasn't being purposefully cruel but was trying to convince Valerie to see the reality of the situation. Whatever promises Ted had made to her didn't matter much now.

"What we felt for each other matters!" she wailed, looking around at everyone for a consensus.

But Ted Winslow's friends, acquaintances, and coworkers remained silent.

"Why don't I walk you to your car?" Grant asked calmly.

Valerie could apparently see her outburst had set her apart from everyone else. After another long look at the polished walnut casket, she let Grant lead her away.

Caprice put her arm around Roz's shoulders. "Are you all right?"

"Other than being humiliated and embarrassed, I'm fine."

"Grief can do strange things," Nikki said, casting a pitying glance toward Valerie.

"Do you think she could have staged that on purpose?" Caprice wondered aloud. "To throw any suspicion away from herself?"

"Grant can probably answer that. Vince always says he's a good judge of character," Nikki reminded Caprice.

"Except men can be fooled by someone like Valerie," Roz said. "They don't always think with their brain."

Caprice heard the bitterness in her friend's voice because she was putting the blame for Ted's infidelity where it belonged—with him.

When one of Roz's neighbors stepped up to say good-bye and tell Roz how sorry she was for everything that had happened—including Valerie—Caprice and Nikki moved away from the canopied area. Out of the corner of her eye, Caprice could see Dave Harding speaking to Roz after her neighbor stepped away. It was nice of him to come.

"I really have to go," Nikki said. "I'm looking forward to tonight and seeing a *happy* couple." After a hug and a promise to call soon, Nikki left Caprice alone, studying the group that was still waiting to speak to Roz.

Caprice was particularly interested in the man who'd just taken Dave Harding's place and was now holding Roz's hand. He was one of the expensively suited men Caprice had wondered about earlier.

She heard Roz say, "Chad, thank you so much for coming."

Chad's response was, "Ted was a wonderful colleague. We'll all miss him."

Caprice could hardly keep from rolling her eyes. "Ted" and "wonderful" weren't two words she'd use in the same sentence. Was this the Chad Thompson whom Ted had been talking to the day Caprice had overheard the "If-he-does-that-I'll-kill-him" conversation?

Grant's tall, broad-shouldered physique caught Caprice's attention as he walked toward her. His charcoal suit fit him well. He glanced toward Roz, saw she was still occupied by Ted's coworkers, and came to stand beside Caprice.

"Did Valerie drive away?" Caprice asked.

"She did. But before she did, she gave her number to a reporter lurking on the fringes."

"Terrific. Is anyone else talking to the reporter?"

Grant shook his head. "Most people know not to go near a journalist, especially when murder is involved. And the reporter knows someone like Roz has enough clout to have her escorted off the premises." Without missing a beat, Grant asked,

"Who's that? You're watching him like you want to know more about him."

"That's Chad Thompson, I think." Caprice told Grant about the conversation she'd overheard.

"You really saw what Ted said as a threat?"

"You should have heard him. He was really upset."

"And you're still planning to go to PA Pharm to fish around, even though it's a bad idea?"

She looked directly into Grant's stormy, gray eyes. "I am. The question is—do you still plan to go with me?"

Caprice had offered to stay at the house with Roz this evening—she could pick up the kittens another time—but Roz had insisted she get them. Kittens could give them both a distraction from the draining day. One of the reporters at the funeral had tried to elicit comments from Roz as they'd walked to Grant's SUV, but Grant had intervened. Caprice could hear his deep voice now in her head as he'd warned them all—"There is an ongoing investigation and you'd better not interfere in that. Mrs. Winslow is *not* making comments to the press."

And he was going with Caprice to the drug company. However, he still disapproved.

Thank goodness, the press hadn't yet figured out Roz was staying with her. Taking a circuitous route home from the funeral, Grant had again made certain they weren't followed. Roz could have gone back to her castle-like home now if she'd wanted to, but she didn't want to, and both Caprice and Grant believed rambling around that mansion alone with a killer on the loose seemed like a very bad idea.

At the funeral, Caprice couldn't help thinking that any one of the mourners could have been the murderer.

The first place Caprice stopped after she made certain Roz ate some dinner was Perky Paws, Kismet's pet-supply store, to pick up a litter box just for the kittens, kitten food since they required different nutrition than adult cats, and a few toys. Sophia might not want to share hers.

There was a particular strategy when introducing a new cat or cats into a family that a veterinarian had shared with Caprice when she'd first begun taking in strays. Roz would be helping her with it. At Caprice's phone call, Roz would secure Sophia in Caprice's bedroom and take Dylan out back to play until Caprice gave her the signal to bring him in. She said she'd take one of Caprice's paperbacks with her and wouldn't be bored.

Less than an hour later, Caprice listened to the two adorable kittens—she guessed they were about ten weeks old—as they meowed in the carrier on the floor of her van.

She saw the taupe sedan parked in front of her house as soon as she turned the corner onto her street. Pulling up beside it, she recognized the auburn-haired woman inside. She was Marianne Brisbane, the reporter who had interviewed Caprice a couple of months ago about her home-staging business, as well as taking in strays. As a human interest article, it had attracted readers.

The reporter didn't simply stick to the lighter stories. She'd broken the scoop on a scandal in Kismet too.

But whether Caprice sort of knew this reporter or not, a reporter was the last person she wanted to talk to.

Where was Roz? She'd called her just five minutes ago to start the new-kittens-in-the-family ball rolling. She picked up her phone and pulled into her driveway wondering how fast she could text.

Fast enough.

She turned off the ignition and quickly typed in—Lay low with Dylan out back. Reporter in front. I'll get rid of her.

Roz texted back—OK.

Never more grateful for the poplars along the sides of the house camouflaging the fence, Caprice opened her door and climbed out. After sliding open the van door, she lifted the carrier holding the kittens.

Marianne Brisbane met her on the path to the front door.

Caprice could have gone into the garage, up to the back porch, and into the house that way. But the reporter would still be sitting outside in her car, watching and waiting.

"Hello, Miss Brisbane. How can I help you?"

One of the kittens meowed.

Caprice shifted the carrier from one hand to the other so the reporter would understand she wouldn't be standing here long.

"We meet under different circumstances than the last time. Can I come in?"

They had done the interview in her house over coffee and biscotti. But Caprice wouldn't be inviting her in today.

"This isn't a good time. I'm bringing home stray kittens, and I don't know how my cat will accept them."

"I'll get straight to the point then. I believe your car was parked at the Winslows' the night of the murder."

Caprice kept silent. That night she'd been parked to the side of the garage and suspected it would have been difficult for anyone to see her car unless they'd breached the crime scene perimeter.

"One of my sources saw your car in the police garage. And you are Rosalind Winslow's friend. You even arrived with her today at the funeral."

"With her lawyer."

Marianne's green eyes narrowed. "Mrs. Winslow isn't staying at her house. Is she here with you?"

Both kittens were meowing loudly, and Caprice didn't blame them. "Do you see her?"

Dusk was falling now. No lights were on in the house, but a person walking past the windows would have been noticed.

"No, but—"

"Look, Miss Brisbane. I just picked up two stray kittens who need a home. I'd like to get them settled. Mrs. Winslow has other friends too, some with a lot more conveniences than I have. If you want to find her, maybe you should stretch your net. But keep in mind, if you do, she's still not going to answer any questions."

"And what about you? Were you at the crime scene?"

"Whether I was or wasn't isn't an issue. Because I'm not answering your questions either."

"I could help," the reporter suddenly said.

"Help with what?"

"I could help find out who the killer is. I don't think Roz Winslow did it, even though she's the prime person of interest."

Caprice kept silent again. Most people didn't like silence and rushed into the vacuum. Maybe she could learn something.

"Word on the street says she had means, motive, and opportunity."

Everything in Caprice urged her to pose a denial and do it loudly. But she kept quiet. Maybe she could trust this woman and maybe she couldn't. But she wouldn't risk saying the wrong thing to the wrong person.

Marianne blew out a long breath. "All right. So you're being loyal to your friend. Believe it or not, I admire friends who stick up for each other." She took a business card from the pocket of her slacks. "If you change your mind, give me a call."

Caprice just stared at the card. "Miss Brisbane—"

She extended it farther. "We were on a first-name basis when we did your interview. It's Marianne. You never know when you can use my help. And . . . I'm always looking for a good source. I'll warn you now, I've heard the D.A. is building a case against your friend. If I hear anything else, do you want me to let you know?"

She was not going to make a deal with the devil. Grant had contacts in the D.A.'s office. He'd gather the same information as this reporter, wouldn't he?

As if Marianne Brisbane read her mind, the reporter said, "Lawyers don't always have the skinny first."

Caprice took the reporter's card but didn't commit.

Marianne Brisbane gave her a conspiratorial smile and returned to her car.

Not glancing around, Caprice heard the engine start. She hurried up her porch steps and unlocked the front door. Once inside, she set the cat carrier in the middle of the living room and waited, murmuring to the kittens. A few minutes later, she saw the reporter's car pull away. As soon as it did, Caprice closed the blinds in the living room and the dining room's bay windows. Once Roz came back inside with Dylan, she didn't want anyone to know her friend was here. Thank goodness, Roz hadn't picked up her car after the forensic team had finished with it and the crime scene.

Going to the back door, she called to Roz, "The coast is clear for now. I don't know if she'll be back. I closed the blinds."

"I hate hiding out. Maybe I should go back to the house so you don't have to deal with this kind of thing."

"I'm okay, Roz. You can't stay in that house."

"I just can't believe anyone would want to hurt me too."

"You can't take any chances."

After a long, silent moment, Roz said, "Let Sophia meet her new housemates. Dylan and I are playing ball. Just give a shout or text me when you want us to come back in."

After stopping in the laundry room to change her blouse—she been handling the kittens and she didn't want Sophia to smell them on her yet—and then washing her hands at the kitchen sink, Caprice went upstairs to her bedroom to fetch Sophia. The cat was sprawled on Caprice's bed on her side, her paws stretched out as if she was reaching for one of the shoestrings Caprice used as a teaser when they played. She'd heard the door open and lifted her head from the quilted spread. In moments she was on her paws.

Caprice sat beside her and fluffed her mostly white ruff. "You're such a pretty girl. And you take such good care of yourself." Her ruff was usually pristine white. She was a fastidious cat.

After her cat was purring happily, Caprice said, "Let's go downstairs and see what Dylan is doing."

As Caprice stood, Sophia jumped from the bed onto the swirled pastel, hand-braided rug. Her bedroom was colorful in a more muted way than the downstairs, but she'd chosen each piece of furniture with the same enthusiasm and fervor—from the brass four-poster bed to the antique yellow armoire hand-painted with hummingbirds and roses.

She and Sophia jogged down the steps together, Sophia making it to the bottom of the stairs first. But she immediately went on alert.

As soon as Caprice had set the carrier on the floor, the kittens had quieted. But now as they heard her and sensed another cat, they began meowing once more.

"What's this?" Caprice asked with surprise in her voice. "Someone must have left us a present!"

Sophia turned her head slightly toward Caprice, then slowly padded toward the carrier. Suddenly she crouched low, examining the case with the newcomers.

"Aren't they adorable?" Caprice asked Sophia. "They look like they need a friend."

Sophia made a complete circle around the carrier

while the kittens meowed. Finally she stole closer and sniffed. She sniffed again. Padding around to the other side, she did the same.

"What do you think?"

Sophia sat beside the carrier, peering in at the furry, meowing creatures. Then she stretched out beside the kittens and Caprice took that as a sign. "Want to meet them?"

Sophia stared up at her with her beautiful golden cat eyes, looking almost eager.

Caprice bent down and opened the door.

After a minute, the kitty nearest the door realized she was free. She ran out and took off in a streak across the living room. Sophia streaked after her.

Caprice kept a close eye, but kitten and older cat raced under the end table, circled the coffee table, and around the perimeter of the room. Kitten number two tentatively ventured out of the carrier and meowed at Caprice. All she wanted to do was scoop her up into her arms, but she wanted Sophia to acknowledge her first.

The chase ended when kitten number one almost ran headlong into the carrier. Suddenly Sophia was aware of the second newcomer. She stared at her for a few moments, sniffed her back, then meowed.

"Do you like them? We'll have to name them. Who wants to chase a ball?" Out of her pocket,

Caprice produced a plastic ball with a bell in the center and tossed it.

Kitten number two came to life and raced to Sophia, pawing the ball first. While the three felines pushed around the ball with playful abandon, Caprice went to the back door.

At her call, Roz brought Dylan inside.

In the doorway to the kitchen, Dylan shook his fur out as he usually did, then sensed something was different. He spotted Sophia on the coffee table . . . and then he saw them—two orange, yellow, and white fur balls who hadn't been in the room before he left.

He didn't even glance at Roz or Caprice. He took off toward the kittens. At the base of the coffee table, they scattered.

Caprice wasn't sure how to handle this introduction. She knew cats better than dogs. But she could see almost instantly that Dylan didn't mean the newcomers any harm. He wanted to get to know them and play.

When Dylan barked, they moved deeper under the sofa and meowed.

Caprice ordered in a firm voice, "Dylan, sit."

He looked up at her and wiggled his tail with excitement.

She held out her hand and waved downward. "Sit."

After another bark and wiggle, he did what she'd asked of him.

She praised him with several repetitions of "Good boy," and said, "They might come out if you're quiet."

"Or they'll fall asleep under there," Roz said, sitting in the wide fuchsia armchair and crossing her legs. "What did the reporter want?"

"She found out my car had been at the police garage. She saw me at the funeral with you and put two and two together. She believes I know where you are. She's the reporter who did that article about me, and she wants an exclusive. Her name's Marianne Brisbane. Do you know her?"

Roz thought about it. "Isn't she the one who broke the scandal on the town council a while back?"

A bribe had been paid to a member to have a property rezoned. "That was her. Great reporting. Not supposition, but all facts."

Dylan rested his head on his paws as if he'd decided he was there for a long wait.

"I guess she wanted to talk to me about what happened. Grant said I shouldn't talk to anyone. But maybe it would help if I got my side out there."

"Your side?"

"Yes. That I came in from running and found Ted—" Abruptly, she stopped.

Grant would blow his stack if Roz did that. "Talking to anyone isn't in your best interests."

"Even if someone came forward who saw me running?"

One of the kittens scurried out from under the

couch and darted across the living room. Dylan jumped up, yipped, and scampered toward the kitten, who suddenly turned and faced the dog. Dylan went still as the two animals eyed each other warily. Dylan inched closer, and the cat's back arched, her tail fluffing fuller. After two sniffs, Dylan sat and just watched his new friend. The kitten's tail became its usual size. She came forward out of the corner and sidled up to Dylan.

Caprice watched in fascination as dog and cat became friends.

Roz said, "I think they're going to be okay here together. Do you think the other one will come out?"

"I have to set up their litter box. And I'll put out some food. She'll come out. If she sees her sister and Dylan are getting along, she'll be okay."

Sophia had settled on the coffee table, her tail curled around her, and was watching all with a knowing eye.

Caprice turned to Roz to continue their conversation. "I don't think you should talk to the reporter. Let Grant and me learn what we can at PA Pharm tomorrow. After that, we'll decide what to do next. Going public could do more harm than good."

Roz didn't look convinced. Caprice hoped she'd take her lawyer's advice. Her freedom could be the price she paid if she didn't.

Chapter Twelve

"Security isn't as tight as I thought it would be," Grant said to Caprice as he held the door that led into a two-story office building.

"I did some research on PA Pharm last night," she told him. "Research and Development takes place in that separate building in the back. You can't get in there without pre-authorization."

The lobby was expensively appointed with tan ceramic-tile flooring, muted brown wood paneling, and deep chocolate leather captain's chairs around granite-topped side tables. A high counter with a clipboard and sign-in sheet overlooked the reception desk.

But no one was stationed there at the moment. The sign-in sheet was devoid of signatures.

"No visitors today," Grant noted as he and Caprice both peered down at the sign-in sheet, their elbows brushing.

Caprice glanced up at him. They'd met in the

parking lot. As always, she'd noticed his well-tailored suit, crisp white shirt, and striped tie. He looked like the consummate lawyer. But was he? Did all that intensity under the surface stem from losing his family? Had he still been in love with his wife when they divorced? Or had *he* been the one who had stopped loving?

Bringing her focus back to the task at hand, she said, "I wonder where the receptionist is."

"Bathroom break?" Grant suggested with a slight smile.

She smiled back, feeling a little extra thump in her heart rhythm. That wasn't because of Grant. Their mission was important and maybe even a little dangerous.

"Let's explore." His smile faded as he was again a lawyer with a busy schedule and a limited amount of time to spare.

A doorway led to the first-floor offices. But the three small offices in a row before them were empty. None of them had Ted's name on a window. In fact, there were no names on those three windows.

Caprice moved to the right while Grant headed to the left, where corridors led to more work spaces.

"Do you want to split up?" Caprice asked.

"We can cover more territory," he agreed matter-of-factly.

She gave him a little wave and started down the

hall, imagining they'd meet at the south end of the building where the corridors converged.

Where was everyone?

The offices along this longer hall were bigger, and names were painted on the doors. She recognized one—Chad Thompson—and paused. That was the man Ted had been speaking to on the phone the night he'd gotten upset and then abruptly left. Chad Thompson's title was Vice President—Sales.

After passing another office on her left and one on her right, she found where everyone had gathered. In the conference room, she counted fifteen men and women seated around a large table. The voices that came through the door were agitated as several conversations seem to zing across that table.

This was a perfect time to explore.

At the corner office at the end of the hall, she spotted Ted Winslow's name painted on the door— not in black like all the others, but in gold.

She tried the knob on the door.

It turned.

Just like that she stood inside his office. Now if she just knew what to look for. If she had time to switch on the computer and scroll through files . . . None of it would probably make any sense at all to her.

She'd walked around the L-shaped desk and was

staring at a photo of Roz and Ted on some tropical island when a woman's voice cracked sharply into the office. "Can I help you?"

Caprice spun around ready to spurt out the cover story she and Grant had decided on. At the last moment, before her tongue went into action, she realized she knew this woman. Well, actually she didn't know her, but she'd met the slim honey-blonde at Roz's open house and seen her yesterday talking to Roz at the cemetery.

With a smile she said, "I think we've met, haven't we? At the Winslows' open house. I'm their home-stager, Caprice De Luca. And you're—" This was not the time for her memory to blink. Then she remembered. "You're Lonnie Hippensteel."

She never knew when an open house attendee could become a client so she had to remember names . . . and personalities. Lonnie had been friendly and talkative, telling Caprice all about her mother, who painted the rooms in her house a new color almost every year.

"I do remember you," Lonnie admitted, coming to stand beside Caprice. "I just can't believe Ted was there that night and now we've buried him."

She actually looked broken up about it. Had Ted showered extramarital charm on her too?

"I was his assistant," Lonnie explained as if she needed someone to talk to. "Now they don't know what to do with me until they hire someone else.

For the past few days they've been running me around town on errands and using me as a go-between with R&D and the managers."

"If you were Ted's assistant, you must have been important to him. Who's taking over his responsibilities?"

Lonnie seemed to like the idea that Caprice had recognized her importance to Ted. "Mr. Thompson and Mr. Jimenez are splitting the job load. But they don't seem to want any input from me. I feel extraneous, and I guess I could be let go. They sent me to R&D to ride the back of one of the lab techs about a late report while they called a meeting here. That's where everyone is—in a strategy meeting about the glitch."

The hairs on the back of Caprice's neck prickled. Nana had told her that was a sign of her sixth sense at work. Whether it was or not, Caprice asked, "What glitch?"

Lonnie shrugged. "I don't know." She lowered her voice. "Ever since Ted died, everyone seems so secretive."

Knowing a good contact when she saw and heard one, Caprice opened her yellow vinyl purse and extracted a business card. Not knowing how much to say, she finally settled on, "Ted's wife, Roz, is in a tough place right now."

"Do the police think she killed Ted? Everyone knows they suspect the spouse. We all watch enough cop shows."

There didn't seem to be any jealousy attached to Lonnie's comment or her demeanor. She really did just seem curious and interested.

"The police have questioned her. We're just trying to piece it all together." She handed Lonnie her card. "If you would happen to find out what that glitch is, I'd really like to know. Call me anytime. Both my cell and home numbers are there."

Lonnie was just about to respond when Grant suddenly appeared in the doorway, accompanied by a security guard. The security guard wore a scowl and glared at them all.

Grant tried to appear unruffled and calm. Maybe he was practiced at that demeanor.

"Seneft . . ." He gestured to the guard's security ID badge. ". . . doesn't believe I have a good reason for being here." Nodding to Caprice, he went on, "But I told him you're Roz's best friend, and she gave you permission to come here and collect any personal mementoes Ted kept in his office."

That was their cover story, and they were sticking to it.

Immediately Caprice picked up the photograph, then pointed to a stein on a shelf. "They bought that on their travels to Luxembourg." Roz had told her about their vacation there and the set of steins she'd had shipped home. Caprice assumed this was one of them.

The guard studied the photo and the stein.

Looking to Lonnie, he asked, "You know these folks?"

Caprice held her breath as Grant's mouth tightened with worry.

But Lonnie answered easily, "Caprice was Roz and Ted's home-stager."

Seneft looked blank.

"To help them sell their house. Caprice and this man were with Mrs. Winslow at Ted's funeral."

"I'm Mrs. Winslow's lawyer," Grant reported to Lonnie. Then with one of those crooked half smiles, he said, "It's good to meet you, Miss—"

"Lonnie Hippensteel. Ted's assistant." She turned to Seneft. "Certainly they can take Ted's personal things, can't they?"

But the security guard shook his head. "I'm gonna pull someone out of that meeting. I don't want to lose *my* job."

The emphasis he put on *my* told Caprice he was pretty sure Lonnie would lose hers . . . as others had.

"Don't wander anywhere," he ordered in a stern voice.

Caprice felt like wandering just to spite him, but that was her rebellious nature kicking in. Instead she reached to the shelf for the stein while quickly taking inventory of everything in the office.

Grant seemed to be doing the same as he asked, "Is the wall art Ted's or does that belong to the company?"

Caprice's gaze lifted to the painting Grant was asking about—an oil painting of a rustic barn set amid rolling green hills.

"Ted bought that last year," Lonnie responded. "He said the painter was local."

"He is," Grant confirmed. "He had a show right after I moved to Kismet."

"You go to art shows?" Caprice asked with some surprise.

Grant looked a big discomfited by her question. "I was getting used to life in Kismet and at loose ends one weekend."

What else did Grant do for recreation? Or had he preferred any distraction—even an art show—rather than being alone with his thoughts?

Glancing down the hall, Lonnie said, "I'd better scoot. My next task is to make copies of the year-end profit projections. I don't want anyone to think I'm not busy."

Caprice reminded her, "Call me if you hear anything about that glitch."

After Lonnie checked the card in her hand, she didn't respond, simply scurried down the hall in the opposite direction of the meeting.

"What glitch?" Grant asked.

"That's what I want to find out. If we do, maybe we'll discover what Ted was upset about work-wise before he was killed."

Follow-up discussion with Grant had been on the

tip of her tongue, but she went silent as Chad Thompson came in with the security guard.

Thompson didn't begin with pleasantries. After giving Grant and Caprice a quick once-over, he stated, "You have to leave. You're unauthorized."

Stepping into the man's personal space, Grant argued, "We were authorized by Rosalind Winslow to pick up Ted's personal items. Why would we have to get permission for that?"

Thompson was apparently not used to being contradicted, because his frown lines cut even deeper around his mouth. "Not just anyone can wander around these offices."

"We're not wandering."

"You *were*," Thompson snapped.

Males locking horns, Caprice thought. Her brother and her dad did that now and then, though less often now than when Vince was younger.

"Mr. Thompson." Her tone was conversational and nonconfrontational. "Roz would have come herself, but we felt this was something we could do for her. Is there any reason we can't take the obviously personal items, maybe look through Ted's desk for her? That is, if the police haven't already confiscated everything."

Thompson bristled. "The police were here asking questions, but they couldn't take anything. They would need warrants and subpoenas."

She waved to the desk with its one long top drawer and its three side drawers. "So I can look?"

"Quickly. I have to return to my meeting."

In case he changed his mind, Caprice moved around the desk and opened the top side drawer—envelopes and a stapler. The second drawer didn't hold anything of significance either, just stacks of Post-it notes, a container of paper clips, and a bag of rubber bands. Before Thompson could stop her from opening the bottom drawer, the file drawer and the one Caprice most wanted to scope out, she pulled it out.

It was empty. Absolutely empty.

Of course, it was. If anything shady was going on here, the upper echelon of managers would have covered their tracks before the police arrived.

From across the desk Grant was watching her. He gave a what-did-you-expect shrug. "Try the top one."

She did. The long drawer slid out easily, and she didn't expect to find more than she saw at first glance—a calculator, a highlighter, pens, and pencils.

Impatient, Thompson was checking down the hall. For raised voices?

Caprice slid her hand across the back of the drawer. She felt . . . a business card.

Thompson was half turned toward her and half turned away. Without even glancing at it, she palmed the card and slid it into her pocket. It might be nothing. It might be something.

"Finished?" Thompson called across the office.

Straightening, Caprice shut the drawer. "Yep. So we can take the painting on the wall too? I understand Ted brought that in."

His eyes narrowed. "Do you think Rosalind Winslow needs a painting when she has a house full of collectibles?"

Thompson probably had been at the Winslow house for cocktail parties and the like over the course of Ted's employment here. On the other hand, maybe he'd had a close-up look at Ted's sword room when he'd killed his colleague. The idea that Caprice could be talking to Ted's killer gave her chills.

"I think if it belonged to her husband, she'd like to have it."

"Fine," he said with a resigned sigh and a nod to Grant. "Take it. Seneft will escort you out. Don't ever come back here again without authorization from the front desk."

It was on the tip of her tongue to retort that they shouldn't leave the front desk unattended if that was their policy. But she didn't.

Thompson returned to the conference room while Seneft escorted them not only to the front desk but out the front door.

Once outside, Caprice asked, "Wasn't that a little over the top?"

"Possibly." Grant's long stride kept her hurrying to keep up as he used the remote to unlock his SUV. However, he passed it and finally stopped at hers, two spaces away. "Do you want this in the backseat?"

Taking her keys from her purse, she unlocked the front door, then pushed the passenger seat forward so that Grant could deposit the painting inside.

When they were face-to-face again, he returned to her question. "If a visitor to our law offices didn't stop at Giselle's desk and just walked into our back offices, we'd be alarmed or at least cautious."

"We don't look like thieves."

He gave her a wry smile. "Most corporate thieves don't. Whatever's going on there, I don't think you can fault Thompson for being a little put out."

"More than a little," she muttered. "I wish I could have switched on Ted's computer."

"It's probably wiped clean. Especially if there was anything on there they wouldn't want his replacement to see."

"I'm surprised the police didn't confiscate it."

"It's not that easy. That computer wasn't Ted's property. It belongs to PA Pharm. The police have Ted's home computer . . . and probably his laptop, for that matter."

Remembering the card she'd fetched from Ted's desk, she withdrew it from her pocket. "I found this in that top drawer."

Grant came closer as she turned the card right side up. At the name on the card her eyes widened and she gave a little, "Oh!"

"What?" Grant had moved beside her and was looking over her shoulder.

"It's from Isaac's shop—Older and Better. I shop there all the time." Turning the card over, she saw "1700s Ottoman Empire Turkish dagger."

"Something he was thinking about buying?"

"Or already bought. I didn't realize Ted dealt with Isaac, but that would make sense—at least on a local level. I think I'll drive over and talk to him."

"Caprice—"

"Don't give me that look," she warned him.

He checked his watch. "I can't come with you. I have an appointment in half an hour and I haven't gone over the client's case yet."

"There's no need for you to go with me. I've known Isaac for years."

"Don't tell him Roz is the main suspect."

"I wouldn't do that!"

"So what are you going to say?"

"That Roz is a friend and I'm looking into things. He knows I'm curious."

"I know I can't stop you. But helping Roz shouldn't become your second job."

"Why not?" she asked flippantly and didn't wait for an answer as she rounded her car's hood and unlocked the driver's side.

He followed her and kept his hand on her door as she slid inside. "You will call me if you discover anything?"

"Maybe," she tossed out, right before she closed the door.

At Older and Better, Caprice found Isaac hunkered down before a cupboard, rummaging on the lower shelf.

"Searching for something?" she joked.

After shooting an impatient glance over his shoulder, he responded, "Yeah. One of those early-sixties Woolworth's five-and-dime teacups and saucers. Pink flowers. Customer called, left a message, and said it was in the oak china cupboard, bottom compartment. Like I don't have more than one oak china cupboard."

At least five of them were spaced at regular intervals around the room.

"Pay dirt!" he grunted and rose to his full height, cup and saucer in hand. "Did you come over to see if I found any more crystal? There's a place in Philly where I can get a few of the plates. You were on my list to call tomorrow."

"That's great that you found them, but that's not why I came over."

His brows arched. "Looking for props?"

That's what he called her staging furniture, and he wasn't far off. "Not that either. I want to talk to you about daggers and swords and Ted Winslow's collection."

Isaac carried the fragile-looking teacup and

saucer to his cashier's desk and motioned her behind it. There was a small sitting area there with two walnut captain's chairs that had red and black plaid upholstered cushions tied to their seats.

"Coffee?" He nodded toward the pot on a narrow table against the back wall. It was half-filled.

She knew she probably wouldn't sleep tonight, but coffee and conversation went a long way with Isaac. "Sure. Lots of milk, though."

Opening the mini-refrigerator under the counter, he pulled out a plastic jug of milk. "Terrible thing that happened to Winslow. You go way back with his wife, didn't you say?"

"We were friends in high school." She poured coffee into two mugs that looked as if they'd seen years of caffeine stains.

"So why do you want to know about Winslow's collection. Is someone thinking about buying it?" He poured milk into his own mug and capped the jug.

"Could be. Did you procure any of the swords or daggers for him?"

"Sure I did." Isaac put the milk away. "But Winslow found a lot of them himself too, at private auctions."

"You mean physical private auctions or online?"

"Both." Isaac picked up his mug and took a long swallow. "I know he sometimes planned his business trips to coincide with them. Chicago. New York. L.A."

Caprice sipped her coffee and wanted to make a face at the stale taste but didn't. "So if you found a piece for him he wanted . . ." She trailed off so Isaac could fill in.

"I got a finder's fee. Winslow did tons of research and knew what he wanted." After a thoughtful pause when they both drank coffee, the shop owner asked, "He was killed with one of them, wasn't he?"

Could Isaac possibly know she was there that night with Roz? Not necessarily. The police had released the information Ted was stabbed, so everyone was inventing his own scenario. Isaac's happened to be right.

She kept silent.

"It's out that his wife found him or—"

"She did *not* do it."

"Spoken like a friend. And you think you can figure out who did?"

"Possibly."

He laughed. "If anyone can, you can. So what do you really want to know?"

"About a few of Ted's daggers. Roz has given me the history on some of them. The one with the rubies, diamonds, and emeralds in the handle interests me."

"Did he get killed with that one?"

She kept silent once again.

"Okay. There's things you can say and things you can't."

Not confirming or denying his conclusion, she answered, "Roz said Ted gave it to her for her birthday since rubies are her birthstone."

"Now I remember." Isaac squinted his eyes together as if he was thinking really hard. "Rubies, diamonds, emeralds, and a hilt covered with gold. A sheath of pierced gold."

"Wow. So it was worth a lot?"

"I got into a bidding war over it. Winslow kept egging me on. He really wanted that one."

"Did he say why?"

"Because it was for the Mrs.'s birthday, I suspect. There was provenance with it. But I don't specifically remember what. Indian Khanjar dagger, I think. I might have a copy somewhere. Those papers, from a couple of years ago, are all in boxes in the attic. Now it's different. I put everything on the computer."

While she thought about what he'd said, Isaac continued, "He had quite a collection. It wouldn't surprise me at all if he was murdered for one of the pieces in it."

Her thoughts exactly—rubies, diamonds, emeralds, gold. The question was—who knew about that dagger? Who killed Ted for it?

Chapter Thirteen

The following morning Caprice stood in the warehouse of the rental company she used, examining a white wicker settee with two high-backed arm chairs. The set would be perfect for her client who had decided on a tropical theme. The whole house would be reminiscent of a luxurious beach house in the Florida Keys. All pastels, floaty fabrics, bamboo, rattan, and shades of the sea. Besides what Caprice had chosen here, she could find the rest online. She'd encouraged Roz to come along with her today, but instead her friend had just wanted to stay at the house with the animals. The kittens were adorable, and the furry family seemed to be getting along . . . for now. This evening she hoped to start a phone chain to find homes for those kittens. And she hoped to nail down a family meeting with her sisters and brother for Monday night. They had to make plans soon; their mom's birthday was only ten days away. She'd be able to pull everything together in a few days, but she wanted them all to agree on the details.

Now, however, she had another errand. Dave Harding had been at the Winslows' open house as well as at Ted's funeral. She wondered if he'd heard any scuttlebutt about the murder or Roz that she hadn't. A friendly catch-up visit wouldn't be out of the question as she shopped for a new garage door. Hers was the original that came with the house. It was wood and high-maintenance; the paint chipped and had to be scraped every summer. They could talk garage doors, and she might get some information to boot.

Her cell phone played as she ran between parked cars in the direction of Dave's store. She checked the screen and smiled—Dr. Seth Randolph. He hadn't forgotten about her.

Her voice carried a lilt she couldn't hide. "Hi! I was thinking about you last night."

"I hope you have caller ID," he teased. "So exactly what were you thinking?"

"I do have caller ID, and I was just wondering if you'd forgotten about our date."

"Obviously not," he said seriously. "I wanted to make sure you were still available."

"I'm available." She realized how happy she sounded and how flirty. What was it about this man that caused that fluttery sensation in her stomach? She didn't even know him.

"Is two o'clock still good? Why don't we meet

there? Then, afterward, we can get a bite to eat somewhere."

"Two o'clock is fine. That should be a good time to play. The afternoon crowd will be thinning out and the evening crowd won't have started."

"Exactly what I thought," he said. "See? We think alike."

She laughed, "At least in matters of miniature golf."

"We'll find out in what other ways when I see you. I'll meet you in the parking lot."

"I'm looking forward to it." As she ended the call, she really was.

She was still smiling as she approached Dave Harding's storefront. It was crisp and clean, with a placard of hours on the door. When she walked inside, she spotted the long desk across the back and Dave behind it. To the right there were several displays with miniature garage doors and pamphlets with the history and explanation of each brand. To the left she spotted an actual garage door that she supposed would go up and down with a remote. That way Dave could explain its workings to his customers. It was a double-window model and was something like what she was looking for. She guessed it was his most popular style.

When he spied her, he raised his hand in greeting. "Hi there. How are you?"

"I'm good."

"Do you need a garage door?" he asked.

"Actually, I do. I hope to pick up some brochures and decide on the style."

"Maybe we can trade services. I'd like to do some redecorating at my place and I hear you're the go-to person for that."

Trading services. She'd be open to that. "If you're serious, I can drop by sometime."

He moved from behind the desk out into the open part of the showroom. Then he walked with her over to a stand with brochures. "Sounds like a plan." He started plucking out a few of the pamphlets. "You're looking for a traditional garage door?"

"I suppose, but one with some of those pretty hinge-looking things might be good too."

He laughed. "Only a woman would describe them that way." He plucked out another pamphlet. "How's Roz?" he asked. "I saw you were with her at the funeral. I only had a short time to talk with her because of all the people. It was hard to tell how she's really holding up."

"I think she's coming through this remarkably well."

"She's staying with you, isn't she?"

When Caprice remained silent, he shrugged. "I know you probably don't want to say, reporters and all that, but I certainly won't tell anyone."

Caprice made a calculated decision to trust him. After all, he'd already guessed. And it really wasn't that much of a stretch to figure out Roz was staying with her. At least not for any of her friends.

But rather than actually confirming it, she said, "Roz is keeping a low profile."

"And you're helping her do that?"

"Any way I can."

"So is it true the police suspect her?"

"I hope they're looking at lots of suspects."

"At the funeral I heard some of those men from PA Pharm talking."

"About what?" she asked, knowing this could be the information she was hoping for.

"The one said Ted had a lot of enemies. Another one, the guy talking to Roz after I did, looked really troubled about a detective calling some of them in for questioning."

"Chad Thompson?" Caprice murmured.

"Yeah, that's the guy. I heard somebody say his name."

"I should have circulated more," Caprice admitted. "But I didn't want to get too far from Roz."

"You're a good friend. That guy you were with, so he's her lawyer?"

She remembered Grant had announced that when Valerie came on the scene. "Yes, he is."

"Is he good?"

She said simply, "He'll steer Roz in the right direction." If Grant couldn't help Roz himself he'd make sure he'd hook her up with someone who could.

"I can't believe that woman barged into the funeral." Dave's brows furrowed and his lips pursed. "So Winslow was having an affair?"

"That's what it looks like."

"Maybe his mistress killed him."

"I suppose that's possible. We can only hope the police sort it out soon. Since I was occupied most of the time at the open house, I didn't wander around. I wondered if you might have heard anyone arguing with Ted."

Dave thought about it. "I didn't see him much that night. After I spoke with Roz, I left. That's what I told the police too, when they called me. I guess they were talking to everybody who was there."

"That's what I heard."

Dave handed her the pamphlets. "All we can do is hope everything turns out okay."

Caprice nodded. Yet she knew everything was not going to turn out okay for someone.

Caprice was on the first hole of the miniature golf course Saturday afternoon ready to swing when she felt Seth's gaze on her. She'd worn the blouse she'd bought at Secrets of the Past with lavender capri pants that were the same color as a shade in the blouse. Her hair swung over her shoulder as she adjusted her sandals on the green turf, ready to tee off.

"You look incredible today," Seth said, right before she swung.

The ball careened off the side barrier of the green, and she didn't know whether to be annoyed with him or totally flattered. "Did you say that so that my first shot would go wild?"

He grinned and came closer to her. "It just came out because it's what I was thinking. Don't you believe me?"

He was close enough that she could almost feel his body heat. She could definitely smell his after-shave. He was dressed in khakis and a short-sleeved, cranberry-colored Henley shirt. He was so good-looking she still couldn't believe she was on a date with him.

"I don't trust easily," she said casually.

"Hmm. I'd like to hear *that* story. But I'm not sure this is the place for it. Maybe later over an early dinner you can tell me why trusting is hard for you."

She liked the fact he was willing to listen. She liked the fact he was talking about later. Speechless for a moment, she realized he was looking at her as if he wanted to . . . kiss her.

But he didn't reach out to touch her. Instead he said, "Since I distracted you, you could take the shot over."

She studied her ball, which had stopped on the wrong side of a miniature mountain. She'd have to go around the mountain before she could shoot up a little bridge, over a lake, and into the cup. "I don't need an extra shot. If I don't make up the stroke on this hole, I'll make it up on the next."

"Confidence," Seth said with a chuckle as he stooped and put his own ball down. "I like that. But we'll see how confident you are after I play this hole under par."

"Have you been practicing?" she demanded when his ball zoomed through the mountain and halfway up the bridge.

"I've only been here a few times in the last couple of months. But my photographic memory records every hill and bump."

As she walked to her ball, she asked, "Seriously? A photographic memory?"

"Close to it. It's not a talent. It's a gift."

"A gift most people would like to have." She whacked her ball so it lined up with the hole through the mountain.

"I think what *you* do is a gift. I can't imagine staging a whole house. Do you move everything out and what you want in?"

"Sometimes. But usually I just modify what the owner already has. I switch it around a little, add different throw pillows, maybe drapes and accent pieces."

"Is that what you did with the Winslows' mansion?"

"Pretty much. Why?"

"I stopped for coffee at the Koffee Klatch yesterday. I heard your name mentioned."

"Do I want to know why?" she asked jokingly.

"I'm not sure. Two men were talking and I heard 'Caprice.' You've gotta admit that's not a common name. So I listened."

"And."

"The one man said you were snooping around PA Pharm and no one there liked it."

"I wasn't snooping. I was just collecting Ted's personal items for Roz."

"Did you ask questions?"

"A few. But that was natural under the circumstances, don't you think?"

He studied her. "I don't know. I do know Ted Winslow was murdered. If that was in any way connected to something going on at his company, you could be stirring up a hornet's nest."

"Well, somebody has to," she muttered. "This murder won't get solved any other way."

"Aha! So you are snooping."

"Are you going to tell me I shouldn't be?"

This time he approached her slowly. This time he did touch her. He brushed her hair from the front of her shoulder to the back, his long fingers causing a tingling sensation where he'd touched. "I'm not going to tell you what you should or shouldn't do. But I do know those two guys in suits looked seriously ruffled. So you might want to try asking your questions more discreetly."

Maybe going to PA Pharm like that with Grant

had been a mistake because their questions had put Ted's colleagues on notice.

"Do you go to the Koffee Klatch often?"

"I run in and out practically every morning. Why? Do you like the place? I could rise and shine a half hour earlier and meet you there sometime."

That sounded like a nice idea. Maybe even a second date.

Stepping away from her, Seth went to his ball, adjusted his stance, and hit it into the cup.

She had the feeling Seth Randolph was going to be terribly hard to beat . . . and terribly hard to resist.

Some holes on the course were more challenging than others. She made par on hole five, with its windmill. But at hole six, the course had too many sand traps *and* . . . she was distracted by Seth. Although his attention was on her a lot of the time, he still managed to maintain his focus. On hole nine—at a waterfall—they both studied it, planning their strategy. He played first.

But after he set his ball down, he glanced at her and asked, "So what house are you staging next?"

"A country theme. The open house is next weekend."

"A country theme. Let me guess, flowers and distressed wood."

"And you said you don't know anything about home-staging."

"My mother likes the country look."

"Does she live around here?"

"In Virginia. Dad's a GP there."

"So you followed in your dad's footsteps?"

"I was in and out of his office a lot as a kid. I can remember being fascinated by his stethoscope. He didn't push me into medicine or anything. I know he'd like me to join him in his practice."

"But you don't want to?"

"I needed to be out on my own for a while. I'm still not so sure I might not like to get involved in trauma medicine. I was thinking about applying for a fellowship."

If he applied for a fellowship, he'd probably move to a city where there was a teaching hospital. Johns Hopkins wasn't too far away, but he could be thinking of a fellowship anywhere. "So why Kismet?" she asked, becoming more curious about him the longer she was with him.

"It's not too large and not too small. At urgent care, I get a taste of emergency medicine."

"So this is temporary for you." She suddenly thought of Craig in California and his "Dear Caprice" letter.

"I'm not sure yet," he said honestly.

Their gazes met.

He seemed to forget about his ball. Instead of playing the hole, he took hold of her hand, pulled her toward him, then let go of her hand, and slid his hand under her hair. "Everything's in flux, but my life is mine to make. My choices depend on what happens next."

"Are you talking about opportunities?" His fingers were light but warm on her neck, his hold a bit possessive.

"I'm talking about *everything*," he said.

When he tipped her chin up and ran his thumb over her lower lip, she felt as if she'd collapse right there on the green.

But he didn't kiss her. He just tapped her on the nose, gave her a sly grin and went back to considering how he'd play his ball.

She felt totally rattled. Why hadn't he kissed her? Because he wanted to prolong the tension for them both? Or because he wanted to find out why she didn't trust easily first?

Maybe *she* wanted to rattle *him* a little. "What was your longest serious relationship?"

He stopped mid-swing. "You'd like to have that conversation *here* . . . right now?"

A family of four had approached the green behind them. As the scents of freshly mown grass rode on the air, she responded, "It only requires a two-word answer."

"If I give you the two-word answer, you'll stop there?"

The question seemed light-hearted, but she couldn't be sure. "I'll stop there . . . for now."

"We have caves, more waterfalls, and dogleg

holes up ahead. I don't know if I can concentrate with questions like these."

"Your lack of concentration means I'll win."

He burst out laughing. "All right. But I have to give you five words, not two. My most recent serious relationship lasted a year and a half."

Her next question popped out. "How long ago . . . ?"

"Remember," he warned her. "You said you'd stop for now. No more serious stuff until we finish these eighteen holes. Then we can get down to business at the Blue Moon Grille. Okay with you?"

The Blue Moon Grille was situated in the oldest part of downtown Kismet. It was located on the second floor above an arts-and-crafts mall, and there were tables on the deck that were usually packed full, especially when the moon was out. She liked the idea of sitting there with Seth . . . a lot.

"The Blue Moon Grille it is. I'll try to keep any more questions from popping into my head. Does the winner buy dinner?"

"You couldn't stop asking questions if your life depended on it. Yes, the winner gets to buy dinner."

Seth's blue eyes twinkled in a way that told her he was definitely going to be the winner.

And he was.

An hour later, they were standing at their cars in the parking lot, weighing the pros and cons of taking one car or two to the restaurant when Seth's cell phone beeped. He checked the screen, then said, "Sorry, I have to take this."

She nodded that, of course, she understood.

He paced about ten feet away, listened, then secured the phone back on his belt.

With a frustrated expression, he approached her. "The questions will have to wait. So will the Blue Moon. I'm needed at the clinic. We're short-staffed, and when it's quiet, that's fine. But they have about ten patients waiting, and since I'm due in there in a couple of hours anyway—" He stopped and assessed her expression.

Sure, she was disappointed. But she did understand. "It's okay, Seth. It's your job. It's what you do."

"You won't delete my name from your phone's contact list?" he joked.

"Not for this," she assured him.

"That's a relief. I'll call you. Maybe we can have that coffee some morning . . . before I get called in to see patients."

"Sounds good."

He could have kissed her then, she supposed. But they were standing in the middle of the parking lot with evening golfers parking, climbing out of their cars, flowing in a stream of families and couples toward the cashier's kiosk, ready for an evening of fun.

So Seth didn't kiss her. He climbed into his car, gave her a wave, and in a spit of gravel drove away.

On Monday morning, Caprice ended the call on her cell phone and glanced over at Roz, who was sitting at the kitchen table examining a list of possible apartments. Dylan sat at her feet, while Stripes—one of the kittens—nestled in her lap. Sophia and Creamsicle—that's what they had named the other kitten—were batting about a tin-foil ball in the living room.

Roz looked up and saw Caprice's smile. "Good news?"

"Great news! An offer came in on the vacant house I staged."

"Wonderful! You are so talented. I wish I had your knack."

"You have talents too. I will never look as put together as you do. Your fashion sense is impeccable. Maybe you should open a boutique."

Roz considered Caprice's suggestion as Stripes jumped off her lap. "Maybe when this is all over, I'll look into it. What's on your agenda this morning?"

"I'm meeting with Teresa Arcuri around noon. At your open house she asked me if I could redo her kitchen and dining room. Her theme is sun-flowers. It was a cinch to gather up ideas for that.

I don't do much just plain decorating anymore. Dave Harding asked if I'd consider doing his place."

"Did he? He has a cute little house over on Sunset."

"You've seen it?" Caprice asked.

"No, but he was telling me about it. It was good reconnecting with him at the open house. He was very kind when he came to the funeral. He didn't go running off after Valerie's appearance, like some people did. We're going to have lunch sometime."

The doorbell rang.

"Stay here," Caprice said. "Just in case it's Marianne Brisbane."

"If she pushes her way in, I'll duck outside."

Caprice hadn't seen the reporter again, nor received any phone calls. She'd wondered if she'd given up. Yet she knew reporters didn't give up.

As Caprice opened the door, she had a pleasant surprise. The young man standing there carried a vase filled with red roses and baby's breath, along with a few ferns. "Caprice De Luca?" he asked.

"That's me." Glancing around for the animals, she saw Stripes had clawed her way up the cat condo and was lounging on the first shelf. Creamsicle scampered after Sophia up the stairs. Caprice didn't want any of them darting out the door.

The man with the flowers handed her the vase and said, "Have a good day." As he returned to his van, she saw the flowers had come from Posies, one of the two local flower shops.

Closing the door, Caprice carried the vase into the kitchen. She suspected whom it might be from but didn't want to jump to any conclusions. After all, her clients might have been glad about their sale and sent her the bouquet to thank her. Or the real estate agent might have done the same. It wouldn't be the first time.

Still they were red roses. Not mums or carnations, not even something exotic.

"So what's this?" Roz asked with a quirked blond brow.

"I'll soon find out." Caprice plucked the white envelope from the plastic card holder and found her heart was beating way too fast for early morning. She just held it between the tips of her fingers for a few seconds.

"Open it," Roz coaxed. "We know who it's from. Let see what he said."

When she'd returned home after her date, Roz had given her the third degree, and Caprice had happily related every detail about it. "We don't know that it's from Seth."

Roz gave her a get-real look.

Caprice slid the card from the small envelope. The scrawl was difficult to read—a doctor's handwriting. She smiled, feeling an excited warmth fill her.

Caprice—Thinking of our date and the next one.
Seth

She read the message aloud, knowing Roz would expect nothing less.

"What a great start. I hope you two can go out again soon."

Taking the vase to the sink, Caprice filled it with a little more water. "I don't know. His schedule sounds heavy. But it's possible we could have an early morning coffee date."

"At least the flowers show you he had a good time."

"Is that what they show me? I'm not very experienced at starting new relationships, Roz. When I'm with Seth, I'm afraid I'll put my foot in my mouth."

"That's because you like him. And my guess is you feel some vibes coming back from him too."

Caprice thought about when he'd almost kissed her. At least she thought he'd almost kissed her. Not only didn't she trust men, but she was unsure of her self-confidence when she was with them. Was past experience a good teacher? Or did past experience just cause doubts and uncertainties that could derail a future relationship? She certainly didn't have the answers.

"I know this is probably something you haven't thought of. It's so soon after Ted died. But do you think you'll ever be able to trust a man again?"

When Roz stood, Dylan trotted into the living

room to find animal company. Going to the sink where the vase was sitting, she picked it up and took a whiff of the roses. "I can't believe everything Ted and I had was a sham. What we had at the beginning seemed so real. So perfect. My guess is when something is perfect, you really should doubt it."

Caprice was old enough to know nothing was perfect, at least for not very long. "I've been thinking about you and Ted a lot. I don't think he would've built that house for you if he didn't love you. He put so much attention to the details in it, details that he thought would please you. A man doesn't do that for a woman he doesn't love."

"I don't know when he stopped loving me," Roz said in a small voice with a catch in her throat.

"Maybe he didn't stop loving you."

"Do you think he loved me *and* Valerie? That's hard to swallow. And when I think about the time we spent together in New York, I wonder if he was pretending to love me."

"Maybe he didn't love Valerie. Maybe she was just a distraction because of everything else going on in his life—the troubles at work and the tension that caused with you."

"She was some distraction. But she thinks he loved her."

"Is that so unusual when a man has sex with a woman? Doesn't the woman sometimes delude herself that it's love?"

"I did. But we'll never know in their case."

"If you never know, then you'll have to choose what you believe about Ted. Wouldn't it be better to believe that he really loved you and just got off on the wrong track somehow?"

Roz's face showed surprise. "I never thought you'd stand up for him."

"I'm not standing up for him. I'm standing up for you. There's a big difference."

"Yes, I guess there is," Roz said. "But to answer your question—"

Caprice's cell phone sounded from her pocket. "I don't have to get that."

"Go ahead. It could be important."

When Caprice took her phone from her pocket and glanced at the screen, she looked again to make sure she was seeing correctly. She didn't recognize the phone number, but she did recognize the name—L. Hippensteel.

She quickly put the phone to her ear. "Lonnie."

Lonnie's voice was low. "Can you meet me somewhere?"

"Where?"

"Someplace inconspicuous. How about the parking lot at Country Fields Shopping Center?"

"What time?"

"How about three, at the south end?"

"I can do that. Do you want to tell me what this is about?"

"I'm still at PA Pharm. Not from here. See you at three." Lonnie ended the call.

"What was that about?" Roz asked. "You look a shade paler."

"Because this afternoon I could get some answers as to why Ted was murdered."

Chapter Fourteen

The May day was balmy, and the curbside planters were lush with pink petunias. Silver maples towered over landscaped islands meant to give the shopping center a garden appeal.

Since both Caprice's car and van were highly recognizable, she'd borrowed Nikki's less-conspicuous sedan. The car had lots of dings and could belong to anyone. When Caprice had told her sister why she wanted to borrow it, Nikki's eyes had lit up as she'd asked, "An adventure? Can I go with you?"

But Caprice had nixed that idea because Lonnie had sounded nervous enough. Bringing someone else along could make her even jumpier. It was possible that she might not even show up.

Caprice parked in the south end of the lot near an island . . . away from any other cars. She was a good distance from the back doors of the shopping center but could spot shoppers coming and going.

In the middle of the afternoon, when the weather was almost summery, mall retail traffic was minimal.

Suddenly Caprice was aware of a white, late-model, compact sedan pulling into the parking lot. The driver made a circle around the lot, wove around a few islands, then slid into the slot next to Caprice. Lonnie was wearing a straw hat that hid her hair. She must have piled it on top of her head. Although she was also wearing sunglasses, Caprice could still recognize her. This disguise wouldn't go much further than Roz's had.

Lonnie glanced over at her and motioned Caprice into her car.

That was easily accomplished. Making sure her phone was clipped to her wide leather belt, her keys in her pocket, she transferred to Lonnie's car, climbing into the passenger seat.

"Are you okay?" Caprice saw that Lonnie was pale under her sunglasses.

After checking right and left, seeing no one else in the vicinity, Lonnie removed her sunglasses. "I don't know. I realize I'm being paranoid. But I'm sitting on a powder keg."

"At PA Pharm?"

Lonnie took her hands from the steering wheel and shifted toward Caprice. "I'm no longer working there."

"You quit?"

"No, I was let go today. Mr. Thompson said they're not going to replace Mr. Winslow so they no longer need me. Ever since Mr. Winslow died, I felt they were keeping a close eye on me. They wouldn't give me any computer tasks, just odds and ends of secretarial work. Nothing important like I used to work on for Mr. Winslow."

"What did you consider important?"

"Typing up R&D memos, printing inventory reports from our warehouses, taking notes at department meetings, making sure the monthly report didn't have any errors."

"So why do you think they took you away from what you usually did?"

"Because they knew they were going to let me go and they didn't want me to see something I shouldn't."

"Do you have any idea what that was?" Caprice guessed Lonnie wouldn't have called this meeting unless she did.

"I was in Mr. Winslow's office before I left—just sort of saying a last good-bye to everything there— when I saw Mr. Thompson's line light up. I was furious they were letting me go, and I guess I just wanted to be difficult. So I picked up the phone and listened in." She said it defiantly, still obviously piqued.

"They couldn't tell you listened in?"

"I don't know for sure. Those lines are set up for conference calls. Mr. Thompson, Mr. Pendergast— he's one of the pharmaceutical reps in Delaware—

and Mr. Bodine from our Texas warehouse were talking."

Caprice caught the "our" reference. Lonnie had been a loyal employee, and apparently she found it hard to separate herself from the company.

"There was lots of background noise coming from the warehouse, so I think the click when I picked up might have gone unnoticed. I was real careful when I clicked off, but I suppose they could have heard that."

"But they wouldn't know you specifically had listened in."

"I don't think so. The line is set up so any department head can conference."

"Tell me what you heard."

After hesitating and glancing around the parking lot again, she admitted, "They were talking fast. And they were all worried and sharp with each other. With good reason. They changed the expiration date on antibiotics to move inventory! Mr. Bodine was worried they'd go to jail because that's illegal. But Mr. Thompson seemed more worried that if what they did was ever found out, PA Pharm's stock price will plummet. From what they said, I think Mr. Winslow was ready to blow the whistle to save himself."

If what Lonnie had surmised from the conversation was true, it could have meant financial ruin for PA Pharm, and that was a strong motive for murder. "You have to go to the authorities with this."

"Oh, no, I don't. Are you kidding? If someone at PA Pharm killed Ted, they wouldn't hesitate to come after me."

"If you go to the authorities and they begin an investigation, the whole scandal will be broken wide open. Once it's public knowledge, you won't have anything to fear. But if they know you know and you're a threat, that's something else."

Wringing her hands, Lonnie looked unconvinced. "I don't know. I'm not sure what to do. I could go stay with my sister in Virginia for a while . . ."

"If you run from this, Lonnie, what happens next?"

"I don't know. But I don't have any real evidence. Just what I heard. That won't hold up anywhere, will it?"

"Probably not. I'll have to ask Roz's lawyer." She saw increased worry on Lonnie's face. "I won't tell him anything specific for now. I'll just give him a hypothetical."

Lonnie still looked worried.

"You came to me because you didn't know what to do with the information. Right?"

Lonnie slowly nodded.

"Let me look into this. I'll be discreet."

After she blew out a breath, Lonnie pulled her hat down over her brow. "Talk to Mrs. Winslow's lawyer. But I didn't hear anything. I don't know anything."

* * *

Caprice thought about merely calling Grant. But she was on the way to a loft address downtown to meet with a perspective client and she could just stop in and see Grant on the way. If he was out, she'd leave a message for him to call her.

When Vince rented the first floor of the old house he'd turned into professional offices, he'd furnished his space in a practical rather than showy way. Of course, he hadn't asked her to help. She would have taken advantage of the older home and moved in a few antiques, woven drapes, Tiffany lamps. He'd gone to an office-supply store and purchased laminated desks and chrome lamps, although he had sprung for a wool rug he'd found at an outlet for the reception area. However, there wasn't an overall theme or welcoming effect from any of it.

"Practical" seemed to work for Vince and Grant, but she could have developed the space with so much more feeling.

Vince's response to her offer to redo it for him sometime was, "No one who's making a will, getting a divorce, settling an estate, or closing a deal on a house cares what my offices look like."

She wasn't convinced that was true.

A staircase to the second floor was located in the small foyer. She passed it and opened the door into Vince's space.

Giselle was stationed at her desk, her posture perfect as usual. Her wiry, gray hair was spiked in a style usually worn by women who were much younger than her fifty-four years. She wore the latest trends in makeup too behind her round tortoiseshell glasses. Today green eyeliner and shadow matched her blouse and slacks.

Noticing that her unexpected visitor was Caprice, she smiled. "I haven't seen you for months! Burning the candle at both ends?" Giselle liked proverbs and old sayings. Her commentary was loaded with them.

"I've been busy." Caprice leaned closer to the office in a conspiratorial gesture. "And we both know Vince doesn't like to be interrupted." His office door was open now. "He's not here?"

"You just missed him. Can I help?"

"Actually, I'm here to see Grant."

"I'll buzz him," Giselle said without blinking an eye. That's why she was such a good office manager. Nothing seemed to fluster her.

When Grant emerged from his office, he looked so . . . lawyerlike, even though he'd discarded his suit coat. His white dress shirt was pristine, his blue striped tie perfectly knotted and centered. "Unflappable" was a term she'd apply to him.

She remembered how expertly he'd defused the situation with Valerie Swanson at Ted's funeral. Possibly smoothing over sticky situations was all in a day's work for him.

"I have a few minutes," he told Giselle. "Hold my calls." He motioned Caprice inside.

Although Grant's office hadn't been professionally decorated, it had character. Two wine-colored leather club chairs with brass fittings down the seams faced his desk. A painting of the Grand Canyon hung on one wall, accompanied by two sand-painted plaques with Native American symbols. Although his desk was a laminate, twin to the one in Vince's office, his pottery pencil holder was hand-painted with images of wolves. His blotter complemented the chairs.

"Do you handle divorces?" she asked him.

"I didn't know you were married," he quipped. "Do you have a husband hidden away somewhere?"

She waved off his question as she plopped into one of the chairs. "I was remembering how you appeased Valerie at the funeral. You handled her expertly, as if you're used to dealing with distraught mistresses."

"I handle a few divorces. Vince does most of that. But I also have to facilitate estate settlements, and sometimes family members can become irate, even hostile. A good lawyer knows when he has to be a mediator."

After stopping beside her chair and gazing down at her for a few seconds—as if he was getting used to her presence in his office—he went to his high-backed leather desk chair and lowered himself into it. His gaze was as direct as his question. "What are you doing here?"

"I was going to call, but . . ." She hesitated. Maybe she shouldn't have come. Maybe sharing what Lonnie had told her wasn't a good idea. What if Lonnie *was* in danger?

Grant studied her intently and waited.

Finally, she came to a decision. Grant was Roz's lawyer, so she had to give him a clue as to the dealings at PA Pharm. "What if I told you there were several people with a motive to kill Ted?"

His face was expressionless. "I'd ask you to name them."

"What if I told you someone at PA Pharm had given the order to do something illegal, and some of the management heads were afraid of the problem going public?"

"Where did you get this information?"

"I can't say."

Grant's eyes narrowed. "You *won't* say." His line of vision shifted to the window and the brick row house next door. Then he redirected his focus once again to her. "What did PA Pharm do?"

"They changed the expiration date on antibiotics so they could sell them."

With a low whistle, Grant shook his head. "On many drugs that wouldn't matter. But with antibiotics . . . Just how much do you know about this?"

"Not much."

"Is there evidence?"

"No. Just an overheard phone conversation."

"Did Ted's secretary give you this?"

Caprice didn't answer.

"Right," he muttered. "You can't say. But that answer is obvious."

"If someone has this information, should he or she go to the authorities?"

"There is no evidence."

"But if the person who gave the order knows someone overheard him—"

"If we're talking about Ted's secretary, and if the person who killed Ted was someone from PA Pharm, she could be in danger. Let me look into the reporting procedure."

"Ted was going to blow the whistle, maybe to save himself."

Grant leaned back in his chair. "I might have to visit the D.A.'s office. This would shift the heat from Roz."

"My source doesn't want to come forward."

"It could be the safest thing for her if she did."

"I didn't say my source was a she."

"You didn't have to. You're going to have to work on your poker face, Caprice. Your eyes give too much away."

They sat gazing at each other for a very long moment.

Caprice glanced away first, down at the purse in her lap. "I don't want to regret telling you."

"I understand. I realize how explosive this information is. I won't put Miss Hippensteel in danger. I'm more concerned about you. You're asking questions. If you ask them of Ted's killer or he feels threatened, you're the one in danger."

She thought she heard real caring in Grant's voice, and that freaked her out. So much so that she stood. "I'll be fine."

"Famous last words. If anything happens to you, Vince will blame me. Your family will blame me."

Was he only worried about being responsible? That thought irked her. "No matter what happens, I absolve you of blame. No one's going to stop me from asking questions or getting to the bottom of this."

She swung around, intent on exiting his office and shutting the door behind her. But he caught her arm before she reached the door.

There was some kind of apology in his eyes, but she wasn't sure what it was for. However, he didn't express it.

"I won't do anything stupid," she promised him.

"You'd better not," he warned her and stepped away.

On her way to her car, she wondered what would happen if she did.

* * *

"So what do you think, Roz?" Vince asked, as the De Luca family—all except their dad, mom, and Nana—sat in Bella's living room discussing their mother's birthday.

Caprice had jumped in automatically, ready to protect her friend. "Don't put her on the spot." Roz hadn't even wanted to come tonight, saying she wasn't part of the family. But Caprice had convinced her she needed to get out, whether they had to confront reporters or not. They could always say "No comment" and go on their way.

Like any news story, though, Ted Winslow's death had lost steam and public interest. Unless there was a break in the case and until someone was charged, there wouldn't be much news coverage.

"Do you feel put on the spot?" Vince asked Roz in his smooth lawyer's voice.

Caprice could have clunked him on the head. Roz would see through that fake charm in a minute.

"Yes, I do," she admitted honestly, and his grin faded. But then she added, "I can tell you what I think, but I don't want to impose my ideas on any-body here."

Sitting beside Bella on the sofa, Joe nodded in agreement.

Bella still hadn't told him about her pregnancy, and Caprice didn't understand that at all. Holding this news close to her heart wasn't going to settle anything.

"So what do you think?" Vince prompted. No fake smile this time.

"I think your mom would appreciate a party in her honor with all the frills and trimmings." She glanced at the rest of the family, and then her focus went back to Vince. "You have to realize where I'm coming from. I lost my mom. So anything you can do to show yours that you appreciate her is monumentally important. I don't think you should pass up the opportunity."

Everyone in the room went quiet. Bella's children were asleep. The evening breeze blew in the front windows, rattling a blind. Each of them were taking in what Roz said, maybe realizing for the first time what it would mean if they were to lose their mother.

Nikki, on the carpet beside Caprice, broke the silence. "That decides it. We should bring Roz to all of our family meetings."

"Exactly what does it decide?" Joe asked with a frown. "Sure, you want to have a party. But just how elaborate are you gonna get? We can only stretch our budget so far."

"Joe!" Bella looked humiliated he'd said such a thing.

"I'm just being honest. Vince, Caprice, and Nikki—they have their own businesses. They're pulling in good money. We've got a family. On the other hand, I don't want to shortchange your mom, either. We'll chip in our fair share. Just putting it all out there on the table. We sure can't afford to rent a ballroom somewhere."

As much as Joe irked her sometimes, Caprice realized he had his pride. "My mom wouldn't want us to go overboard. Nikki and I talked a little bit about this."

"Well, of course you did," Bella murmured. "You always talk to Nikki."

Caprice felt shocked and a little hurt. She wanted to shoot back—*Maybe that's because Nikki can keep secrets and you can't.* But she didn't. If Bella was pregnant, her hormones could already be in an uproar, which would account for that little outburst. On the other hand, maybe it's what she'd been thinking for years.

Vince and Joe looked uncomfortable, like guys who didn't want to be involved in a sisterly crisis. What else was new?

"We didn't want to go ahead with anything," Caprice explained calmly, "until we all decided what we wanted to do. Isaac found a place that sells Fostoria crystal, including some of the dishes Mom has wanted. So we can all go together for that. Once that's split up, it should fit into your budget," she said to Joe. "As soon as Isaac tells me the price, I'll call you and we'll figure it out. Okay?"

Joe gave a shrug as if that was suitable.

"But as far as the party itself, we considered the church's social hall but thought my back-yard would be even better. Mom's birthday falls on Memorial Day this year, and the weather should be okay. So I can provide my place for the party and get a great deal on canopies. I won't even have to pay for setup if we have our own manpower." She gave a direct look at Vince and Joe.

"No problem there," Vince said.

"Same here," Joe agreed.

"I can call or e-mail everyone Mom would like to see there," Bella offered.

Nikki pulled her knees up and wrapped her arms around them. "That just leaves the food. I'll be glad to cover that. And everybody can chip in whatever they want."

"So you'll treat it like a buffet?" Roz asked.

"That would probably be best. You have electrical outlets out back, don't you, Caprice?"

"Two of them. We can even string lights."

"I'm pretty good with flowers," Roz said. "Let me cover the table decorations. I'm grateful Caprice has let me stay with her, and your family has been very kind. I want to contribute."

"Mom loves roses. Dad sends her some on any occasion that's important to her."

"That's good to know. I'll keep that in mind for the tables."

"What *about* the tables and chairs?" asked Joe.

That started another whole discussion about whether or not they should use picnic-style tables or cafeteria-style tables.

While the others were talking, Nikki nudged

Caprice. Bumping shoulders was something they'd done since they were kids.

"What?" Caprice asked.

"I've been thinking about the murder, and the dagger you said was stolen."

"You haven't told anybody about that, have you?"

Nikki looked around at the gathering; nobody was paying any attention to them. "No, of course not. I understand the police wouldn't want the news of what was stolen to get out. Did you ask Roz if there was anything special about that particular one?"

"Just that Ted bought it for her for her birthday and it was more valuable than some of the others."

"Ted's whole collection made me curious," Nikki said. "So I was fishing around on the Internet. I discovered that some of the antique pieces have legends with them. You know, like Excalibur. With Excalibur, whoever pulled it out of the stone would be the next king. Maybe Ted's dagger had a legend attached to it."

"A legend," Caprice murmured. "Do you think that could have something to do with the murder?"

"It could have something to do with why that particular dagger was stolen. I don't know. I'm just guessing. But there's history behind those pieces and that history could matter."

"I'll call Isaac tomorrow and ask him. Maybe it's time Roz and I went back to the house and looked for the provenance on the piece. I'll talk to her about it later."

After they ironed out all the details of the party, Bella served iced tea and homemade cookies. Caprice noticed she didn't drink the tea nor eat the cookies. Did she have all-day nausea instead of just morning sickness?

After they chatted a little longer, they thanked Bella and Joe and said good night. Caprice thought about taking Bella aside and asking her why she was keeping her secret, something she couldn't usually do if her life depended on it. But she wasn't sure what would happen if she did. Bella seemed on edge, and she didn't want to push her over it. When Bella was ready, she'd do whatever she was going to do. Maybe in spite of what Bella had said, Joe would embrace the idea of a larger family. There was no way to know until she told him. Could she be afraid that the news of a baby coming would damage her marriage irrevocably?

Nikki drove off first. Vince walked Roz and Caprice to Caprice's car. Caprice thought he was hovering just a bit with Roz, and that was unusual for Vince. He waited at the curb until they were safely inside the car with seat belts fastened before he went to his car.

"You have a wonderful family," Roz said.

"Even when we squabble?"

"Sure. That's what families do. But you all want the best for each other and it shows."

Caprice slid her key into the ignition and started the car. But then she glanced at Roz. "How would you feel about going back into your house?"

Roz sighed. "I know I'll have to do it sometime. Why?"

"Because I think we need to find the provenance on the dagger that was stolen." She told Roz what Nikki had said.

"I can see your point. There's only one problem."

"What?"

"The provenance for that dagger is probably in Ted's office safe. I don't have the combination."

Chapter Fifteen

"It's empty. Just like you said it would probably be." Roz crossed her arms over her chest, obviously uncomfortable with being in a house she'd once called a home.

Before they'd arrived this morning, Caprice should have realized the investigation would probably have taken the forensic team into this particular space in Ted's office closet on the first floor.

There was still fingerprint dust everywhere, drawers standing open. The worst part—

Roz knew everything had been touched.

She'd called a service that specialized in the type of sanitation she needed for the sword room. They'd peered into every other room downstairs, except for that one, finally ending up in Ted's office.

"Let's go upstairs," Roz murmured, obviously resigned to what she'd find there.

A few minutes later, they were entering the

master suite. It was easy to see the bedroom had been rifled through. Roz wrinkled her nose, then seemed to lose all her self-control and courageous starch as she sank onto the bed. "I can't stay here, let alone live here. I know that."

Tears came to her eyes and she swiped them away. "Life as I know it is destroyed. The bed reminds me of—" She stopped again. "Both loving times as well as Ted's infidelity. I'm going to pack clothes to take to your place and call in my cleaning service so the real estate agent can show the house again. Though now, it's going to be even harder to sell."

"Someone might want to buy an infamous house. You never know." Caprice glanced around the room. "Do you want me to help you?"

Roz shook her head. "No, I'm okay. I think I want to be up here alone for a while."

"I'll look around downstairs again."

Although Roz couldn't stand to go into the sword room, Caprice wanted to. Did that make her morbid . . . or just a sleuth?

Downstairs once more, Caprice took her time, peering into each room again with a discriminating eye. When she migrated down the hall, she found herself holding her breath as she approached the sword room.

She prepared herself, then stepped inside . . . not knowing what she'd see or feel.

After a quick look around, she realized it was just

a room with a sword collection. No unusual vibrations or woo-woo feelings. It was simply a room with
no evidence of what had happened here.

However, she remembered. The sight of Ted
dead on the floor with a dagger in his back was a
picture that could haunt her for a long time . . . if
not forever.

Stepping deeper into the room, Caprice studied
the glass curio case that housed the smaller and in
some cases more expensive collectibles. She crossed
to it, questioning why the door had been hanging
open that night. Because Ted had shown the killer
something inside it? Because the dagger that had
been stolen had questionable provenance? Because
someone who'd bid on it wanted it so badly he or
she would kill for it? But that would have had to
have been someone Ted knew, wouldn't it? Or had
he gotten a call from another collector and let the
person in?

Could Valerie have done this? Was she capable of
stabbing the man she loved? Why would she have
been with Ted in the sword room? Why would she
have taken the dagger? Because it had been the
one he'd bought for Roz? Could she have been jealous that Ted still had feelings for his wife?

Then there were Ted's cohorts at work. Had one
of them come over? Been chummy? Talked about
Ted's collection? Then killed him because of something Ted knew? Or killed him because he was
going to do what would have been bad for the

company? Maybe the murderer just stole a dagger, any dagger, to make it look like a robbery. Was Chad Thompson the culprit?

Caprice hadn't forgotten about Monty, either, and his argument with his employer.

Leaving the sword room, she went down the hall that led to Ted's office and the back door. After she opened the door, she peered outside.

Monty had apparently been taking care of the place. The yard was mown and the bushes trimmed. Spirea and peonies bloomed in one of the rear gardens. But today Caprice wasn't interested in the gardens. She spotted the break in the hedge that Monty had spoken of.

Going outside, she left the patio and crossed the grass to the hedge. Anyone could have pushed through there. Had the police found footprints or any evidence someone had been there? Had that break been there all along? Maybe Monty even used it. Yet the murderer fleeing out the back door and sliding through a break in the hedge made sense. Caprice just couldn't figure out who that person had been.

She'd been thinking through all of it, absolutely everything, when she was playing with the kittens, taking Dylan for a walk, not sleeping at night. She had come to one conclusion. Lonnie needed to come forward and talk to Vince and Grant. Grant was Roz's lawyer, so it might not be a good idea for him to advocate for Lonnie.

But Vince—Maybe he could convince her that she had to reveal what she knew. Maybe he could convince her that she could be a witness if she had to be.

Bits of what she'd seen and what she'd heard swirled around Caprice's head. She whimsically believed if she could just snatch the right ones out of the air, then maybe she could put all the pieces together.

She'd returned inside the house ready to make a cup of tea for herself and Roz when she heard Roz bumping her suitcase down the stairs. It was a large suitcase.

"I've made some decisions," Roz announced when she reached the first floor.

"What decisions?" Caprice asked.

"First of all, I'm going to drive my car back to your house, then stop hiding as if I've done something wrong. I have to build a new life and get around on my own."

"You can find a condo or an apartment if you want. But I still don't think you should live there alone. Not until this is solved."

"It might take me a while to find a place. You can decorate for me," Roz said with a small smile.

"I'll be happy to, you know that."

Roz rolled her suitcase to the door. "I also made another decision. I think I'm going to do what you suggested. I want to find space to open a boutique. I do have fashion sense and I can share it. The mall is fine for ordinary shopping, but most stores don't have that personal touch anymore. I can give that to women in Kismet."

"Yes, you can. I know you'll be a great success at it."

Roz threw her a wry look. "That's a good friend talking."

Caprice just smiled. Anything she said wouldn't matter. Roz wouldn't believe she could be a success until she was. Being Ted's wife hadn't led to independence and self-confidence. Maybe now those qualities would grow.

"Are you ready to leave?" Roz asked. "I really want to get out of here."

But before they could move either down a hall to the garage or out the front door, the doorbell chimed.

"Did you tell anyone you'd be here?" Caprice asked Roz.

"No. Did you?"

Caprice shook her head and crossed to the peephole. "It's Marianne Brisbane. My car's in the driveway, so she knows we're here. Do you want to not answer the door? Sneak out the back?"

"No point," Roz answered with some resignation, letting go of her suitcase handle. "Let's see what she wants."

"You know what she wants."

"I have to face this sometime, Caprice." Roz

put her hand on the doorknob and opened the door wide.

Marianne actually looked surprised. "I didn't think you'd come to the door," she said.

Roz didn't let the reporter inside. "You'll keep hounding me or Caprice until I see you face to face. So here I am. But I don't have anything to say. So just go away!"

Marianne shook her head. "I'm not going away, and you know it. Even if you're cleared of all suspicion and go back to a normal life, I'll still want a story about what happened, how you felt, and what you're doing. I can put together information I received from other sources. Or you can give it to me straight yourself."

Caprice stepped in. "She can't talk to you now. You should know that. There's an ongoing investigation."

"And anything she says can be used against her. I know. But can't we just talk? Can't you just show me where it happened?"

Both women exploded at once. "No!"

"But I've heard it's all cleaned up. What's the harm?"

"Pushy doesn't begin to describe you," Caprice muttered under her breath.

"Of course, I'm pushy. I'm a reporter. Now come on. Give me something. If you do, I promise I'll let you alone, either until you're charged or until the murderer is found. I already know you're staying with Caprice. I could see you both in Caprice's car when you pulled out of her driveway."

"Have you been stalking me?" Caprice demanded.

"I've been parked down at the end of your street now and then waiting for the right time. Obviously today was the right time." She spied Roz's suitcase behind her. "Are you going somewhere? Flying off without permission?"

"No!" Roz erupted, now outraged herself. "I just needed some clothes."

"While you're staying at Caprice's."

Roz sighed, "Yes, while I'm staying with Caprice. But she doesn't need more reporters parked down the street. So you don't know that."

"Then give me something I do know."

After a glance at Caprice, Roz answered her. "I'm still selling the house. I don't intend to ever live here again."

"Are you moving away from Kismet?"

"No, in fact I have plans to open a business here."

"What kind of business?"

"A fashion boutique. In the upcoming weeks I'll be looking for a space and gathering some ideas. And that's all I'm going to say."

Marianne tried to see farther inside the house. "Are you sure you won't let me come in? If I had known there was going to be a murder here, I would have toured it the day of the open house. I've seen the floor plans and the pictures of the rooms on the real estate site. If you let me see the sword room, I promise I'll let you in on anything I find out about the investigation."

Caprice exchanged a glance with Roz and had to admit it would be great to have a source.

"Won't Grant tell us what he hears?" Roz asked her, obviously thinking the same thing.

"Possibly. But Grant doesn't know everyone. And Marianne has her contacts."

"I sure do!" The reporter bobbed her head vigorously.

"All right, two minutes," Roz agreed. "That's it. One look around and out."

"Deal." Marianne looked elated.

But she stuck to their deal. In those two minutes, her gaze seemed to record absolutely everything in the room.

Caprice wondered if, like Seth, she had a photographic memory.

Seth. Their date had seemed so long ago. This murder scene seemed so removed from her ordinary life. But was it really? Just what was her ordinary life? Dinners with her family . . . walking the dog . . . staging houses? But Roz was part of her ordinary life now too.

At the door Marianne said, "Thanks. I really mean it. I'll call you if I hear anything. And if you want to spill your story, you do the same." She handed her card to Roz. "I gave one of these to

Caprice, but she might have thrown it away. You keep it. You never know. You might need it."

After the reporter left, Caprice turned to Roz. "I hope that wasn't a mistake."

A shiver crept up Caprice's spine that evening. She felt almost as paranoid as Lonnie had looked in her car at the shopping center. She couldn't shake the feeling someone was watching her.

After she and Roz decided to make dinner later, she'd driven her van to the storage compartment in order to pick up a few pieces she'd stored there for a new client she'd taken on yesterday. Leo Heinz wanted to sell his high-end loft quickly. The best way Caprice knew to have a fast turnover was to turn it into a bachelor pad.

Leo and his wife already had lots of leather and chrome that would work, but Caprice wanted to add a few more luxurious elements to the rearranging she intended to do. She could find an alpaca rug at the rental company. But she had a few glass art pieces that would work perfectly, as well as a Quoizel lamp and a painting with broad geometrical shapes. The theme for the loft was, of course, Bachelor's Night In. She was looking forward to working there this week. Bob Preston and his crew were tied up, so Monty would be painting the kitchen cabinets a subdued sage that would counterpoint the gleaming black appliances and gray granite counter.

After Caprice exited her van and shut the driver's door, she opened the two back doors so she could carry the pieces directly into the van. Dusk was falling and everything around the rows of storage compartments was shadowy. She thought again about her and Roz's encounter with the reporter that morning, still wondering if they'd done the right thing by letting Marianne inside the house. But Caprice usually was a good judge of character. She didn't feel Marianne Brisbane was vindictive or simply out to make a splash. She wanted to know the details and the truth.

Just as they did.

If they'd made a mistake, so be it. They'd have to live with whatever came of it.

But ever since Marianne had told them she'd been sitting down at the end of her street, Caprice couldn't shake off the prickly feeling she could be in danger, along with Roz and Lonnie. Had Grant's warnings finally taken root?

Was she being watched now? Who would want to watch her? Who would care if she went to her storage compartment?

Night was rapidly falling, and only Roz knew she was here.

Suddenly Caprice heard the low hum of an engine. She couldn't see beyond the storage compartment area to know if anyone had followed her in. To be realistic about the whole situation, she was asking questions about a murder, ruffling feathers at PA Pharm, secretly meeting Lonnie, and hiding Roz.

Taking her phone from her pocket, she quickly texted her friend. "Keep the doors locked and the shades drawn." Moments later Roz texted back, "Will do. Dylan will protect me."

Caprice smiled. Then she heard that low rumble again. Had a car braked and then accelerated? Was it searching through the rows of compartments looking for *her*?

All of a sudden she panicked. Up until now she'd been dealing with the murder as if it were a puzzle or maybe a game. But this was no game. Ted had lost his life. Panic wasn't a feeling she usually knew, and it overcame her before she figured out what had happened. She was breathing fast and her hands were shaking. Who could she call that would have her back? Who could she call who would tell her what to do?

Without thinking twice, she pressed speed dial for Grant's number.

"What's up, Caprice?" He'd obviously seen her number on caller ID.

"I'm not sure, I just feel . . . creepy. I'm at my storage compartment and I hear another car or something. But it's like it's searching through the rows. Or else it's coming after me slowly. Or maybe I'm having a nervous breakdown."

"Do you have your compartment opened?" Grant asked.

"No, why?"

"Open it. Get inside. Shut the door and pick up something you can use for a weapon. Now. Don't even think about it. Just do it."

There was something in his voice that urged her rebellious nature to quiet and to follow his orders. Taking out her key, she quickly undid the padlock. Was the growl of an engine coming closer? Was it in her row?

She didn't even take time to look. She hiked up the door, ducked inside, and quickly lowered it again. That's when she realized she was standing in the dark, except for the light from her phone.

"Are you inside?" Grant wanted to know.

"Yes, but I don't have a flashlight or anything."

"I'm on my way. Don't open that door for anybody but me. The dark won't hurt you, but somebody outside could. What do you have as a weapon?"

His voice rose and fell as if he was walking somewhere. Then she heard other sounds—his car door, his SUV's engine starting.

She thought about her storage compartment and what she had stored there. She transferred her phone to her left hand, sidled along the compartment to one wall, and wrapped her fingers around a tall vase. "I have a vase."

"I'm on my way. If someone actually tries to lift

that door, just shout at them that you already called 9-1-1. Shout it over and over again. And then tell them you have a gun."

"But I don't."

"Doesn't matter. He or she won't know that. Give me your compartment number and PIN number to get into the storage compartments."

Apparently he knew about that. She rattled off the info he needed.

"Listen again and see if you can hear anything."

Was that a vehicle slowly coming up the row? The compartment door muffled what she was hearing. But, yes, that was a car, a truck, something. It slowly idled outside the compartment. Should she start yelling now?

No, she told herself. Wait. Wait.

She put the phone on speaker and set it on a stack of boxes. Then she took the handle of the door and pushed down with all her might. If anyone was going to try to get in here, they were going to have one heck of a fight. She'd taken a course in self-defense a few years ago. She even remembered some of the moves. She put all her weight into holding the handle of the door down.

The vehicle was still idling out there. She didn't hear a door opening and closing. Could anyone do that silently? Of course, they could open their door and just leave it open.

Were those footsteps on the macadam? She started sweating in the damp night air, more scared than she'd ever been in her life. No puzzle or game now. This could be life or death. Not only for her, but for Lonnie, maybe for Roz. Just what had they tapped into?

It seemed like forever until she felt the slight tug on the door.

She began shouting, "I called 9-1-1. I called 9-1-1, and I have a gun."

The pressure on the handle stopped. She thought she heard someone swear. Then she did hear a car door. She did hear an engine. Her hand on that handle was starting to ache.

She heard Grant's voice coming over the phone. "I'm in the lot, Caprice. A couple of minutes. I just have to find your row."

"There's a car outside. Someone tried to get in."

"I see row G. Whoa, a black SUV just rolled out of F. He's headed out of the lot, but I'm coming into your row. I wish I could've gotten that license number."

She wanted to tell him the license number didn't matter right now. She wanted to tell him that all she cared about was seeing his face and knowing there was someone else with her who could fight whatever demons came along.

After she heard another car door open and shut, Grant was shouting at her from both the phone and outside. "I'm here."

He was trying to lift the door, but she was still holding it down.

Feeling foolish, she released her hold as he raised the storage compartment door. The night floodlights had switched on and backlit him.

When she saw Grant, she had the weirdest reaction. She wanted to throw her arms around him! But that was just because he meant safety. He meant rescue. He meant everything she didn't want to need in a man.

So when he braced his hands on her shoulders, looked into her eyes and asked, "Are you all right?" she backed away. "I'm fine. Really."

He shook his head and scolded her. "Yeah, you look it. You're white, you're sweaty, and your eyes are as big as bowling balls."

"Bowling balls?" she asked as relief washed over her and she felt the panic begin to fade away. "Really, Mr. Weatherford, can't you do better than that?"

"How can you joke? Remember, I saw the SUV zooming out of here. The one that obviously followed you."

"I told whoever it was I had a gun and they ran away," she responded flippantly.

But Grant didn't like her flippancy any more than he liked her "fine" answer. "You've stirred up trouble."

"I didn't have to stir it up. It was already there. Ted Winslow was murdered, remember?"

"Oh, I remember. And you should have done what any self-respecting citizen would do. Let—it—

a—lone." He drawled out each word so she got a clear message.

"I'm sorry I called you," she murmured under her breath.

"Why did you? I'm sure your brother's name is in your phone too."

"I thought you might have a gun," she shot back. "I know Vince doesn't."

That seemed to take Grant by surprise. "I do have a gun. Right now it's locked in my glove compartment, which is the best place for it. But what made you think I would?"

"You worked in a big city. I have no idea what kind of cases you took on, but it was a possibility. Besides, I called you because you have a stake in this. You're protecting Roz's interests."

"I'm not sure your reasoning made logical sense. But then I've found lots of women's reasoning doesn't."

One woman in particular? Caprice wondered. Grant's ex-wife?

"What were you doing here anyway at this time of night?" he asked impatiently.

"I need something for tomorrow that I have stored here."

Grant assessed the dark space. "What do you need? I'll help you pull it out."

"You don't have to do that."

"Do you think for an insane minute that I'm going to leave you here in a dark storage compartment?

I'm following you home, Caprice De Luca, and making sure you are safe inside. So find whatever you need, and let's get it packed up."

A half hour later Caprice pulled into her driveway, while Grant parked along the curb, letting his engine idle. Roz's car was now in the garage with Caprice's Camaro. Her friend's car was worth a heck of a lot more than her van, even with everything packed inside it. While she and Grant had been loading the van—not talking, just doing what had to be done—she'd been thinking. It was hard for her to believe someone had intended to harm her tonight. Her experience had taught her to stand up to fears and confront foes. But she'd never before had to confront a foe who might be a murderer.

Had tonight's little escapade just been a warning? Maybe Ted's murderer wanted her to stop asking questions and stop poking around.

She couldn't do that.

Grant had said he'd wait until she was safely inside the house. Instead of hurrying toward the house as he expected, she jogged toward his car and stood in the street at his window.

He pressed the button and the window eased down.

"Come inside. There's something I want to talk to you about."

"Concerning the murder?"

What did he think this concerned? "Yes."

He shifted his gearshift into park, then switched off the engine. She didn't wait for him but started toward the house, ready to give Roz a heads-up that he was coming in.

But Roz was dressed in a blouse and jeans, curled on the sofa with Dylan, using a highlighter on the papers on her knee.

Although Dylan stayed beside Roz, the two kittens scooted from wherever they were playing and ran toward Caprice. She managed to scoop them up before Grant opened the door.

She held one close to her neck, the other in the crook of her arm.

"Who are they?" he asked with a half smile as she nuzzled them and cooed to them.

"This is Stripes, and this is Creamsicle. They need a good home if you know of one."

She crossed into the living room, expecting him to follow. He did and settled into the armchair. When she went over to sit beside Roz, the kittens wiggled out of her grasp and meowed, running off. One hopped over Dylan, who didn't seem to mind all that much. The other flashed by Sophia, who was lounging on the back of the couch, paws crossed in front of her like a dainty lady.

"Are you going to tell Roz what happened tonight?" Grant asked Caprice.

"I suspected something did to bring you in

together. Caprice is supposed to be at her storage compartment."

Caprice quickly outlined what had happened with as little drama as possible. She didn't want to frighten Roz.

"So what are you going to do?" Roz inquired. "Ask for police protection?"

"There's no specific threat against me. Whoever was in that SUV could have come to my compartment by mistake. Maybe he wasn't following me. Maybe I panicked over nothing."

"If he tried to raise the door to the compartment without using a key, he knew you were inside," Grant said. "He wasn't a bystander or an innocent renter. Don't soft-pedal this, Caprice. You have to seriously consider what you're doing."

"I am. That's why I invited you to come in. We need to talk about my hypothetical person in PA Pharm."

"You weren't over there again, were you?" he demanded.

"No, I wasn't there. But I think we should try to nail down the witness. Even though she doesn't have specifics about what's going on, I want to try to convince my hypothetical person to possibly talk to you and Vince."

Stripes rounded the corner of Grant's chair and started climbing his jeans' leg, one paw after the other.

"Hey, you," Grant said with a chuckle, probably

feeling the claws on his skin. He scooped up the kitten and raised her up in front of him. "You're about as precocious as your owner."

Stripes looked down at him and meowed. Grant shook his head and settled the kitten on his lap.

"Are you sure you don't need a cat?" Caprice asked.

"I'm positive. I'm not home enough to have pets. It wouldn't be fair to them."

It wouldn't take a psychologist to deduce that Grant worked as hard as he could to escape the memories of his wife and child. He looked comfortable with the kitten, who was curling up in a ball near his belt buckle. Grant looked as if he was comfortable with animals, and the kitten certainly seemed to like him.

Animals were a great judge of character, she reminded herself, then returned to their conversation. "So, do you have time tomorrow to meet with my witness? Do you think Vince might?"

"Why do you want Vince there too?"

"Because you're representing Roz. If I bring somebody else into this maybe she or he should have another lawyer."

"The FDA is the agency overseeing pharmaceuticals. I haven't probed deeper."

"You could stay for dinner while we discuss all this," Roz suggested, giving Caprice a look.

"Sure." Caprice felt a little uncomfortable, wishing she had made the suggestion herself. "I was going to make a chicken stir-fry. There's always enough for one more."

Grant seemed to hesitate. But then he decided, "No. I'd better get home. But thanks for asking. Are you going to try to get hold of your witness now?"

"What time will you be free?"

"Better make it around nine. I don't think Vince has any appointments tomorrow morning. Giselle keeps us apprised of each other's schedules."

"Okay." Caprice agreed. "I'll call now."

As she went to make her phone call to try to convince Lonnie that talking to Vince and Grant was the best way to proceed, she regretted the fact that Grant wouldn't be staying for dinner. She regretted the fact that he wouldn't accept the meal as a thank-you for coming to her rescue tonight. She'd never thought of Grant Weatherford as a white knight.

Should she think of him that way now?

Chapter Sixteen

Lonnie looked scared to death as she sat in Vince's wood-paneled office early Wednesday morning, her gaze zipping back and forth between him and Grant. "You mean I have to tell somebody important what I heard?"

Caprice felt sorry for the pretty blonde, who just wanted to do her job and do it well. She'd never intended to be caught up in intrigue or blow the whistle on the company she'd worked for.

Vince's posture, his concerned expression, and the way he was leaning toward Lonnie as he sat beside her on the sofa told Caprice he was sympathetic too. Grant, however, was stunningly silent. And she couldn't tell much at all from his expression.

"You'll have to talk to someone in CDER, the Center for Drug Evaluation and Research. It's a center of the FDA where you report a problem," Vince explained. "I don't know how important he or she will be. But this is a vital matter—life and death, really."

Vince wasn't exaggerating for drama's sake. He went on to convince Lonnie of the seriousness of the situation. "Do you have any children?" he asked.

She shook her head. "I'm not married."

"Do you have someone you care about a lot?"

"My parents and my sister."

"All right. Now imagine they're very sick. The physicians diagnosed them with an infection of some kind and there's an antibiotic that will cure it. Most antibiotics you take for a certain amount of time, and the effect is that the drug will kill particular bacteria. If the expiration date has run out, maybe that antibiotic won't work effectively. Maybe it's just not quite strong enough to kill the bacteria. Maybe your sister or your parents figure they finished the prescription so they're well. But the bacteria isn't killed and they get sick again. This time maybe worse than the first time. Do you see where I'm going with this? These are people's lives were talking about—their suffering and well-being. And you have knowledge that could prevent something bad from happening. Don't you agree you should do something with that knowledge?"

Caprice's respect for Vince grew. He really was good. Maybe he should have been a defense attorney.

Now it was Grant's turn. He sat forward on the gray upholstered chair that was similar to the one Caprice was using. They both were usually positioned facing Vince's desk. But today he'd turned them around, so there was a grouping by the sofa. She'd love to take this office apart and put it back together again.

"I think Caprice told you that the police have had Rosalind Winslow in for questioning. That's not widespread knowledge, but she could be a prime suspect. What if she was arrested and charged for her husband's murder and she didn't do it?"

"What does me telling someone about the expired drugs have to do with that?" Lonnie wanted to know.

Now Caprice weighed in. "If the police have other suspects, they won't just analyze Roz's motives. Pharmaceuticals are a huge business. We're talking millions of dollars. Those dollars might be worth killing for. We can make sure the D.A. knows that Ted Winslow's murder might not have anything to do with simple passion."

However, Caprice had to admit passion was never simple. And maybe they were all wrong and Monty did it. But they couldn't get to the bottom of anything if Lonnie didn't come forward.

Vince laid his hand on Lonnie's. "Don't you want to help?"

Lonnie's gaze met Vince's and they stared at each other. Caprice had to wonder if more was going on here than sheer advice. Did Vince feel some kind of zing when he looked at Lonnie? And did she feel the same thing when she looked at him? The same kind of feeling as when Caprice looked at Seth? Or Seth touched her?

Actually Caprice hoped not. She didn't get the sense that Lonnie was the type of girl who would want to date Vince one weekend and not the next. She was the kind of girl who could get hurt quickly. So was Vince pulling out the lawyerly charm or something else?

Finally Lonnie answered him, "I want to help, but I'm afraid."

"If rumors of an investigation go public," Grant said matter-of-factly, "you won't have to be afraid. You heard a conversation and that's all. There are a lot of people involved who know more than you do. Once the FDA rattles this cage, there could be more than one whistle-blower hoping to escape the consequences."

Caprice's phone vibrated. She hadn't wanted to have anyone interrupt this meeting. Checking the screen, she didn't recognize the number. She'd pick up her voice mail later. When she looked up after pocketing her phone, Grant gave her a quizzical look. Then he frowned, and she suspected he wished she had something more to do than stick her nose into this investigation. But she couldn't stop now. Not when she was in this far. Not when she was making headway.

Her cell phone vibrated again. This time she

didn't check it but simply let the call go to voice mail.

"Okay, I'll help," Lonnie said suddenly, squaring her shoulders. "I couldn't live with myself if I didn't. This is wrong on so many levels. And I want to help Mrs. Winslow. Besides that . . . PA Pharm is hurting so many people with its layoffs. It's just not right. What do I do first?"

"I'll set up an appointment," Vince said. "For as soon as possible. Believe me, Lonnie, you won't regret this."

Caprice could only hope that was true.

As Lonnie said good-bye and left Vince and Grant's law offices, Caprice thought about PA Pharm, Chad Thompson, and the rest of the employees who'd sat around that conference table the day she and Grant had gone there. How many of them knew exactly what had happened with the expiration dates? How many of them had printouts with proof? Would they all succumb to PA Pharm's pressure and keep quiet during an investigation? Or would one of them break ranks and back up Lonnie's story?

She stopped in the reception area to check her voice mail, remembering the missed call. There were two now. One was from Roz. She pressed that call to listen to the message first. Roz was supposed to have a meeting with her real estate agent to check on vacant apartments and condos. Listening to the message, she heard Roz say, "Caprice, I know you're at the law offices. Joanie and I have been looking at condos. We're at one in Vince's building, second floor, number 204. When you finish up your appointment, stop by if you can. Joanie and I are discussing quite a few things and I'd like your input. Talk to you soon."

She could easily stop by. But before she headed for her car, she listened to her other call. A muffled voice warned her, "Don't ask any more questions or you'll be sorry."

She'd be sorry for asking questions? Which ones?

"What's wrong?"

She'd been unaware of Grant exiting his office. He stood beside her now, briefcase in hand, suit coat back on, looking as if he was on his way out. She, of course, could tell him nothing was wrong, but just how wise would that be?

She started with, "I had a message from Roz . . ."

He cut in. "A message from Roz made you go pale and then red? I doubt that. Not unless—Is she okay?"

"She's fine. She wants me to meet her to look at a condo. But I had a second message."

"From?" he asked impatiently.

His impatience made her just want to say forget it. She almost did.

"I'm on my way to the hospital to meet with a family whose mom is critically ill. I don't have a lot of time," he explained, apparently realizing he'd been abrupt.

"Someone warned me about asking questions."

"Exactly what did this someone say?"

She found the message again. She hadn't deleted it. She gave it to Grant so he could listen. His brow furrowed and he frowned. "Don't delete that message. We can probably trace it."

"My guess is that call was made from a prepaid phone or a pay phone."

"Do you want to call Detective Jones?" Grant asked.

"And say what? Someone told me to not ask questions? He could think I had a friend do this to move their investigation away from Roz."

"I don't like it, Caprice. Between the SUV and the phone call—"

"We know nothing."

Grant rubbed his forehead. "No, we don't. Really, you're better off that way. It might be even better if you don't go anywhere alone in the dark for a while."

She didn't have to say what she was thinking.

"You don't want any of this to affect your life, but it is. Give it a rest, will you?"

She let out a sigh. "I'm going to be preoccupied with getting everything ready for Mom's birthday party on Monday. In the meantime, I'm staging a loft to sell. My theme is Bachelor's Night In. Maybe you should take a look at the place."

"I'm not your usual bachelor. I'm happy with what I have."

He wasn't your usual bachelor because he didn't date? Or because he didn't feel like a bachelor? Did he still feel married?

Grant checked his watch. "I've got to get going or I'm going to be late." He started toward the door, then turned around. "By the way, I received an e-mail invitation to your mom's birthday picnic and RSVP'd to Bella. Do you think your mom would like chocolates? Truffle Delight has great raspberry truffles."

"I'm sure she'd like them. Like all of us, she has a sweet tooth." She paused, then added, "I'm glad you can come."

"The way you De Lucas throw a party, I wouldn't miss it."

On that note he left.

Although Giselle seemed to be engrossed in work, she said, "I RSVP'd to Bella too. I hope the weather holds for you."

"Rain or shine, we'll make it work. The De Lucas always do."

"You're lucky," Giselle said. "My son lives across the country. Bill and I wished we had more kids. But Jason was it. As we're getting older . . ." She stopped. "Sometimes we think about moving to Texas where he is."

"Do you want to do that?"

"We're not sure. We have good friends here. But he's our son and we miss him."

"I understand. I know Vince would certainly miss you if you moved."

"He could replace me."

"Certainly not easily. When you come to Mom's birthday bash, we'll make you feel like you're part of our family. Then you won't want to leave."

Giselle laughed. "Tell me what your mom might like for her birthday."

"Anything pretty. She loves pretty things."

"Does she collect anything?"

Caprice thought about her mom's favorite things. "She'll be putting out hummingbird feeders. I got her interested last year when I started hanging them in the backyard. I'm sure she'd like another one."

"Now that sounds like a great idea. I'll see what I can find. You have a good day."

"You too."

As Caprice left Vince and Grant's office, she knew Giselle would be irreplaceable. If she left, Vince would miss not only her work ethic, but also her presence. She was a positive force in his office, and it would be hard to find someone else to fill her shoes.

Grant was already gone from the small parking lot when Caprice went outside. She thought again about the warning she'd received. Had the voice sounded just a little bit familiar? It had been disguised and it sounded like a man. But it could be any man. Besides that, she might be mistaken that she'd heard it before. Between clients, open house guests, the employees at PA Pharm, and the mourners at the funeral, she'd have a lot of voices to sort through. But if she played it again and again and again, maybe a memory would kick in.

After climbing into her car and leaving the parking lot, Caprice headed deeper into the downtown area of Kismet. Its charm was definitely rooted in its early-1900s heritage. Many of the red-brick buildings displayed white trim around the windows and under the eaves. Several of the shops sported oval signs hung on wrought-iron brackets. Vince's building had once been a two-story elementary school. More than five years ago, it had been renovated into condos, four on each floor. Vince's condo was on the first floor.

Caprice headed into the side parking lot and pulled into a visitor's space. The residents of the condo had their own row of garages to the rear of the building, and a walkway led from the eight garages to the condos.

After walking to the front door, she ran up the stairs and went inside. A small lobby housed mailboxes to the left, and double doors led upstairs to the right. She took those stairs quickly and strolled down the hall until she found 204 and rang the bell.

When Joanie came to the door, all smiles, she said, "Roz is ready to sign the lease, but I think she wanted you to look around first."

The best feature of these condos was the tall windows divided into nine panes by white grids. With the southern exposure, the windows let in streams of afternoon sunlight. Roz's condo was laid out differently from Vince's. Her brother's was a two-bedroom unit. But his kitchen, living room, and dining area were parts of one open space. This unit's foyer led into a high-ceilinged great room. The walls were cream-toned and sand-textured. An archway to the left opened into the kitchen, and Caprice could see another archway from there and a dining room beyond. The bedroom hallway could be negotiated from either the living room or the dining area.

Caprice estimated the unit occupied about fifteen hundred square feet. Certainly not what Roz was used to. The condo was empty, and the wood floors gleamed with recently polished splendor. Roz sat in a corner of the living room at a card table with two folding chairs, papers spread before her.

When she saw Caprice, she smiled. "Take a look around and see what you think. Don't analyze staging it. Just think about me living in it."

After Caprice studied the bedrooms and the amount of light pouring into each, the master bathroom, and the powder room off the hall, she came back to Roz and asked, "You'll be okay in this amount of space?"

"I was used to a lot less before I met Ted. Even in our house, I mostly lived in our bedroom, sitting area, and the kitchen. Just how much space does one person need?"

Caprice had often asked herself that when she staged monstrous luxury homes.

"How would you decorate it?" Caprice wanted to see if Roz really pictured herself here.

"I don't care if something is in or out. You know me. I like curvy furniture, nice thick rugs, jewel colors. I know you'll do a good job for me."

They exchanged a look, and they both laughed.

"Tell her your other news," Joanie prodded. "I'll see if I can get hold of the manager." Taking her phone out, she went into the kitchen so Roz and Caprice could talk.

"What other news?" Caprice studied Roz, trying to figure out if it was bad or good.

"An offer came in on the house."

"And . . ."

"It's a low offer." She named the price. And low-ball or not, it was more than enough to fund anybody's retirement.

"Have you decided what you're going to do?"

"I can either take the offer, counter, or wait for something better. The real question is whether or not I want to sell the house and move on."

Caprice was glad to see that Roz had clarified it for herself. "Still . . . you know counselors give the advice not to make life-changing decisions the first year after a spouse dies."

"I suppose that's good advice. But my situation is

a little different, don't you think? Why would I want to hold on to it and have that reminder of what happened? I can remember the good times in my marriage to Ted without the house."

"Why don't you consider it overnight, at least?"

"I'll think about the offer on the house. Later you and I can discuss it more. And I'm having lunch with Dave tomorrow. Maybe he can give me an unbiased opinion too. But I'd like to sign the lease on this condo. If I get arrested, well, I guess I'll have to forfeit the security deposit."

Although Roz was being flippant, Caprice could sense the real worry underneath her cavalier attitude. "I think an investigation with PA Pharm is going to take the pressure off the case against you. But I'm not sure you should move in any place by yourself until Ted's killer is apprehended."

Roz looked around the room, as if by imagining herself here, she could have an optimistic outlook. "Did you mean what you said about me taking Dylan?"

"He's adopted you. He follows you around, sits in your lap, and sleeps with you. I want to see you both happy. So yes, I meant it. I know you'll give him a good home."

Roz's eyes glistened with unshed emotion. "I don't know what I would have done without you through all of this." She stared down at the papers again. "You know this is only the second place I've looked at. And if I take Dylan, he really should have a yard. Maybe I shouldn't be so eager to sign."

This was exactly why a person with any kind of loss shouldn't make a major decision the first year. Roz had to be hurt, angry, and maybe even confused by everything that had happened. But an impulsive decision could definitely cause her more stress.

Or could get her killed.

"I'm sure Joanie won't mind showing you other properties."

Roz lowered her voice. "But she's calling the manager."

"She is. But you haven't signed anything yet. You're not committed. Be sure, Roz."

"I'll stop at your house before I visit more properties, so I can let Dylan out. What are you up to?"

"I have to drop off furniture and a few art pieces at the Heinz's loft. I'm going to have tea with Nana around two. Do you want to come?"

"I don't think so. I don't know how long I'll be tied up with Joanie. And then I think I just want some time to chill with Dylan and Sophia and the kittens. Your grandmother is a sweetie, but—"

"But you need alone time. I get that. Give the furry brigade cuddles for me."

Since Roz looked like she needed a cuddle herself, Caprice gave her a hug. "I'll see you around supper time, and we'll create something brilliant with a pound of ground beef."

When Roz laughed and hugged her back, Caprice knew her friendship with Roz was becoming almost as strong as her friendship with her sisters. What would happen if she was arrested? What would Caprice do then?

Her friend wasn't going to get arrested. She was going to figure this out. Had Isaac found the provenance of the dagger yet?

That was her next clue on her list to investigate.

Caprice cherished her teatime with Nana Celia. She and her grandmother had shared a cup of tea as often as they could since Caprice was around ten. When she was sick and had to stay home from school, Nana took care of her and always brewed tea. When she had good news to share, she'd visit her Nana, and her grandmother would bring out a box of wonderful flavored teas. As a child, the idea of strawberry or blackberry or peach tea had been a treat like a piece of candy. But even more than the tea, she enjoyed her grandmother's stories. Caprice had asked over and over again why Nana had married when she was only seventeen. She'd enquired about her grandfather's barbershop and studied old photo albums. Nana Celia embodied family history, Old World charm, and all the best traditions. She was cooking and laughter and comfort and joy.

She'd called Isaac before she reached the door

of Nana's suite but had only reached his machine at the shop. She'd have to try again.

Fifteen minutes later Caprice was sitting with Nana in her parlor. At least that's the way she thought of the small living room. Nana's taste ran to antiques, lace, and small, flowered patterns in lilac, yellow, and pink. Her grandmother was regal. Only five feet three, Nana always held her head up high and her shoulders straight. They were seated in wing chairs near a window, sipping from delicate teacups, munching on biscotti laid out on the tray on the marble-top Victorian table between them.

"So tell me what you've been doing since our dinner," Nana invited. "You haven't called."

Caprice felt a pang of guilt. No, she hadn't, except to confirm they were having tea today. "Mostly, I've been thinking about Mom's party and turning a loft into a bachelor pad."

"That will be great if you sell it to a bachelor. Narrow market, isn't it?"

Caprice had to laugh. "It might be. But I think it will work. There are unmarried men in the area."

"Then why aren't you dating them?" Nana asked in a serious tone.

Her grandmother never let her get away with anything. So she revealed, "I am. I had a date last weekend."

"Tell me about him."

"He's a doctor at the urgent care center. So his

hours are all over the place. We played miniature golf, but then he got called away."

"Do you like him?"

"I do, and I think the date went well. He sent me red roses."

"Flowers! A traditionalist. Maybe men do still know how to court a woman." After sips of tea, Nana said, "I saw you and Grant discussing your friend."

So why had Nana brought up Grant?

"Is Roz still staying with you?" her grandmother asked.

"Yes, she is, but she's looking at apartments and condos."

Nana studied Caprice thoughtfully. "But you're still worried about her?"

"I am. The police haven't found the killer yet. She wants to move into her own place . . . alone."

"I've heard talk that you're trying to figure out who killed her husband."

"Talk from whom?"

Before Nana could answer, the door that connected Nana's suite of rooms with the main house opened and Bella walked in.

Nana responded to Caprice's question, "Bella told me."

Caprice glared at her sister. She didn't want her grandmother to worry. "And just what did Bella say?"

Sweeping into the room like royalty, Bella took

a biscotti from the dish. "So you're probably talking about the murder. Nikki says that's all you have on your mind. I told Nana you're asking questions at Curls R Us and PA Pharm. That's true, isn't it?"

Crossing to the small table where they sat, Bella dragged one of the chairs with needlepoint seats over next to Caprice.

Caprice automatically warned, "You shouldn't be moving furniture." If Bella was pregnant she should be careful.

But Bella gave her a baleful look, and Caprice knew her secret still wasn't out. Just when was she going to tell Joe? When she started showing?

"So tell me what you found out," Nana said. "Don't leave me in the dark."

"I haven't found out anything concrete."

"And who are your suspects?"

Caprice ran through the list from Monty to Chad Thompson, to disgruntled employees at PA Pharm, to Valerie.

"Do you know what your problem is?" Nana asked.

"No. But I'm sure you're going to tell me, aren't you?"

Her grandmother shot her a smile. "Always. Your problem is that you need to find the missing link. If you pinpoint the missing link, you'll find your murderer."

Chapter Seventeen

"Maybe Valerie is the missing link," Bella offered as she took another bite of biscotti.

"I don't even know if she's a viable suspect," Caprice responded, then sipped her tea.

"Oh, she's a suspect. I heard there was a ruckus over at Curls R Us. Valerie was back at work on Monday. The police came in, wanting to ask her more questions. Apparently they'd met with her once before. She put up a fuss at first . . . said they shouldn't be hassling her when the killer was out there somewhere. But Detective Jones told her she could talk to him there or go down to the station with him. I heard she was fit to be tied. Red-faced, blustering, even a few tears. But she might really miss Ted, and all of it is upsetting. Valerie's a hard one to read."

Was Valerie hard to read on purpose? Caprice wondered. After all, she'd been having a secret affair with a married man. It wouldn't be so far-fetched to jump to the conclusion that she could be hiding being a murderess. Maybe she was so upset because her veneer was starting to crack. Had it been a crime of passion? Committed in anger? Was she feeling guilty?

The recognizable ringtone from her phone disrupted Caprice's train of thought. She slid it out of her pocket to see if Roz needed her. "It's Seth," she murmured.

"Your young man?" Nana asked.

"The doctor," Bella explained. "Go ahead and take it. We can listen in."

Caprice wrinkled her nose at her sister, stood, and went to the farthest corner of the small kitchen to have a conversation.

Seth asked, "How about tomorrow morning for a latte at the Koffee Klatch? Is six-thirty too early for you?"

An excited feeling tingled up Caprice's spine. "Six-thirty's just fine."

"I have to be at the clinic at eight, so that should give us a little time. Sorry this is on the run."

"I'm not sorry. I'm just glad you have time at all." Had she just given away the fact that she was really looking forward to seeing him?

"I'll say it again, Caprice De Luca, I like you. See you tomorrow morning."

When she slipped the phone into her pocket, she was smiling.

"Well, I think I see a flush on your cheeks," Nana said. "A date?"

"Early tomorrow morning for coffee."

"I suppose that's safer than late-night drinks at his condo," Bella concluded.

"Bella!" Caprice cast a glance at her grandmother.

But her grandmother was already brushing the remark away. "I'm not too old that I don't remember what goes on. When your grandfather and I met—" She gave an exaggerated sigh.

To deflect further attention away from herself, Caprice checked the teapot on the tray. "I'll heat up more water. We really have to discuss shopping for Mom's party. Maybe you and Nikki and I can go for supplies tomorrow afternoon."

"Remember, your mom's favorite color is pink," Nana reminded them. "And speaking of her birthday celebration, why don't you invite your doctor to come?"

Caprice hadn't even considered that. "He probably has to work."

"But if he doesn't . . ." Nana gave her a conspiratorial wink.

Bella said slyly, "Grant's coming. I got his RSVP."

Yes, Grant was coming. But what did that matter? Why would he even care if Seth was there too?

* * *

Later that evening while Roz watched TV, Caprice worked in her office. Her paperwork had mounted up over the past week, and she had follow-up visits to schedule. Sophia was sprawled across her lap as she worked, tired of kitten play. Caprice was ready to pick up her office phone to schedule a consultation when it rang. To her surprise, it was Grant.

"I found a home for your kittens."

There was a note of achievement in his voice, and Caprice realized, for the millionth time, that most men just wanted to accomplish a goal.

"Will I approve of this home?" She wouldn't let Creamsicle and Stripes go just anywhere.

"I think so. My neighbor in the town house next door is looking for a pet for her little girl who's ten. I convinced her that two kittens are better than one because they can keep each other company. If you're going to be home, we can be over there in fifteen minutes."

"That soon?" She suddenly realized she loved Stripes and Creamsicle. It would be hard to let them go. But that's how she felt about any stray she brought in and found a home for.

"I'll be here," she said. "But if I don't like them, the kittens don't go."

Grant's voice was filled with wry amusement when he said, "I'll tell everyone to be on their best behavior."

"I'd rather see what they're really like."

With an exhausted sigh, he suggested, "Then bring out that biscotti you and Nana make and something to drink. Tanya can play with the kittens for a bit so you can see how they interact. I'm sure her mother will be open to that. Donna's pretty understanding."

Caprice suddenly wondered what Donna looked like . . . if she was single or married . . . if she and Grant were friends. But she didn't ask. She'd simply wait until they arrived.

It was more like half an hour later when Grant's SUV pulled up outside.

Roz peered out the bay window. "She's pretty. I'd say a few years older than you." She gave Caprice a wink, and Caprice didn't know exactly what that meant.

After introductions all around, Tanya, who had beautiful red-blond hair like her mom, gravitated toward the cat condo, where the kittens were curled together asleep.

"Can I touch them?" she asked in a lowered voice.

Caprice thought it was a good sign that she seemed respectful of Stripes and Creamsicle.

Caprice walked over to the cat condo with her. "You can even pick one up if you're careful. They get squirmy and wiggly if they don't want to stay in your arms. Probably the best thing to do is to scoop one up with both hands and then sit on the floor with her."

Caprice showed Tanya how to do that and they both sat on the floor right there.

Both kittens awakened, and Stripes yawned.

Tanya laughed and gently petted her on the head.

"Sorry we're a little late," Grant said. "We stopped to buy a cat carrier."

"I'll get us some snacks," Roz said, "while Tanya and the kittens get to know each other. Come on, Dylan, you come with me."

The dog scampered after her, always eager for her approval.

Sophia now stretched out on the top shelf of the condo, her white paws crossed, and just stared down at all of them, disdainfully wondering what all the fuss was about. But Caprice knew she'd miss her two companions.

As the kittens fully awakened, Caprice showed Tanya how to play with them with a shoestring, wiggling it on the floor and then higher. They were laughing at the kittens' swivels in midair as Roz served iced tea and biscotti that Nana had sent home with Caprice.

"These are great," Donna said. "Grant told me you cook."

"I do. But my grandmother made these."

"I don't do enough cooking and baking. We eat too much processed food. But it's fast. At least we do sit down for supper every night when I get home from work. That's more than I can say for our neighbor."

Grant didn't look the least bit uncomfortable. "I often grab something on the way home."

"Yeah, at nine o'clock," Donna chided. "At least my job's eight to four. You go in early and come home late."

Through body language and conversation Caprice still couldn't get a handle on just how friendly Donna and Grant were. "Where do you work?" she asked.

"I'm a secretary at Tanya's school. After my divorce, we sold our house and I needed to find a job. I've been there two years now, and it's a nice fit."

So Grant's neighbor was divorced. That would give them a lot to talk about. That is, if Grant talked to anyone about what had happened to him. But there was no point going down that road. Whatever Grant did was his own business.

As Stripes scampered over to the sofa, Donna scooped her up and cradled her in her arms. "You are a cutie, and so is your sister. Grant tells me they're both girls, right?"

Caprice nodded, but then asked the next question on her list. "Will you be keeping them inside?"

"I think that would be best. We have a nice big yard, but I think we want them to be mostly indoor cats. I like your cat tree. I saw smaller versions at Perky Paws. It might be nice to put one under a window."

"They'd like that," Caprice agreed, feeling the loss of the kittens already. This little girl and her mom seemed loving and capable. Just the type of home stray animals should have.

After another fifteen minutes of conversation and finished glasses of iced tea, Caprice gave Grant a look that said the exchange was going to be made.

He said, "I'll get the cat carrier."

Over the next few minutes, Caprice said good-bye to Stripes and Creamsicle as she rubbed heads with them, then placed two toy mice as well as a towel into the carrier for them.

After she zipped it up, she swallowed hard. "They're ready to go." She'd given Tanya two of the shoestrings from the pack she'd bought.

Caprice lifted the carrier and followed Grant, Donna, and her little girl out to Grant's SUV, where he strapped the carrier into one half of the back-seat. Tanya fastened her seat belt after she settled in next to the carrier.

After Donna thanked Caprice, she climbed in too.

Grant, however, stood on the walk with her, eyeing her with a bit of concern. "This is hard for you, isn't it?"

"Yep. I've been taking care of them like a mom for the past week."

"But you do this a lot, don't you?" His steady

gaze was curious, and she felt he couldn't quite understand why she did it.

"It's never easy to let go of an animal I become fond of." She felt her eyes welling up a little and suspected it wasn't just letting go of the kittens that caused it. It was everything that had happened in the past few weeks.

She blinked fast and cleared her throat. "Thanks for helping me find them a home."

He squeezed her elbow and held on a few beats longer than she would expect. "You're welcome. I'll see you at your mom's birthday party. Unless another crisis pops up before then."

As he climbed into his SUV, Caprice went back inside.

Roz took one look at her face. "Why don't we make a pot of that flavored decaf you bought and talk about the tension between you and Grant?"

"What tension?"

"Man–woman tension. You light up like a Christmas tree when you talk about Seth. But whenever Grant's around—" She shrugged. "There are thumping vibrations there too."

"Thumping vibrations? I don't think so. We just clash more often than we agree."

"Thumping vibrations," Roz insisted again, moving through the dining room into the kitchen. There she opened a cupboard. "Mocha Cinnamon or Chocolate Candy Bar?"

After a brief inner debate, Caprice released

a breath. "Chocolate Candy Bar. But instead of talking, you can help me make the list for supplies for Mom's party."

Roz took the bag of coffee from the cupboard. "You're in denial."

Maybe she was. But that's exactly where she was going to stay. Grant Weatherford was out of bounds for a multitude of reasons.

Late that night Caprice was almost ready to slip under the covers when "She Loves You" played from her cell phone on her nightstand. Sophia, already napping on the pillow beside Caprice's, opened one eye.

"Go back to sleep," Caprice told her. "It's not for you." Picking up the phone, she checked the ID and saw Isaac's name and number. She didn't hesitate to say, "Hi, Isaac, how are you?"

"Did you think that I'd fallen off the face of the earth?"

"I wasn't sure."

He chuckled. "You try so hard to be diplomatic. I've been on a buying trip for a couple of days in the wilds of Maine and just called in for my messages and got yours. I'll be back tomorrow."

"I'm glad you're safe and sound. Find anything interesting?"

"A fifties cupboard you might like."

"Did you have time to look for the provenance on the dagger before you left?"

He laughed. "Like I said, always diplomatic. Before I left, I narrowed it down to four boxes in the attic, thinking I'd go through them when I got back. But I just found out about an estate sale tomorrow night and I won't have time."

Caprice felt her hopes and clues fading away. "I see," she said, not knowing where to go to next.

"No, you don't. I pulled the boxes down from the attic because anyone looking through them would suffocate up there. You can have a go at them."

"You don't mind?"

"They're just filled with old receipts, old paperwork, stuff I keep in case I ever have an audit."

"I'll be shopping with my sisters tomorrow for supplies for my mom's birthday party. Maybe I can rope one of them into going to the shop afterward."

She had her date with Seth in the morning, then two appointments and a trip to the lighting specialist. She was meeting Bella and Nikki around two at the party-planning store.

"Will someone be there around three-thirty or four?"

"Julie Ann will be covering the shop tomorrow. The boxes are in the back storage shed. You're welcome to stay as long as you want."

"Thanks so much, Isaac. I don't know if anything

will come of this, but if I find another clue, it could help solve the murder."

"If anyone can figure it out, you can. Let me know when you catch the killer."

There was humor in his voice as if he didn't expect her to do it. Probably no one expected her to do it.

Catch a killer. Why did she even think she could?

The party-planning shop was an array of colors—red, blue, yellow, white, silver, black. There were patriotic themes and displays for over-forty birthdays, as well as tables with the newest and brightest decorations for kids' parties. Nikki had decided on a heavy, paper-coated dish with pink roses around the edge for their mom. Of course there were matching napkins and cups. They could have gone with plastic instead, but they didn't want to skimp.

"So what about balloons?" Bella asked.

After another perusal of her sister, Caprice decided she was pale today. Worry about Bella had nudged Caprice the whole time they were shopping. She hadn't even asked about her coffee date with Seth.

"If the weather is windy, that could be a problem, even with canopies," Nikki mused. She'd catered plenty of events. "What if we go with sparkly pink bows or something like that?" She pointed to rolls of ribbon on a high stand in the corner.

"Pink and silver would be a pretty theme," Caprice agreed. "Maybe we could do something with the bows and the chairs too. Mom's really a girly-girl. I think she'd love that."

"We could probably rent white chairs, which would look really nice. How about the table coverings? Fabric or plastic?"

"No plastic," Bella said automatically. "Yuck."

"Speaking of yuck . . ." Caprice began. She glanced around and didn't spot anyone nearby. The store's cashier had even gone back into the storeroom. They were basically alone. "How are you feeling?"

Bella shook her head. Apparently she still hadn't told Nikki about her pregnancy. Caprice believed the time for all secrecy should stop.

She asked, "Have you told Joe?"

Bella sighed and looked away at the party hats and favors on a nearby display. "No, I haven't."

"Told him what?" Nikki asked. "What's going on? Are you leaving me out of the loop?"

"There is no loop," Bella snapped. "I just told Caprice because . . . because I had to tell somebody."

Nikki glanced from one sister to the other. "So tell *me* already."

"You have to promise not to tell a soul. No one. Not Mom or Nana. Because Joe doesn't know yet, and I don't want him to find out until I'm ready to tell him."

"I promise," Nikki vowed solemnly. Caprice knew she'd keep that promise.

"I'm pregnant," Bella whispered.

Nikki blinked and then studied her sister. "Isn't that a good thing? You want more kids."

"I don't think Joe does. At least not right now. He's said some things lately that have really worried me."

"What things?" Caprice asked.

"How we have to cut back on any expense that isn't necessary. He was all over me today about meeting you here. Couldn't one of you pick me up? And the kids' play dates . . . He wants me to stop those so I'm not running around so much. He says music lessons for the kids are out anytime in the near future. I'm just scared about how he's going to react."

"You have to tell him," Caprice and Nikki said at the same time.

Bella's face fell even further. "I know . . . and I will. But Mom's birthday party is Monday, and I don't want my pregnancy to be the topic of conversation. So I'm going to wait until after the party."

"What if he does have a problem with you being pregnant?" Nikki asked.

"He's just going to have to learn to live with it. No, this isn't the best time, but a child is a precious gift. Every time I look at Megan and Timmy, I realize that. Even when they make me crazy up to my eyeballs, I realize that. Any child of mine is going to be loved and loved well."

Caprice gave her a hug. "The two of you will figure it out, I know you will. Nikki and I are going to ride up to Isaac's place, Older and Better. Do you want to come along? You can catch a ride with us and we'll bring you back to your car."

"No. I have to pick up Megan at her friend's and Timmy at school." She checked her watch. "I'd better get going. Go ahead and buy what we decided on and anything else we need. I have some money saved from costumes I sewed for Megan's classmates at Halloween. I stowed the money in a shoe in the closet."

"So Joe doesn't know?" Caprice asked. If Bella was keeping more secrets from her husband, that wasn't good.

Bella's brow furrowed as she frowned. "Don't go all judgmental on me. I just didn't want to face what he'd have to say or what he'd want to do with the money. Sure, if we need it for food, we'll spend it. But we don't. Everything is not as black as he thinks. So anyway, buy what you need for Mom's party. I'm in."

Nikki's narrow-eyed look as she studied Bella mirrored what Caprice was thinking. Bella's marriage was in big trouble.

* * *

An hour later, Nikki couldn't help but stop at almost every display at Older and Better. If she wasn't picking up a lead-crystal vase, she was studying a piece of Depression glass or peeking into an interesting cupboard that was fashioned with two doors and a side piece.

"I think that was used as a refrigerator in the late 1800s," Caprice told her. "They put a block of ice in the bottom cavity."

"Much too pretty for ice. It looks like something *you* might like."

"I have enough furniture for now. Maybe if I re-stage my living room—"

They both laughed.

"Not likely anytime soon," Caprice added. "I've got to admit, once Roz and Dylan leave, the house is going to seem empty."

"Maybe you need another roommate?"

"Or maybe I just need to find another stray pup."

"I wasn't talking about another roommate per se, you know." Nikki's golden-brown eyes danced with mischief.

"Oh, I know. But it will be a long time till I'm ready for anything like that."

"Even if the handsome doctor sweeps you off your feet?"

"I don't get swept off my feet easily." At least that had been true before she'd met Seth.

"Red roses help, don't they?"

"Did Nana tell you?"

"We're looking out for your best interest, that's all. You have to be prodded every once in a while to help you realize you can still have dreams. How was your coffee date this morning?"

Caprice wasn't sure what she thought about having dreams, at least not the happily-ever-after kind. If anything, she was more interested in the here and now with Seth and what could possibly happen with that.

But when she remembered sitting across the table from him at the Koffee Klatch, their knees bumping—

The aroma of brewing coffee had wafted all around their small wrought-iron table. Seth had looked so handsome in khakis and a polo shirt.

Smiling at her, he'd noticed how she'd had her coffee prepared. "So you're definitely a whipped cream kind of woman."

"And you're straight black coffee all the way."

"I've grown up on caffeine. Necessary in my line of work."

"How do you sleep at night?"

From the look he gave her, maybe he was thinking about how *she* slept at night. Then he shrugged. "I've trained myself to fall asleep and wake up on demand."

"Sort of like a soldier."

"I guess you could say that."

"I admire what you do. It's selfless."

Holding her gaze, he took her hand and folded his fingers around hers. "You could give a guy a swelled head."

"Only if he deserves it."

Seth had chuckled and she'd grinned back, and the warm feeling surging through her had had nothing to do with hot coffee. Knowing their coffee date would soon be over, she'd explained, "My family is having a surprise birthday party for my mom Monday at my place. Would you like to come?"

"I would. But I'm working at the clinic until three."

"If you can be at my place by four, you'll be able to shout surprise."

"I'll try to make it by four. If I can't, I'll phone you and come over after you surprise her."

Suddenly she thought of Seth meeting the clan. "My family can be overwhelming. I have two sisters, a brother, Nana—"

He squeezed her hand. "I've worked in a big-city ER. I think I can handle a few relatives."

What she liked about Seth as much as everything else was his ability to put life in perspective.

She'd lost her perspective completely when he'd walked her to her car, pulled her close . . . and kissed her.

Oh, yes, Seth could sweep her away. But was she going to let him?

Julie Ann, Isaac's main clerk, came from the back of the store to greet them, interrupting Caprice's reflection on her date, the heat that still lingered when she relived Seth's kiss.

She whispered to Nikki, "The date was everything a coffee date should be." That was all she was going to say.

"You're Nikki and Caprice, right?" Julie Ann inquired.

"We are. Did Isaac tell you we need to look through some boxes?"

"He phoned me this morning. Right this way. Take the back door outside the shop and go to the storage shed. He doesn't usually have files in there, but he carried the boxes there for you." She looked at Caprice. "He said if you feel like baking him some biscotti, that would be a great repayment."

"I'll do better than that. I'll make him a rum cake."

Julie Ann laughed. "I think he'd carry more boxes down for you for that. Come on. I'll unlock the back door."

Five minutes later, Caprice and Nikki were checking out the old storage shed and Julie Ann had returned to the shop. Shelves with old lanterns and tools, antique tin cans and figurines lined two sides of the shed. In the back, chairs, mostly ladder-back with cane seats, were stacked on top of each other. In the sparse space that was left in the middle of the concrete floor sat four cartons, none of which were labeled. Isaac had laid a tattered rug on the floor and tossed pillows on top of that so they could sit there if they wanted to sort through the contents of the cartons.

As Nikki began to untape one box, she asked, "So do you think Dad's going to be able to get Mom to your place without her asking too many questions?"

"I think Dad can persuade Mom to do anything. He'll just tell her I'm having an impromptu picnic. The only thing she won't like about that idea is she doesn't have time to cook anything for it. Dad and I will stay in contact by cell phone. So this really should be a surprise. Unless one of us lets something slip."

"You mean Bella?"

"I mean Bella. On the other hand, she's not saying much about anything because of her secret. So she'll probably stay away from Mom and Dad until the party."

Nikki began to get bored after sorting through the first two boxes. She'd looked through one and Caprice the other.

"This is dull," she complained.

"Detective work is mostly dull, from what I hear. It's the details that matter. Like Nana says, I have to find the missing link."

Nikki climbed to her feet, put her hands on her back and stretched. Crossing to an ornate table lodged between two chairs, she said, "This is kind of cute."

"It would be more attractive if it were painted

and distressed," Caprice responded, after giving it a quick once-over.

Nikki took a step back and studied it again. "I think you're right."

"I have to be right or my clients would fire me."

"I guess they would. You're always dealing with expectations. If they don't sell their house, I suppose you don't get referrals."

After a thoughtful pause, Nikki asked, "It's been a lot harder for you to get into the home-staging business than you let on, hasn't it?"

A fistful of receipts in her hand, Caprice set them in her lap. "Beginning to stage homes took a ton of research, a lot of footwork, and honing PR skills I didn't know I had. People are people across the board, it's true. But when I went after high-end staging accounts, I had to learn what rich people want."

"What *do* they want?"

"They want me to be right. They want to be able to trust me, not just my skill, but my connections. If I recommend a real estate agent, they want it to be the best real estate agent for them. They want an offer they can live with and be proud of. Early on I learned these clients, especially the entrepreneurs, network like no others. That's how I've been able to get this business up and running so quickly, fitting into their networks."

"You're good at whatever you do, Caprice. We're all in awe. Vince won't admit how much he respects you, but I will. Sometimes, I do think Bella feels intimidated by you."

"Bella isn't intimidated by anything or anyone."

"I think she's intimidated by Joe."

Caprice considered that. "I always thought she just wanted to please him . . . wanted to be the best wife, the best mom. She wants him to be proud of her."

"You're worried about her, aren't you?"

"I am. But after the party, maybe everything will settle down." Caprice rifled through the papers on her lap. "Or maybe it will get all fired up. You know how Joe can be."

"He loves Bella."

"I hope so."

Still exploring Isaac's inventory in the shed, Nikki picked up a figurine of a courtly gentleman seated beside a beautifully dressed lady. "Nana might like this. I think it's a music box." She turned the key and a tinkling melody began issuing from the statue.

"It's 'The Way We Were,'" Caprice said, immediately recognizing the melody. "I've watched that movie with Nana more than once." She hummed along for a few bars with the music box until it stopped.

"Come on," she said to Nikki. "Let's get through the papers. I have research to do tonight on a home builder who is planning a new development. I'd like to stage his model homes."

"Luxury homes?"

"Not exactly. Homes around three thousand square feet. My brand could help his and vice versa."

"Do you have a meeting with him?"

"I haven't set one up yet. I want to know everything about him before I do."

Returning to Caprice and the boxes, Nikki lifted out a handful of papers. For the next fifteen minutes, they sorted, scanned, and particularly studied the sales dates. They were about to give up when Caprice noticed, "These receipts are from three years ago. That's the right time period. And there are notes on many of the invoices . . . descriptions and histories too."

Nikki suddenly stopped flipping through them. Carefully, she examined a paper on her knee. "Describe the dagger to me again."

"It has a gold and jeweled hilt. Did you find it?"

"I think I did! There's a picture too. Hold on. There's another page stapled to it."

Scrambling over to Nikki, Caprice peered over her shoulder. The copy was faint, but still readable. "There's the provenance."

Caprice pointed to the dagger's history and then she pointed to something underneath it that was in quotes, a little bolder than the rest. "And there's the legend that goes with it. You were right about it having one."

They read it silently together.

"What do you think it means?" Nikki asked.

"I'm not sure, but this could be the missing link. I think maybe we've been looking too hard at one place. Maybe we need to look at suspects we haven't considered before."

"Like?"

"I'm not sure. Let me think about it."

"The problem is, Caprice, you don't just think, you do. Promise me if you figure this out, you'll call in help."

"When I figure it out, then I'll know what to do." She knew she sounded confident enough, but then she remembered the other night at the storage compartment. When panic took over, a person didn't know exactly *what* to do.

She would not panic . . . because panic could get her killed.

Chapter Eighteen

Vince had brought Lonnie!

Standing at the buffet table in her backyard on Monday afternoon, Caprice helped Nikki arrange the trays with prosciutto-wrapped cantaloupe, sausage with pepperoni balls, and a lentil and tomato salad served in puff pastry cups. Those were merely the hors d'oeuvres. When she'd noticed her brother descending the porch steps with Lonnie, she'd realized they were among the first to arrive for her mom's surprise party.

"Where is everybody?" Vince asked Caprice.

"They'll be here," she assured him. "Bella asked everyone to arrive no later than four. Everyone will probably pile in at once. The hors d'oeuvres are ready when they do."

"I hope you don't mind that Vince brought me." Lonnie seemed nervous as she glanced from Caprice to Nikki.

"Of course, we don't mind," Caprice assured her.

"Vince told me about your appointment at CDER with the FDA official." Washington, D.C., and the surrounding area was known for its agencies with acronyms. "Vince said your meeting went well. How do you feel about it?" Caprice asked, eager to have Lonnie's opinion.

"The man was thorough. He wanted to know every little detail. But I only knew so much. I only heard so much."

"But they will investigate?"

"As I told you after the meeting," Vince said patiently, "like any government agency, they're close-mouthed. They're not going to tell us what they're going to do next. They probably don't want anyone to know. The element of surprise and all that."

Leaning a little closer to Lonnie, he motioned to the transformed backyard. "So what do you think? Did my brother-in-law and I do a great job or what?"

Lonnie's gaze drifted to the four white canopies, the white folding chairs trimmed with silver and pink bows, the tables covered with pale pink cloths with their pink roses and silver streamer center-pieces. "I think it looks fabulous. I can't believe you did all this yourselves."

"We set up the canopies and had the tables and chairs delivered yesterday," Nikki explained. "While Caprice and I prepared the food trays this morning, Roz covered the tables, worked on the flower arrangements, and attached the bows."

"Bella should be here any minute," Caprice told Vince. "She's taking care of wrapping the presents. Isaac came through for us. I think Mom will be pleased with the Fostoria pieces he found."

Just then the back door opened and Dylan barked as Roz emerged with him. Joe, Bella, and the kids were right behind.

Roz went straight to Vince. "Caprice and Nikki asked me to act as hostess and doorkeeper. What do you think about that? What if your mom's friends—" She stopped, then after a moment went on with, "What if they shy away from me? What if I'm a distraction?"

To Caprice's relief, Vince shook his head. "We've only asked Mom's closest friends. And she would want you here. I'll say the real question is—are you up for it? There could be a whisper or two. Will that bother you?"

"I'd better get used to it," Roz responded practically.

"Then I think it's a good idea. We'll be busy talking to the guests. Your help with the flow of traffic will be a benefit."

"All right. I'll keep Dylan inside with me and Sophia. I don't want anyone to step on him."

After Roz patted her side, Dylan ran up the steps with her and returned inside.

Caprice asked her brother, "So is Grant still coming to the party?"

"He said he was."

Caprice thought about Seth's enthusiastic acceptance of her invitation and her heart fluttered faster. From anxiety because both men would be here? Of course not. She was simply looking forward to seeing Seth.

As more guests filed into the backyard through her house, Caprice tried to greet each one. There was a neighbor of her mother's they had all known since they were kids. Kendra had babysat them when her parents had "date night." A few of the teachers they'd invited piled their presents on the gift table, looking happy to be there. Her dad's foreman and his wife joined the others, as well as Giselle. A special guest, her mom's college roommate, who'd driven two hours to help celebrate, was going to be an unexpected surprise.

When Grant entered the backyard, Caprice gave him a friendly hello, and he migrated to the table where Vince and Joe were standing, probably talking sports stats. They could bore her to death with those conversations.

Coming up beside Caprice, Bella asked, "How do you think the presents look?"

"They're beautiful. You know how to make them look professionally wrapped. Did the kids bring anything to entertain themselves?"

"Timmy has his Nintendo DSi, and Megan brought her drawing supplies. They'll be fine.

Joe gave them his 'You'd better behave' speech, threatening them with taking away privileges if they don't."

Caprice's phone vibrated in the pocket of her coral slacks. She pulled it out to see a text message from her father. "Dad wants to know if we're ready. I'll give him the go-ahead." Even though Seth wasn't here. Maybe he wouldn't come after all. Maybe he would be late. That was the life of a doctor—putting one's personal life on the back burner.

Vince had suggested they leave the house empty now. If one of them escorted their mom outside, even their expression could give something away.

So while guests, family, and friends waited for Fran De Luca's arrival, they kept their voices lowered and milled around in one large group near the buffet table. Vince acted as bartender, pouring wine and soda.

Grant stopped by the punch bowl and ladled in half a cup. After a few swallows, his gaze found Caprice's. "It's good."

He stepped a little closer, so they could keep their voices down, she guessed. "Pineapple, grapefruit, and ginger ale. Mom uses the recipe every New Year's Eve."

He was wearing casual clothes today—jeans and a snap-button shirt. He looked like a guy ready to enjoy a picnic rather than a lawyer.

"Do you know how Stripes and Creamsicle are doing?" she asked.

"I saw Tanya in the yard with them yesterday. Her mom lets her take them outside to romp in the sun. Then they return them to the house. Both mom and daughter are loving them, Caprice, so you don't have to worry."

She lifted her chin. "I'm not worrying."

"The hell you aren't," he said with a wry smile.

Just like her family, Grant seemed to think he knew her. Did he?

Suddenly there was a sound from inside the house. Then a male voice called, "Hello?"

Caprice knew that voice. Rushing forward, she reached the porch just as Seth emerged from the back door, a pastel envelope in his hand.

She ran up the stairs to greet him. "You got here!"

He grinned at her. "I know I'm a little late. Tough last patient. But I made sure no one else was headed in because I didn't want to spoil the surprise."

In a polo shirt and chinos, Seth looked as if he might have jogged from his car. His hair was windswept, his face a little ruddy.

"You can relax now. Have hors d'oeuvres and punch until Mom and Dad—"

On the porch, Caprice heard the phone inside the house ring.

"Do you need to answer that?" Seth asked.

She pulled her cell phone from her pocket. Nothing more from her dad. "No, I'll let the machine take it. I don't want to be on the phone when they arrive."

The phone had just finished its third and last ring when they heard noise inside the house and her mom's, dad's, and Nana's voices. She'd know them anywhere.

To her surprise, Seth grabbed her hand and leaned close to her ear. His breath fanned her cheek as he suggested, "C'mon. Let's crowd with everyone else so your parents don't see us on the porch."

Of course, he was right. She let him tug her down the two steps, and they hurried to stand beside Nikki, who gave her a wink. Bella's smile was knowing too, and Caprice felt herself blushing.

That was crazy! She did *not* blush.

Behind her, in a tone everyone could hear, Vince said, "When the screen door opens, I'll count to three. Then everybody shout 'Surprise!'"

Her dad and Nana must have been stalling their mom a little—maybe they stopped to pet Sophia—because it seemed to take forever for the screen door to open.

Vince counted down and everyone called, "Surprise! Happy birthday!"

Caprice thought her mom might faint. She looked that shocked.

Still holding Seth's hand, Caprice let go and stepped forward with her sisters and Vince.

Bella explained, "We wanted to give you a birthday to remember. You always do so much for us. Happy birthday, Mom."

Everyone else formed a circle around Fran, offering loving words and kisses and hugs.

Breathless and beaming, she hugged each guest, squealed like a teenager when she spotted her college roommate, and thanked everyone for being there.

After the rush of good wishes died down a bit, Caprice introduced Seth.

"So this is your doctor!"

Okay, so she was blushing. "Mom—" she cautioned under her breath.

Seth simply laughed and joked back. "I'd have no problem being Caprice's doctor. Happy birthday, Mrs. De Luca." He handed her the card. "Not very original, but I've heard a spa day at Green Tea Haven can reduce stress. Since you're a teacher, I thought you might appreciate that."

Never standing on ceremony, appreciative and excited about the gift, her mom gave Seth a hug. "Thank you so much! I've always wanted to make an appointment for a massage there and just never have. Now I get a whole day. Wonderful. You don't have to return to the clinic tonight, do you?"

"I'm always on call if I'm needed. But this is my evening off."

"Then why don't you and Caprice get something to eat? After I greet everyone, I'll join you."

As Caprice and Seth headed for the buffet table, she said to him, "You know how to make a woman happy."

"I try." His sexy smile was absolutely toe-curling.

Although Caprice helped Nikki and Bella keep the food warmers and trays filled, generally making sure the party was proceeding smoothly, she managed to spend a good bit of time with Seth. He was a great conversationalist and seemed to be able to talk to anyone.

Anyone . . . but Grant. Grant was keeping his distance.

At one point during the celebration, all of the guests were seated at the same time enjoying ice cream and cake. Seated across from Bella, Caprice noticed her sister looked gaunt and wan.

Earlier she'd seen Bella sampling Nikki's sausage and pepperoni balls. Now Bella took a spoonful of vanilla ice cream . . . and turned green. Pushing back her chair, she stood and rushed into the house.

Caprice was almost on her feet, ready to follow, when Joe said to Vince, "Keep an eye on the kids, will you?"

Nikki murmured, "Uh oh. I think the cat's about to leap out of the bag."

No way did Bella want to tell Joe about her pregnancy here at the party before the presents were opened. Caprice didn't know whether to stay out of it or make sure Bella was okay.

Seth's elbow grazed hers as he asked, "Would you like me to check on her?"

Caprice shook her head. "She doesn't need a doctor, at least not to tell her what's wrong."

Leaning closer to her, his shoulder brushing hers, Seth asked, "Is she pregnant?"

"I'm sworn to secrecy."

At the other end of the table, Grant pushed his chair back, stopped briefly by Fran, and said a few words to her. Then he gave Caprice a very long look, holding her gaze long enough to make her forget ice cream was melting on her plate, raised a hand in a good-bye gesture to everyone else, then climbed the porch steps.

Caprice tapped Seth's arm. "I'll be right back."

Maybe she could catch Grant to say good-bye and check on Bella at the same time.

As she passed Nana, her grandmother caught her hand and warned in a low voice, "A man's jealousy can make him sullen."

Grant, jealous? She doubted that.

After giving Nana a quick kiss on the cheek, Caprice went inside. She would have hurried through the living room to catch Grant—she heard the front door close—but raised voices suddenly erupted from her downstairs powder room.

Bella's voice was shrill and unintelligible.

Joe's response was angry as he asked, "Why didn't you tell me as soon as you knew?"

Caprice took a step forward, then a step back. Should she join the fray? Shouldn't husband and wife work this out on their own?

She didn't have to make a decision because seconds later Bella shot out of the bathroom into the living room and ran by her out the front door.

Joe followed her but stopped when he saw Caprice. "Did you know?"

Caprice kept silent.

Obviously frustrated and more than a little angry, he said to the ceiling, "Of course, you knew! Nikki too probably. Maybe your whole family. When is she going to realize I should come first?"

So Joe was worried about himself and his pride, not Bella and her condition. Although she should keep her mouth shut, Caprice just couldn't. "You do come first, Joe. That's why she *didn't* tell you. She's upset and scared and needs reassurance."

As Caprice had guessed, none of what she said helped. "Stay out of it, Caprice. And Nikki too. This is for me and Bella to settle." He brushed by her and left the house, letting the front screen door slam.

Caprice called after him, "I'll watch Megan and Timmy."

Bella and Joe were definitely a couple in crisis. Caprice just hoped their children could be protected from the fallout.

Nikki stood at the back door when Caprice crossed from the living room through the dining room into the kitchen. "Is everything all right?"

"I don't know. Are Megan and Timmy occupied?"

"Timmy and Vince are playing catch. Megan is coloring. I'll keep an eye on them." She opened the door and handed Caprice the sugar bowl. "Can you fill this? Everyone must have used it in their coffee. By the way, I think your doctor is a catch."

"He's not *my* doctor!"

"He could be," Nikki disagreed with a sly glance as she disappeared off the porch into the yard.

Caprice wanted to get back to Seth, but she was also concerned about why Grant had left so abruptly.

When she went to the canister on the counter for sugar, she noticed the message light blinking on the phone. She might as well check to see who had called.

Playing the message, what she heard gave her pause for a moment. She jabbed at the button to play the message again. Several puzzle pieces clicked into place in her head.

Why hadn't Roz told her—

Maybe because Roz had no idea what was really going on. As Caprice reconsidered what she'd thought was an innocuous legend attached to the stolen dagger, the clues she had uncovered suddenly all made sense. After all, there were no coincidences with murder, were there?

She just might know who'd killed Ted Winslow.

The following evening Caprice sat in her car at the curb of a one-story house in a quiet neighborhood. Around seven P.M., with the sun sinking lower, she was nervous . . . but not over-the-top nervous. She'd be taking precautions. She just hoped she was right about her deductions. She just hoped this worked. She just hoped the man she'd muted on her phone in mid-conversation would have her back if things got dicey.

A black SUV cruised down the street and pulled into the driveway. Exiting her car, Caprice made sure her phone was still on speaker. After patting the other pocket in her gauzy maxi-skirt for her pepper-spray gun, she took a few deep breaths.

The man she suspected of murdering Ted Winslow climbed out of his SUV, waved at her, then met her at his front door.

"I'm glad you called to schedule this appointment," he said with a smile. "I'm eager to get started."

She bet he was. He wanted a life with Roz. Had he simply waited for his chance to make it happen? Or had he planned the murder all along?

After he unlocked the door, he motioned her to precede him inside.

Caprice stepped into Dave Harding's living room,

repeating the mantra in her head that she had to remain calm. When she'd heard his voice on the answering machine, she'd realized why the man who'd warned her to stop asking questions—though his voice was somewhat disguised—sounded familiar. Besides that—

She was here for a confession, that was all. If not a confession, some admission that the police could use to close in on the murderer.

If she was wrong? She'd leave, looking foolish.

Dave's living room was a mishmash of conflicting styles. It looked as if he'd bought one piece of furniture here, one there, not much caring how the room looked. She imagined the rest of the house would be furnished in the same way.

He looked a bit embarrassed as he motioned to the flat-screen television, the brown corduroy recliner, the gray-patterned sofa. "Drab, I know. That's why I need to spruce it up. Maybe paint? Some curtains?"

Right now, a lopsided blind hung across the front plate-glass window, half up, half down.

"Have you lived here long?" Her voice wasn't quivering just a bit, was it?

"Since the store started turning a profit. About six years."

"Why did you decide to redecorate now?" she asked in what she hoped was an ingenuous manner.

He gave a small shrug. "I'd like it redesigned for

a couple. I'm hoping not to be a bachelor much longer."

Their gazes met and held.

The legend attached to Ted's dagger should have alerted her sooner to what had happened to him. That dagger out of all his collector's items had been stolen. The legend accompanying the dagger stated, "Whosoever owns this dagger will own his heart's desire."

When she'd heard Dave's message for Roz on her answering machine yesterday, she'd had one of those "ah-hah" moments. Dave had said, "I really enjoyed our lunch together, and I believe you did too. Whenever you need a listening ear, I'm here. Maybe we can find our hearts' desires. Call me and we'll do it again soon."

Chills had raced down Caprice's spine when she'd heard the phrase "hearts' desires." Could it be a coincidence that the phrase was used in the legend? She didn't think so. Dave wanted to be more than friends with Roz. Caprice suspected Dave had wanted Roz to be his since high school. He'd lost her once. He wasn't going to lose her again. And she'd recognized the cadence of his voice. He was the one who'd phoned her and warned her to stop asking questions. Anyone could get her cell-phone number because it was printed on her business cards. She'd handed out quite a few at the Winslow open house.

Dave broke eye contact and crossed to a single-drawer occasional table beside the recliner. He glanced at it, then back at Caprice. "I'm hoping you can incorporate ruby red into your design for this room. It's her favorite color. Ruby is her birthstone."

Silence dropped over the room, and Caprice knew she had to take hold of and direct the flow of the conversation. One of her hands lay over her pocket, feeling the solidity of her phone. The other brushed over the pepper-spray gun. How long would it take for her to pull it from her pocket? She should have practiced.

However, maybe this was just a man in love and he hadn't done anything wrong.

"Red's a color trend right now and should be easy to work in."

"You know I want Roz to move in here with me, don't you?"

"I guessed. You liked her a lot in high school."

"I *loved* her in high school." The vehemence in his voice revealed the intensity underlying his declaration.

"A first love is hard to forget," she empathized, thinking of hers and how she'd felt when Craig had walked away.

"I don't want to forget. If her mom hadn't gotten sick—"

"That was a difficult time for Roz."

"I wanted to help her through it. But she stopped dating while her mom was going through treatment.

Then Roz ran off to flight attendant's school, started flying everywhere, and met Winslow. I couldn't believe she fell for someone slick like him." His voice had deepened, the expression on his face growing dark and fierce.

"Ted was rich and could give Roz everything she wanted." Caprice understood she was goading him. She just hoped the man on the other end of the call could hear.

Dave slashed his hand through the air. "She didn't care about his money. She just wanted his love, and he was the kind of man who couldn't give it."

"You heard things about him?" Caprice prompted, searching for even more motivation for murder.

"My sister has her hair done at Curls R Us. Valerie Swanson is her stylist. One night after an appointment—she was Valerie's last one for the night—she saw them kissing out back. Everyone knew Winslow on sight. His picture was in the paper often enough—donating to charity, getting promoted to senior vice president at PA Pharm, flying off to third-world countries on PR trips because the company donated medicine. But he was a class-A, unfaithful jerk!"

Dave seemed to be on a roll now. He was definitely passionate about the subject. Maybe she should just go for the confession if he was ready to spill the whole story.

"I think Ted did love Roz," she theorized. "I think that because of the dagger that was stolen."

"I heard about that," Dave muttered. "It had jewels in the handle."

Caprice had caught him now. The police still hadn't released the information that a collectible had been stolen, let alone a description of it. "I can't remember what kind of jewels decorated it," she said.

Automatically, Dave responded. "Rubies, diamonds, and emeralds."

Now she had him. Going for broke, she hurried on. "I found out that Ted bought it through an auction. Isaac Hobbs told me Ted had looked for something like it for Roz for a long time. When Ted saw the legend attached, he had to have it . . . for Roz. *Whosoever owns this dagger will own his heart's desire.*"

Almost as in a Jekyl and Hyde nightmare, Dave's face contorted with anger. "He wanted to own her. Like a *possession.*" He spat out the word as if it were a profanity. "I met with him that night in his sword room. We'd set it up at the open house. I convinced him I wanted to know more about his damn collection when what I intended to confront him about were his feelings for Roz. He said Roz would never divorce him. He showed me that dagger and patted it into his palm. He told me the legend. When I brought up Valerie and what I knew about that, he said Valerie was just a playmate to let off steam with. He said he loved Roz and she loved him. He said he had his heart's desire and he'd never let her go."

Trying to be as sympathetic as possible, Caprice

urged Dave on. "I imagine you tried to reason with him because you wanted Roz to have better than him . . . to be happy!"

"I thought we could talk man to man. I thought he'd let go of her if he didn't really love her. But he showed me that dagger on purpose. He wanted to rub salt in my old wound. He was so arrogant . . . acting like he owned the world and everything in it. And when he turned around to put the dagger away—"

"That's when you took the dagger from its scabbard and stabbed him."

"He deserved it! It was so satisfying to jab that dagger into him—"

Dave had been lost in his passion, his old hurts, his story. And he still was. Until the realization that Caprice had guessed exactly what had happened splashed over him.

He went for the drawer at the recliner, and Caprice panicked that he might have a gun. Her fingers fumbled in the folds of her skirt until she finally plunged her hand into her pocket for the pepper spray.

But Dave was quicker. He didn't have a gun in his hand, but he brandished the ruby and emerald–embedded dagger. Extracting the blade from its gold sheath, he came at her. Quickly she sidestepped him, finally closing her fingers around the pepper spray.

When he slashed at her, she remembered a defensive move, eluded him, and knocked over his poor excuse for a pole lamp. He tripped over it and fell. With Dave on the floor, she closed her eyes and brought her foot down on his wrist just as the front door burst open. Chief of Police Mack Powalski, along with Detective Jones and two other officers, charged in.

Thank goodness her dad had a good friend with a badge who owed him at least one favor!

Detective Jones had Dave Harding cuffed in a matter of minutes.

As Chief Powalski surged toward Caprice, he looked as worried as her father would have been. "Are you okay?"

Shakily, she nodded. She'd been connected to the chief's line the whole time. Even though she'd muted him, with the phone on speaker he'd been able to hear her.

Detective Jones crossed to the chief while Harding was read his rights by one of the officers. Pulling latex gloves from his pocket, he snapped them on and addressed Caprice. "The chief should arrest you for obstruction of justice."

"You didn't have a case," she protested.

"We were keeping an eye on him."

"And on Roz too," Caprice tossed back, determined not to let the detective intimidate her.

With a frustrated shake of his head, Jones stooped to pick up the dagger.

The jewels glimmered in the end-of-day light streaming through the bottom half of the window.

As Harding was led toward the door, the chief said, "Nobody's heart's desire is worth murder."

Caprice stared at the dagger, suddenly realizing how dangerously close she'd come to being murdered herself. Her knees wobbled and Chief Mack Powalski, who'd pushed her on a swing when she was a child, caught her before she sagged to the floor.

Epilogue

The open house on Sunday was as much fun as a Caribbean vacation. While Nikki served frozen strawberry and banana smoothies, waiters in flowing white shirts passed trays of roasted pork with pineapple, brown sugar and mustard–coated salmon, and coconut-garnished fruit salad. Caprice's multicolored dress floated around her as she made sure all ran smoothly.

Often she was stopped by an attendee who recognized her from the photo that accompanied the article Marianne Brisbane had written. The piece had been picked up by several newspapers and the story had fleetingly flown by on cable news—AMATEUR SLEUTH HELPS POLICE IN STING TO CATCH AN ALLEGED KILLER. Caprice knew the furor would die down soon, though the Office of Regulatory Affairs, another center within the FDA, was starting a field investigation into PA Pharm's practices.

The capiz-shell chandelier tinkled above the

guests' chatter, jiggled by the huge ceiling fan in
the adjoining room. Back in her element, Caprice
felt like her old self again—her pre-sleuthing self.
She was ashamed her nerves hadn't held up until
she'd left Dave Harding's house and gotten home.

Soon Roz and Dylan would be moving into a
town house with a yard and Caprice would be living
with only Sophia again. This whole crisis had
changed her friendship with Roz. They were best
friends now, with a bond that would last.

She was hoping she and Seth were working on
another bond that would last. They'd had another coffee date, discussing everything that had
happened—not only her confrontation with Dave
but Bella's situation too. Everyone had seen the
tension between her and Joe when they'd returned
to the party. Caprice just hoped they could talk
about their problems instead of letting them come
between them.

As Caprice threaded through prospective buyers
to the atrium with its wicker furniture, pastel fabrics, and sisal rug, she was grateful for a bit of
solitude. Everyone else seemed to be looking and
mingling in the more expansive rooms at the front
of the house. Caprice was still a bit introspective,
still considering everything that had happened,
including the police finding the key to Ted's
curio cabinet in the drawer where Dave had kept
the stolen dagger; she stood at one of the floor-to-
ceiling windows, peering into the sunny, late-

afternoon view of a pool and patio that stretched across the backyard.

"Thinking about going for a swim?" The deep male baritone was easily recognizable, though in this setting Grant's voice seemed foreign.

"I don't have my swimsuit. What are you doing here? Thinking about buying a house?" When she turned toward him, their gazes locked.

He shook his head. "Not yet."

Not yet? What did that mean? She hadn't seen or spoken to Grant since her mom's birthday party.

Grant broke the sudden silence. "I stopped by because I wanted to see what you do. Quite a shindig!"

"I try."

"I know you do. I'm impressed." He shifted on his Docksiders, then came a little closer. "I also wanted to congratulate you on solving Winslow's murder. But . . ."

She held up her hand to stop him. "My family, Chief Powalski, and Roz have already raked me over the proverbial coals many times. You don't have to do it too."

She held up a tray of little coconut-walnut pastries for him to sample one. But he took the wooden tray from her and set it down again.

"I didn't come to eat. I came to get your promise that you won't do something that dangerous again."

Everyone who'd cared about her had been afraid

for her. Had Grant felt that moment of fear when he'd learned what she'd done?

She still wasn't sure if she'd done something foolish or something brave. Yet seeing Ted's murderer in handcuffs, knowing Roz was in the clear, hoping her friend could move on, she knew she had to be honest with him.

"I have no intention of solving another murder."

"But?" he prompted.

"But I can't promise that, given the chance, I wouldn't do it again." There had been both an adrenaline rush from the danger and satisfaction in helping a friend. But how often in a person's lifetime did anything like this happen?

Grant studied her for several moments. Then he nodded. "That's what I thought you'd say." He headed for the doorway that led to the hall and the part of the house where the open house was most successful.

"Grant?"

Stopping, he waited.

"Friends accept each other for who they are."

"Is that what we are? Friends?"

"I hope so."

After a half smile that seemed truly genuine, he left her alone in the atrium.

She smiled too.

ORIGINAL RECIPES

Nana's Minestrone Soup

2 tbsp. extra-virgin olive oil
1 pound ground beef
1 cup medium pasta shells
1 cup onion, chopped
1 clove of garlic, grated
1 tsp. salt (to taste, depending on the broth
   you use)
½ tsp. oregano
A pinch to ⅛ tsp. crushed red pepper
2 cans diced tomatoes with juice (14–16 oz.
   each)
1 cup tomato juice
1 quart chicken broth
1 quart beef stock
½–1 pound fresh endive or escarole,
   snipped or cut into ½ inch pieces (leafy
   green part only)
1 can Great Northern beans (drained)
1 cup celery

1 cup shredded carrots (I buy them this
   way)
1 cup shredded cabbage (I use cole-slaw
   mixture)
1 cup sliced zucchini
1 cup cut green beans (fresh or frozen)
1 bay leaf
Romano cheese to sprinkle on top

Brown ground beef on medium heat in olive oil in an 8-quart soup pot. When browned (no pink remaining), add chopped onion, grated garlic, oregano, and crushed red pepper. Stir for a minute to mix flavors. Add tomato juice, tomatoes, and salt, and stir. Add beef stock and chicken broth, then bring to a boil. Stir in Great Northern beans, celery, carrots, zucchini, cabbage, and green beans. (If using frozen green beans, bring soup to a boil again before adding endive.) Add endive last.

Bring soup to a boil again, add bay leaf, then simmer, covered, on low for 30 minutes. Bring to a boil again, remove bay leaf, add pasta, stir once more, and cook until pasta is the way you like it, usually 10–12 minutes, without lid. Stir a few times while pasta is cooking.

Sprinkle each serving with Romano cheese and serve with crusty bread. Makes 12–15 servings.

Caprice's Tuna Cups

2 5 oz. cans chunk light tuna in water,
   drained
2½ tbsp. mayonnaise
2 hard-boiled eggs, chopped
2 tbsp. pickle relish
½ cup celery, chopped
1 cup shredded Monterey Jack cheese
10 slices of bread

Preheat oven to 350 degrees. Mix tuna, eggs, and celery in bowl with mayonnaise and pickle relish until well blended. Press one slice of bread into each cup of a regular-size muffin tin. Fill each cup with tuna mixture. Bake for 15 minutes at 350. Remove from oven and sprinkle each cup with cheese. Bake another 7 minutes.

Nikki's Pasta, Sunflower Seed, Avocado & Tomato Salad

Salad Ingredients

½ cup sunflower seeds
¼ cup chopped red onion
¼ tsp. salt
1½ cups piccolini (wheel) pasta (boil in 4 quarts of water)
2 cups (about 30) cherry or grape tomatoes
1 avocado
1 tsp. salt (for pasta water)
½ cup crumbled feta cheese
1 tbsp. fresh oregano minced, or ½ tsp. dried

Dressing Ingredients

½ cup white balsamic vinegar
½ cup olive oil
¼ tsp. pepper
½ tsp. sugar

Mix vinegar, oil, pepper, and sugar

Pasta

Bring 4 quarts of water and 1 teaspoon salt to a boil. Add 1½ cups of piccolini (wheels) pasta. Boil for 7–8 minutes. Drain. Run cold water over it and drain again. We don't want it to melt the feta!

Halve cherry tomatoes. Add to large bowl. Halve avocado, remove seed, scoop from shell, and cube. Add to tomatoes. When pasta has cooled (you can run cold water over it and drain), add that and then the sunflower seeds, salt, onion, and oregano. Mix dressing, stir, and pour it over all. Toss lightly. Add crumbled feta cheese and toss lightly again. Refrigerate.

Serves 6–8.

Please turn the page
for an exciting sneak peek of

Karen Rose Smith's

next Caprice De Luca mystery
coming in June 2014
from Kensington Publishing!

Chapter One

"It's a crime to cover that up!"

Caprice De Luca watched Eliza, with her symmetrically styled, sleek ash-blond hair, anchor her hands on her slim hips and pout.

As a home-stager, Caprice often had battles with her clients about de-cluttering their homes to present them in the best form to the buying public. In this case, however, de-cluttering wasn't the issue . . . color was. Eliza Cornwall had decorated her mansion in countless shades of purple. The deep purples especially had made Caprice's eyes roll more than once.

Before she could respond with just the right amount of tact, Bob Preston ordered, "Stop complaining, Eliza." The painter was balanced on a ten-foot ladder, but that didn't stop his flow of words. "Caprice told me Baroque Bedazzle is your theme. Everything will show up better with this cream and pale green as its backdrop."

"It really will, Eliza," Caprice reassured her client. "You know we've discussed this color scheme backward and forward." Caprice thought about the hours she'd invested in this particular home-staging process.

"And upside down too, I imagine," Bob wisecracked with a wink for Caprice.

Caprice often used Bob and his painting crews. Bob himself wasn't averse to personally picking up a paintbrush and working hard when he was shorthanded. He had light brown hair and myriad muscles, and was six feet tall. He could also charm the paint off the wall. Caprice knew about his lady-killer tendencies because her sister, Bella, had dated him seriously years ago. Today he wore a red, chesthugging T-shirt and jeans that weren't any too loose.

The way Eliza was looking at him . . . the way Bob spoke to her with familiarity . . . Caprice suddenly wondered if Eliza and Bob had hooked up. Eliza was in her late thirties, so she might be six to eight years older than Bob, but in this day and age, that difference didn't much matter.

"What if the house doesn't sell?" Eliza asked with panic in her voice. "What if I have to stay in Kismet instead of moving to L.A.?"

"I can't imagine Christmas in L.A.," Bob remarked laconically, as he expertly wielded the paint roller toward the ceiling. "Are you sure you want to trade Pennsylvania's seasons for sunny weather all year, not to mention mudslides, earthquakes, and wildfires?"

When Caprice saw the corners of Bob's mouth twitch up, she knew he was teasing. Another reason to believe he and Eliza could have once been involved . . . or were maybe involved now.

"I won't miss the ice and snow, or Kismet's small-town gossip mill. Not one little bit," Eliza muttered.

Caprice thought about Eliza's comment. Kismet, located outside York and a bit farther from Harrisburg, did have a grapevine that tangled through its neighborhoods with more accuracy than most residents gave it credit for. But the town also had community spirit. Neighbors helped neighbors. Eliza had moved here about five years ago and started Connect Xpress, a video and online dating service. If the worth of this mansion was an accurate indicator, she was a multimillionaire.

Caprice had dealt with quite a few of those in her high-end staging business. Before she signed on with a client, they decided on a unique theme that would help the house stand out and sell more quickly than others in the same price range.

Bob, who had been born and bred in Kismet, must have agreed with Caprice's assessment of the town rather than Eliza's because again he quickly said, "Give it a rest, Lize. Kismet's been good to you."

Lize? Caprice had never heard the entrepreneur called by that nickname . . . or any other.

Eliza moved closer to Bob, ready to give as good as she got, when a reverberating *gong* traveled through the house. In the empty living room, the hollow sound echoed off the walls.

"No housekeeper," Eliza said, as if reminding herself. "I gave her the week off because of all the rearranging and painting." She started toward the front of the mansion.

Bob peered down at Caprice and lowered his voice. "She must be low on estrogen today."

Although Bob's attitude was friendly and conspiratorial, she wouldn't be drawn into a discussion of her client. Uncomfortable with Bob's comment, thinking about the best way to be diplomatic, Caprice brushed her straight, long, dark-brown hair over her shoulder. The seventies hairdo with bangs was a nod to the retro-fashion sense she appreciated the most.

As Bob eyed her fifties-style summer dress and white sandals, he considered her silence and shook his head. "You women know how to stick together. But that's a good thing, I guess." He grinned as he stretched to reach an unpainted area close to the ceiling.

Changing the topic of conversation, he asked, "Taken in any strays lately? That article the reporter did on you a few months back was pretty good. Of course, the tie-up of the murder you solved at the end of May was even better. You sure do know how to get press for your business."

"What an awful thing to say!" Caprice erupted, tired of trying to be diplomatic. "I take in strays because they need a home, not to get publicity for my business. And as far as the murder—Roz was a good friend and I had to help her."

"Whoa," Bob said, holding up his roller to stop her. "I was just yanking your chain. Maybe Eliza's mood is rubbing off on you. Or maybe we're behind schedule and you're freaking out."

Yes, they were behind schedule, but she was not freaking out.

He went on, "Think about that doctor you're dating. That will mellow you out. I spotted the two of you at the Koffee Klatch the other morning. You didn't need caffeine to get revved up over each other. *That* was obvious."

Caprice felt a flush creeping into her cheeks. She'd been "dating" Seth Randolph for almost two months, but they hadn't enjoyed many full-fledged dates. With his schedule at Kismet's urgent care center, a morning coffee or an evening ice cream was about all they'd managed after their initial miniature golfing date. She'd fallen for Seth quickly, and most of the time, the depth of their attraction and their rapport scared her.

Bob laughed. "When a girl blushes about a guy, she's hooked."

Caprice was about to tell Bob he was out of line today in several respects, but she was kept from doing so by the voices approaching the living room.

Eliza's voice was the loudest, but she thought she recognized the other one—

Eliza and Bella, Caprice's sister, entered the living room, chattering. Caprice didn't think they were acquainted. After all, Eliza Cornwall and Bella Santini didn't move in the same circles.

Bella was saying, "I always wondered about matchmaking services and how you pair people up."

Caprice took a deep breath. Was Bella wondering about matchmaking because her marriage was in trouble?

"I have a sophisticated computer program that does the initial matching," Eliza explained. "But I also use my instincts with the video footage we shoot."

"They must be great instincts if you're going to open a Connect Xpress in L.A. How exciting that must be. And moving to California—I've always wanted to take a vacation there."

"You should," Eliza encouraged her.

"With two kids and a budget, that's not in the cards right now." Bella's hand went to her stomach, and Caprice knew her sister was thinking about the child she carried. She wasn't showing yet at three and a half months. But she was looking tired and a bit frazzled. In jeans and a wrinkled blouse with her black, curly hair tied back, Bella wasn't her usual well-put-together self.

"Hey, Bella," Bob called from his ladder, then quickly hopped down and laid his roller on the tray.

"Long time, no see. You're even prettier than you were in high school. How have you been?"

Eliza glanced from Bob to Bella, looking perplexed. Caprice was perplexed herself. Why was Bella here? And why was she blushing as if she were back in high school and she and Bob were dating again?

Although Bella and Bob had split up because he'd been unfaithful, the animosity had been laid to rest years ago. The reason was simple—Bella had found Joe Santini, and they'd made a life. If Bella bumped into Bob at Grocery Fresh or at the mall, ignoring him had seemed foolish.

Bella gave Bob a first-class smile. "Busy with two kids."

He gave her another once-over. "You and I will have to talk. Maybe we can have coffee sometime. What do you think?"

She only hesitated a few seconds. "I'd like that . . . a lot."

Bob's smile was rakish as he asked, "Did you come to get decorating tips from your sister?"

"No, just a sister-to-sister consultation. Can you give me a few minutes, Caprice? I just need to talk to you. When I phoned Mom, she said you'd be here this afternoon."

Although Bella had gained color in her cheeks when Bob had complimented her, she'd looked pale when she'd walked in, and there were smudgy blue circles under her eyes.

Not sleeping? Caprice knew there was lots of

tension between her sister and her husband, Joe, because of her pregnancy.

Eliza picked up the clipboard she'd left on one of the tarp-covered tables. "I have to go upstairs and work on the list for the auction people. Caprice is ruthless when she de-clutters, but I probably can't use any of it when I move to the West Coast anyway." With a fluttering wave, she headed for the foyer and the stairs.

Bob crossed to his ladder and said to Bella, "I'll give you a call soon and we'll go for that coffee."

Bella showing up like this was odd, and Caprice really was worried. She said to Bob, "Excuse us," took Bella's arm, and pulled her out of the painter's earshot.

She and Bella didn't always have the most harmonious relationship. Bella thought Caprice's penchant for taking in strays was foolish and that her fashion sense was a horror. Caprice, who liked surprises and knew how to roll with the punches, believed Bella was too rigid.

"Has something happened to Mom or Dad, Joe or the kids?"

"No, nothing like that."

"Then what's wrong? You look—" Caprice didn't quite have the word for it. Ruffled? Unnerved? Anxious? She settled for, "You look upset. And what was that little flirty thing with Bob? What are you doing?"

"I'm just going to have coffee with an old friend. That's not a crime."

No, it wasn't. Still, Bob was an old flame, and right now she could imagine where a cup of coffee could lead when there were problems between Bella and her husband.

After a moment of silence, Bella sighed. "I need to talk to you about Joe. I don't know what to do."

"Where are the kids?" On a Thursday afternoon, Timmy should be in summer camp. But at four, Megan . . .

"Megan's with my neighbor. Nellie's really good with her and in an emergency, she'll watch either or both of them for me."

"So this is an emergency?"

"It feels like it. I can't eat. I can't sleep. I'm so tired all the time."

"Did you say you talked to Mom?"

"Not about any of this. My marriage is too hard to discuss with her. With her and Dad married thirty-seven years and perfectly happy, I don't think she'd understand."

"Not perfectly happy. No marriage is perfectly happy. You know they argue now and then."

"Nothing like this," Bella concluded dejectedly.

Maybe not, Caprice thought. Their mom was a high school teacher, their dad a mason. Money had been tight with four kids and a house that needed constant repair. But most of the time Fran and Nick

De Luca had agreed about their kids and, even more important, about family issues.

"So what's going on with Joe now?" He and Bella had had a huge blowup at their mom's surprise birthday party six weeks ago. That day he'd found out Bella was pregnant. That day he'd also discovered his wife had told her sisters about it before she'd told him.

"He's hardly talking to me. He spends time fooling around with the car, puttering in the garage— He's also been away a lot at night. He comes home smelling like smoke. When I ask him about it, he says he's been out with the guys. I don't know what that means."

"Have you talked more about your pregnancy?"

"I talk, but he doesn't listen. I can tell. He just keeps saying we can't afford another kid. I just keep saying each child is a precious gift. He knows that. I can see it in his eyes when he looks at Megan and Timmy or plays with them. With our Catholic background, he knows there's no way I'd ever consider having an—" She stopped abruptly.

Bella couldn't even bring herself to say the word.

"I don't know what to tell you, Bee." In serious discussions, Caprice always fell back on her childhood nickname for Bella, who was the youngest; her sister's name, Isabella, had been quickly shortened to Bella by everybody. But when they were little, Caprice's nickname for her seemed to give them an added closeness.

Bella looked miserable, and Caprice could only try to imagine how she felt. She and Joe had been married more than eight years, and for the most part, they'd been happy. At least Caprice and her family had thought that was true. Now it seemed as if her sister's marriage was falling apart.

"Is there anyone Joe might listen to? What if you sat down with Mom and Dad to discuss all of it?"

"That won't work. Joe would be defensive from the start. It's not just the fact I'm pregnant. He thinks I got pregnant on purpose. I mean, we got married because I was pregnant, and that was both our faults. We should have known better. He's always said we were going to get married anyway. But maybe there's always been a small part of me that doubted how he felt. And now—I don't know if he believes the antibiotic I was taking counteracted the birth control. I really think he believes I did this on purpose."

"He knew you were taking an antibiotic, didn't he? Did you talk about the consequences of having sex while you were on it?"

Bella blushed. "One night the kids were both at sleepovers and it just happened. I guess neither of us thought I'd be in the small percentage of women who would get pregnant." She paused and collected herself. "So . . . we're not talking. He doesn't want to find solutions. He just wants to be mad. Most of all, I think he's angriest because you and Nikki knew I was pregnant before he did."

"Have you considered going to counseling? Maybe a stranger to talk to would be best."

"We can't afford that. Our insurance doesn't cover it. I checked."

"You might have to afford it if your marriage is at stake. I thought you told Nikki and me you have rainy-day money stashed away that you earned making kids' Halloween costumes."

"But Joe doesn't know about that. The fact that I have it stuffed in a shoe in the closet would make him blow another gasket."

If Bella wasn't going to listen to any of the advice she offered . . . "Why did you come to me today?"

Looking even more dejected, Bella answered, "Because I didn't know what else to do."

After taking a huge breath, Caprice blew it out. "All right. So here's what I suggest. Find a marriage counselor. You need a mediator. Use that rainy-day money. I can help you too, but I know Joe wouldn't like that anymore than the cash you've kept in that shoe."

Suddenly Juan Hidalgo came thumping down the steps, Eliza close behind him. Caprice's right-hand man had broken his ankle. Now it was encased in an unwieldy boot that looked like something an astronaut would wear on the moon. For six weeks, while his broken ankle had begun healing, she'd used temporary help. But Juan managed most of the crews for her, supervised furniture arrangement from her floor plans, and was generally her go-to guy.

Now, however, she glared at him. That look made him slow his progress down the stairs. After all, he was also in physical therapy for that ankle.

"I'm okay," he assured her in response to the glare. Before she could scold him, he continued, "We're ready to move furniture from the second floor to the storage unit. I'm meeting the movers out front." Caprice was about to remind him to be careful again, but he was out the front door before she could. He could move faster on that boot than most people could without one.

Not slowing down herself, Eliza passed by her and Bella and returned to the living room. Caprice knew Bob would shortly be moving his tarps and gear to another room—another glaringly purple, soon-to-be-muted to cream room.

"I feel like I'm in the middle of a cyclone," Bella muttered.

"You're in the middle of a house makeover. I guess you've never been on site while I'm working before."

"I guess not. Did Roz tell you I'm going to help get her store up and running?"

Caprice had helped keep her friend from being charged in her husband's murder back in May. Afterward, wanting to change her life and needing a purpose, Roz Winslow had decided to open a fashion boutique in Kismet.

"Is Mom going to babysit Megan and Timmy?"

"Yes, she is. And when she can't, Nellie can. Roz said it will take a few months to get the store up and running, so most of my help will be behind the scenes. But she feels with my degree in fashion, I was the logical choice."

"You've told Joe about this, right?"

"Yes. And he growled something about not wanting favors from *your* friends. I got really mad and told him I married him instead of pursuing a career in fashion, so I'm well qualified to help Roz. He kept quiet after that."

Bella and Joe seemed to be digging their marriage into a deeper and deeper hole. If they didn't get help soon, there wouldn't be anything left to salvage.

The huge, front door of the mansion burst open. Juan and two burly men bustled in. In their tank tops and jeans and with their bulging muscles, they looked totally out of place in the marble-floored foyer with its two-story ceiling reaching into the second-floor gallery at the front of the house.

"I'd better go," Bella said as Juan directed the men up the stairs. "I feel like I'm in the way."

Caprice wasn't going to admit that Bella *was* in the way. She would never do that. Family was everything to the De Lucas, even when they disagreed, even when they squabbled, even when they saw each other taking the wrong road.

"I don't know what to do to help you, Bella, but you can come to me anytime. You know that."

Bella gave Caprice an odd look, as if maybe she

didn't know that, as if maybe Caprice's opinion mattered more than Caprice had ever imagined.

She gave Bella a hug and held on tight, the way sisters should. When she leaned away, she saw tears in her sister's eyes. Bella didn't cry easily, and Caprice suspected pregnancy hormones were at work.

"Are you and Joe coming to dinner at Mom's on Sunday?" No one missed dinner at their parents, not unless blood and a sudden accident were involved.

"Joe doesn't want to come."

"Then you and the kids come."

"He's never missed a dinner with Mom and Dad, not since before we were married," Bella said sadly.

"Try to convince him to come, Bella. Try to put everything aside for one day at least. Give yourself a break."

"I don't want everybody to gang up on him."

"We won't. I promise. Tell him that. Do you want me to talk to him?"

"Oh, no. I think he's still embarrassed about blowing up at you at Mom's birthday party."

She doubted that. Joe had just said what he was thinking—that he wanted to come first with Bella rather than her family always coming first. What a mess.

"Come on Sunday," Caprice said again. "Seth will be there." She knew her sisters were still curious about the handsome doctor, and dinner with their parents would give them the opportunity to get to know him better.

"Are you serious about him?" Bella asked.

"Trying not to be."

Bella shook her head. "I sure don't have any advice about *your* love life right now."

That one statement proved Bella wasn't really herself. She was always ready to give Caprice advice, and anyone else who would listen too.

After she walked Bella to the door, watched her go down the steps and climb into her car that was parked in the circular drive, Caprice returned inside. She heard men's voices upstairs and lots of noise. Movers at work.

She headed back to the living room, needing to set up a schedule with Eliza. The real estate agent had mentioned wanting to shoot video and still pictures by the beginning of next week. Everything had to be painted, redesigned, and in place by then.

In the doorway to the living room, Caprice stopped cold because she heard Eliza say—

"You have no right to ask Bella out on a date."

How awkward was this? But Eliza and Bob obviously didn't know she was there.

"What I do now is none of your damn business," Bob retorted with what sounded like menace.

Eliza must have heard menace too, because she took a step back and looked as if she might burst into tears. Was that an act? Or did this multimillionaire entrepreneur really have feelings for this painter? Or . . .

Was she afraid of him?